Elizabeth Adams

Unwilling

A Pride and Prejudice Vagary

Elizabeth Adams

ISBN: 1530667801
ISBN-13: 978-1530667802

DEDICATION

For my eldest daughter on the occasion of her tenth birthday. Dream big, baby girl. The world is yours.

ACKNOWLEDGMENTS

I'd like to thank my editor, Lori Todd, for going through this book with a fine tooth comb and making it better than it would have been without her graceful touch. Thank you! You are a treasure.

Caitlin Daschner at Chromantic Studio is a creative genius. She designed this lovely cover and was a big encouragement to me throughout my own crazy creative process.

Thank you Linda and Debbie for the cold reading and the comments and the suggestions. I am truly grateful. Your input was invaluable. Rose and Pamela were encouraging and inspirational.

My husband was endlessly reassuring and supportive throughout this process. He's a catch.

So many friends have been absolute rocks. They've held the bar high and stretched me beyond my comfort zone. Thank you, friends. You make me a better writer.

.

CHAPTER 1

3 December, 1811
5 Days After the Netherfield Ball
Longbourn, Hertfordshire

Thomas Bennet sat in his study facing his old friend Withers, a man he had known since they were boys together and who was a physician in the next town. Once a month, they would meet for a game of chess and a glass of port to discuss old times and new discoveries. Today, after their game, which Withers happily won, Bennet asked his friend if he wouldn't mind giving him a bit of an examination. He'd had some chest pain lately, and though he thought it was likely nothing, it was frequent enough that he thought he should bring it up.

After an examination lying on the divan in his bookroom, Bennet sat up and retied his cravat and pulled his jacket back on while his old friend looked on worriedly. Finally, Withers told Bennet what he suspected, as much as it pained him.

Thomas Bennet's heart was failing and he wasn't long for this earth.

"Are you sure?" asked Mr. Bennet.

"I'm sorry, Bennet. I know it isn't welcome news. But with any luck, you will have another year, possibly two. It could be more. These things aren't always predictable."

Mr. Bennet nodded slowly. "Is there anything to be done?" he asked.

"I'm afraid there isn't much. Relaxation, a calm environment. Some say the seaside is restorative. Perhaps your family is due for a holiday."

Mr. Bennet nodded again, his eyes on the floor.

The physician held out his hand. "Don't hesitate to call for me if you experience further problems. I will attend you as soon as possible."

"Thank you, Withers."

"Of course. Take care, Bennet." The physician left the room and closed the door quietly behind him.

Thomas Bennet sat stunned, staring out the window for he knew not how long, wondering what would become of him. Would he go quietly in his sleep? Would he collapse on his horse in a far off field, not to be found until it was too late? And his girls! Five daughters between the ages of fifteen and twenty-one. What would become of them? What of Jane and Lizzy? His two most sensible daughters did not deserve the life that was about to be thrust upon them.

After a poor night's sleep, Bennet rose early with a new determination.

He may have preferred to ignore the world, but that did not mean he didn't know how it worked. His wife had a meager portion. Her two brothers would surely assist, and perhaps Collins could be worked on for something, but he couldn't be sure. His brother Gardiner was successful, true, but his house was not large enough to suddenly fit in six grown women.

No, he knew how it would be. His wife would become even sillier than she already was and would continue to throw his daughters at every possible gentleman that came within a hundred yards of them. Now was the time to think and plan.

He was ever good at thinking; of thinking, he'd had no lack. But what he thought about before his diagnosis and what he thought about now were very different topics indeed. He must now use his considerable powers of mind to find his daughters husbands—good ones. Ones who would look after his widow when he was gone. Failing that, he needed to prepare them to earn their way in the world, if it came to it. He imagined Mrs. Bennet could live with her sister Phillips, and possibly Kitty and Lydia with her, though it would be tight. His three elder daughters could move to London with his brother Gardiner. If only one of them could marry, even moderately well, it would widen their social sphere and show that the girls were marriageable.

In a fit of industry rarely seen in the master of Longbourn, Thomas Bennet went to his desk and withdrew the estate ledgers. He may only have a year or two left, and he wouldn't be able to save anything significant, he should have started doing that years ago, he knew, but he could do something, surely.

Firstly, he examined the entail papers and made note of everything that was not required to go to his obsequious heir, Mr. Collins—a distant cousin of poor mental powers. Second, he drafted a detailed will, ensuring his wife retained everything she had brought into her marriage and all the gifts he had given her over the years. All of the Bennet family jewelry that could be separated from the estate he divided between his two eldest daughters, knowing they were the least likely to lose it and the most likely to know to sell it if it became necessary. Perhaps he could convince Collins to release the artwork as well.

He then went over the estate budget, and as much as he knew they would not like it, he reduced his wife's and daughters' pin money to a mere pittance, saving the balance for their future. If they stayed in the country, it could go toward a small cottage. If they went to town, he would give the money to his brother Gardiner to invest on his daughters' behalf. Perhaps the man could make more of it than he had.

With that thought in mind, he began his letters. He sent one to his solicitor asking him to finalize the will. Another went to his brother Gardiner, asking if he knew of any seaside towns that weren't too expensive but where he might enjoy a pleasant rest. He also asked his brother if he would consider hosting one or more of his daughters during the season.

It was a conundrum. He knew his daughters needed to marry well and that they had the best chance of doing that in town, but he did not want to part with them when he knew he had so little time left. His most marriageable daughters were his two eldest, Jane and Elizabeth, who also happened to be his two favorite. Of course, he could go to town with them, but he did not find London relaxing and relaxation was what the physician had told him he needed. It was all very vexing.

Finally, he asked his wife to wait on him.

"Yes, Mr. Bennet, what is it?" his wife asked impatiently as she bustled into the bookroom.

"Mrs. Bennet, please sit down. There is something I must tell you."

Mrs. Bennet sat before her husband, her hands clasped in her lap, her cheeks flushed and her white cap with the lace trim slightly askew on her head. She looked at him with pursed lips, clearly ready for him to begin.

"Mrs. Bennet, I have decided to make a few changes to Longbourn. There is news of which you need to be made aware." At that, Mrs. Bennet began to look worried and shifted in her seat. "We did not yield as much as we had hoped with the recent harvest, and our income reflects this." She gasped. "Now, do not fret, my dear, we are not destitute, but I will need to reduce your and the girls' allowances for some time." She opened her mouth but closed it again before any sound came out.

"Now, you may find this strange, Mrs. Bennet, but I believe we need to prepare our daughters for marriage." At this, Mrs. Bennet sat straight up and looked queerly at her husband. "Of course, we don't want any suitors to be put off by our reduced circumstances, so you mustn't say anything to anyone about it. We don't want to ruin their chances now, do we?" he said cajolingly.

"No, of course not, I won't breathe a word of it." She wrung her handkerchief for a moment before asking, "Is it very bad, Mr. Bennet?"

"No, my dear, not so bad. But we want to urge caution, don't we? We'll have to cut back on entertaining, and the meals could be simpler." She nodded vigorously. "Now, about our girls. What say you to a music master for them? I have also thought about drawing lessons."

Not being a very clever woman, Mrs. Bennet never questioned how they could afford masters when they were supposedly in financial straits. And so the conversation continued, Mr. Bennet suggesting he himself would tutor them in literature, something he knew would not be easy but he thought necessary if they wanted to pass themselves off as having any kind of intelligence. Mrs. Bennet suggested French lessons to which her husband quickly agreed and though she did not like it, she agreed with her husband's idea of having the girls learn some basic cookery skills in the kitchen. Finally, he came to the most difficult part of the conversation.

"Mrs. Bennet, I must tell you something you will not like."

She looked at him with wide eyes, surprised after their very pleasant conversation about their girls. It was amazing what having an attentive husband could do for one's nerves.

"What is it?" she asked.

"About Catherine and Lydia, I do not think they are prepared to be out."

Mrs. Bennet began to protest, her voice rising shrilly as she went on about what fun they should be having and how pretty and lively they were. It was almost enough to make Mr. Bennet give up on his plan entirely.

"Now, now, Mrs. Bennet, listen to me." He waited for her to calm before he spoke again in a soothing voice, so unlike his usual acerbic way of addressing her. "Think about it. We have five daughters. Taking them all about and dressing them as they ought will be very expensive. Would it not be easier if there were only two or three of them to dress and plan for?"

She was about to protest again when she saw his serious look entreating her to consider his plan. Silly and petty she might be, but Mrs.

Bennet knew the cost of fabric and she understood his logic, however much she might dislike it.

He could tell she was wavering and decided to add another log to the fire. "If we can successfully reduce our expenditures, and if Kitty and Lydia can focus on their music and studies, I may be able to take you to the seaside for the summer."

"The seaside?" Her eyes brightened suddenly and she sat up straighter in her chair. "Truly, Mr. Bennet? You are not teasing?" she asked hopefully.

Mr. Bennet felt the tiniest twinge of guilt over her enthusiasm and apparent distrust of him, but it was gone almost as soon as it appeared. "Truly. I would like to take a house for the summer. I've already sent out inquiries."

That was enough to convince Mrs. Bennet to agree to even the most stringent changes, and so they continued their plans for the girls, deciding that Kitty and Lydia could attend family functions at home. Until at least one of her other sisters was married or she turned nineteen, whichever came first, Kitty was not to be out, and Lydia must follow suit. Three daughters out was enough for anyone to handle, Mr. Bennet told his wife, and he did not want her to overtax herself. Mrs. Bennet blushed prettily and smiled at her husband, readily agreeing that he knew best.

CHAPTER 2

Over the next se'nnight, Mr. Bennet engaged a music master, a drawing master, and a French tutor. He brought all his girls into his bookroom and told them of the coming changes: he had created a schedule for each of them, and each day they would be expected to study with the masters, practice a bit on their own, and assist their mother in running the household. In addition, they would each meet with him every week to discuss literature and history. They were stunned, and for a full minute, no one said anything; the girls just stared at their father as if they had never seen him before. Jane finally broke the silence.

"I will look forward to the drawing master, sir. Thank you for the consideration."

Her sisters murmured thanks as well and exchanged confused glances. Mr. Bennet held up a hand.

"That is not all. From now on, your excursions and allowance will depend upon your diligence to your daily tasks." Five pairs of eyes widened. "If you complete them satisfactorily and give your masters no trouble, you will be granted privileges. If you do not," he looked at his youngest two daughters steadily, "you will take your meals above stairs and not be permitted in company."

At this, Lydia, the youngest and silliest Bennet daughter, loudly erupted. She complained of how harsh this all sounded and wondered when they would walk to Meryton or visit their friends if they were busy studying all the time. She appealed to her mother who looked at her husband for a moment before calmly telling Lydia that she supported her husband's edicts. Lydia gaped at her father until he told her that her unladylike and childish display had just earned her an afternoon in her room and a meal above stairs.

Lydia stared at her family incredulously, looking to her sisters for support, but their eyes were trained steadily to the floor. Finally, Lydia balled her fists at her side and stomped her way upstairs, loudly slamming the door to her room.

"That will earn her breakfast in her room as well," Mr. Bennet said calmly. "Now, here are each of your schedules." He passed out a paper with a calendar of sorts on it to each of his daughters, who in turn continued to stare at him strangely.

"Music lessons every day!" commented Mary and Kitty, though only one sounded pleased by the prospect.

"Yes. As you can see, your practice times are there as well. You will each spend one hour with the master and another in practice each day, though more would certainly not hurt you." He looked at Elizabeth significantly. She gave him a sheepish look. "I've ordered the pianoforte in the back sitting room tuned and it shall be used to practice while the music room shall be used for lessons. Any questions?"

Mary timidly spoke up. "What do you mean by 'non-religious texts'?"

"I mean that your reading time should be spent reading something other than doctrine and Fordyce. Now," he looked at each of his daughters authoritatively, "you know what needs doing. Get to it."

He turned back to his desk and sat down, his initiative used up for the day. He remained upright, watching them carefully, though, not wanting them to see his weakness. He told himself it would only be difficult in the beginning. Once they had a rhythm going, everything would move along smoothly.

Longbourn was a very noisy house that morning, Mary pounding away on the pianoforte in one room, Elizabeth tinkling half-heartedly in another, Jane huffing quietly as she attempted to draw a bowl with appropriate shadowing and Kitty repeating her French tutor with a very bad accent, though it must be said that she made up for it with enthusiasm.

Sitting alone and thinking about what was to come, Mr. Bennet had a moment of regret for not demanding Elizabeth marry Mr. Collins the month before. Yes, the man was an obsequious toad, but perhaps she could have made something of him. He'd no doubt that she could have managed him, had she set her mind to it. But he had not known then what he knew now, and he wasn't sure which Elizabeth would have hated more: being married to Collins or having to earn her living as a governess or a companion. If another suitor came along, for any of them, he would have to say yes out of simple necessity. As long as the man was good, respectable, and solvent, he saw no reason to withhold his blessing. Had Collins asked after his diagnosis instead of before, he did not know how he would have acted.

He simply did not know.

~

By mid-afternoon, each of the Bennet girls, save Lydia, had spent time with a music and drawing master, had been told by said master what she should work on and accomplish before her next lesson the following day, and had spent an hour learning French with the tutor. The two eldest girls, Jane and Elizabeth, would take their lessons together and be one another's practice partners. Kitty and Mary would continue on individually and practice together in the afternoons, which neither was very happy about, Mary being very serious and Kitty being very silly. When it was time to dress for dinner, Longbourn had never seen four more tired young women trudging up the stairs to change.

Dinner that evening was a subdued affair. The girls were tired and confused by their father's recent actions. The elder were worried that something had occurred to cause so drastic a change—for before, he really had been a very indolent father—and the younger were by turns happy to be studying seriously (Mary) and pleased the day was over (Kitty). It should be said that Kitty did miss her younger sister Lydia, for the first little while, at least. She missed having someone to talk to and giggle with. But it should also be said that while Kitty was a very silly girl, she was also a girl of hidden talents. She had done well with her scales in her music lesson and the master had complimented her high, delicate voice, and to her great surprise, the drawing master told her she was learning the quickest of all her sisters. Though exhausted and confused and missing her sister slightly, Kitty Bennet went in to dinner just a tiny bit happier that day.

~

Lydia Bennet was in a fine mess. She had thought having dinner in her room wouldn't be so very bad. She had a delicious novel to read and everyone at the table would miss her lively conversation and her father would be sorry he sent her upstairs. Come breakfast, they would all be thrilled to see her again. She changed her mind when she saw the tray of lumpy porridge Sarah, the maid, brought to her room. When she asked about it, sure there must have been some mistake, the maid informed her that it was brought on Mr. Bennet's orders and he'd said that proper food was served in the proper dining room to proper ladies. The maid's cheeks burned as she recited the message, and Lydia positively quivered with anger. She balled her fists and stamped her foot and let out a most unladylike grunt. Sarah bobbed a quick curtsey and dashed out of the room, just in time to avoid the heavy spoon Lydia threw at the door.

Mrs. Bennet heard the commotion from upstairs and worried over her youngest and most favored child, but her husband reassured her and said that Lydia just needed time to adjust and would accept the changes in good time. She nodded and attended her meal, imagining how jealous Lady Lucas would be when all five Bennet daughters sang in perfect harmony at the next neighborhood party.

The following morning, Lydia was surprised when the maid came in with another tray for breakfast: porridge again. There was a tiny bit of jam dolloped in the middle, but it was an uninspiring meal. She huffed and sat down to eat, thinking the sooner she was through, the sooner she could leave this room.

"Sarah, you've forgotten the spoon!" she called to the retreating maid.

"The master's orders, miss. There's a note from him there." She pointed to a small piece of folded paper on the corner of the tray and quickly left.

Lydia picked up the note and read, *"Silver is not a ball meant for throwing. See you don't treat it as such."*

Lydia became so angry, the tips of her ears turned red. He expected her, Lydia Bennet, to eat without a spoon? How was she going to manage it? She certainly couldn't put her face in the bowl like an animal. Huffing, she crossed her arms and sat on the edge of the bed, trying to ignore her growling stomach and maintain her ire. It was exhausting.

Finally, her hunger won out and she held the bowl carefully and tipped it toward her mouth. It did not work. The porridge was far too thick. The only thing she accomplished was sliding the jam across the top and onto her own nose. Wiping her face, she poured a little bit of milk from the tiny creamer and stirred it in with her finger. She then licked the digit clean and tried her pouring system again. She was more successful this time and managed to get most of the porridge in her mouth and very little on her chin and only a few drops on her gown. Finally, after several minutes of very undignified eating, she wiped her face, washed her hands in the basin, and left her room to find her sister. Perhaps they could go visit Maria Lucas and walk into Meryton to buy some new ribbons.

Once downstairs, Lydia was met with the sound of Mary practicing the pianoforte in the back sitting room while Jane very painstakingly worked her way through basic scales in the music room. She stepped into the morning room where she found Elizabeth bent over a sketchbook, looking back and forth at a bowl on the table while a thin young man looked on. Searching for her sister Kitty, Lydia wandered back into the main hall where she was quickly met by Mrs. Hill, the housekeeper, who immediately greeted her.

"Miss Lydia, your father has said it's your time for your French lesson. The tutor's waiting for you in the parlor." She quickly ushered Lydia into the room and left, leaving her alone with a portly man about forty years old with a curling gray mustache.

In quick order, Lydia was sitting and repeating words the man told her to say and wondering why she was being forced to undergo such torture when she would so much rather be having fun.

She made it through the first lesson unscathed, but when she got to the music lesson, she refused to sing or play the scales the master instructed her in and stubbornly sat on the edge of the bench, her arms crossed and her lower lip jutting out. Altogether she looked like an angry little duck. Her father was quickly summoned and he sent her to her room, informing her she would miss another dinner and more besides, but she paid him no heed.

Lydia continued to be trouble. By the end of the third day, she had taken every meal in her room, all porridge, and while this did create some small improvement for the times she was downstairs, it was short-lived. Mr. Bennet was forced to admit what he had ignored for so long: his youngest child was a spoiled little beast. Sighing, he rubbed the bridge of his nose and told himself to go ahead and do what needed to be done—putting it off would get him nowhere and might even sabotage the work he'd already put in. Mr. Bennet was not in the habit of putting large amounts of effort into anything, and he had no desire to see what he had already established fall away. Summoning all his reserves of energy and a good bit of stubbornness, he called Hill and informed him of the changes he wanted implemented.

He sent Lydia on a walk around the grounds with her sisters—she really had grown quite plump—and set to work. Lydia's things were removed from her room and taken to the nursery the next floor up. It was accessed by a staircase at the end of the hall and the remainder of the floor was used for the servants' quarters. When each of the girls turned sixteen, she had moved out of the nursery and into her own chamber. When it was time for Kitty to come down last year, Lydia had wailed about being left all alone upstairs and had convinced her mother to allow her to move into the second guest chamber across the hall from her sister's. In the end, Mr. Bennet had allowed it, not wanting to argue with his wife or his very vocal fourteen-year-old daughter. Now he saw that he had done her no favors and that he was reaping the sour fruit of his nonexistent efforts.

So it was that by the time Lydia came back from her walk, hungry, tired, and complaining of poor treatment, she found her room locked up and all her things being put away in the old nursery, which had been closed and under sheets just that morning. A great wail was heard through Longbourn the likes of which had never been heard before. Lydia railed on about the injustice of it all, and Mr. Bennet did find himself sorely tempted to hide away in his bookroom, but when his youngest daughter looked at him red-faced and angry and, in the heat of the moment, cried out that he was an unfair and mean old man, his resolve instantly hardened. How had he let her get so far out of hand? True, she did look shocked at her own outburst and backed away slightly, but there was no excuse for such disrespect.

With great swiftness, Lydia was informed that she would no longer be allowed to visit anyone unchaperoned, not even her friend Maria Lucas, and no matter how well she behaved or how hard she studied, she would not attend family parties nor receive any kind of allowance. She would no longer wear her hair up like a lady, but would go back to the braids and bows of a little girl. All of her gowns would be remade for her sisters as she would now be dressing her age, and until she learned to behave like a lady, she would be treated like the child that she was. If she could not behave, she would not even be permitted to eat with the family, ever.

Lydia was shocked into silence and when she finally regained her senses, she ran up the stairs to the nursery as quickly as she could and slammed the door behind her. She flung herself across the narrow bed and sobbed noisily, hoping her mother would rescue her soon. She couldn't stand this long. She simply couldn't.

Mrs. Bennet stood in the hall twisting her hands and looking worriedly between her husband and the stairs her daughter had just stomped up. Normally, she would console her child or make whichever girl Lydia was fighting with give her what she wanted to shut her up, but in this case, Lydia was fighting with her father, not her sisters, and he *had* promised to take them to the seaside… He had even brought Mrs. Bennet into the bookroom just that morning to ask her opinion on a house he'd received word of and inquired how near to the beach she would like to stay.

That settled it. She would side with her husband. Lydia's wails were not so loud from the nursery and she did so want to spend the summer at the seaside.

~

And so the days established themselves. Each morning, the girls rose and had breakfast with the family, except Lydia who ate in the nursery on her own, then went on to one hour each of music, French and drawing lessons, though not necessarily in that order, followed by an hour of music practice. Once a week they would meet with their father to discuss what they were reading and give him a progress report on their other lessons. Twice a week they sat down with their mother and reviewed menus, looked at ledgers for household purchases and servants' pay, and wrote and answered letters and invitations. Three times a week they met Cook in the kitchen and learned a thing or two about how to prepare food, something that Mrs. Bennet did not want them to learn but that she grudgingly admitted would be useful if one of them married a clergyman or an attorney. Of course, she didn't think that was likely, at least not for Jane or Lydia and possibly not Kitty either, but she did admit it was a possibility for Mary and Elizabeth. At least it kept them all occupied and out of her way for an hour or two. And of course, nobody needed to know.

Kitty had taken the news of her reduced status in stride. Of course, that was largely because she had seen the punishments enacted on Lydia, and she had no desire to return to the nursery or eat nothing but porridge noon and night. And though it was uncharitable, Kitty felt a certain amount of glee in Lydia's set down. Her younger sister had been usurping her for as long as she could remember and Kitty was ready for her own moment in the sun. She thought her chances were good that Jane and Elizabeth would both marry soon, and then it would just be she and Mary out; she could easily outshine her very serious sister. Then it would be a full two years before Lydia was out, and with any luck, she would be married or engaged by then. In the meantime, not being officially out relieved her of making tedious calls with her mother and entertaining bores in the drawing room. No, Kitty Bennet did not mind the change much at all.

CHAPTER 3

By the time the Gardiners, Mrs. Bennet's brother and his wife, arrived from London for Christmas, the household was in a smooth routine. The girls had been practicing with their masters for more than two weeks, and the results were already beginning to show. The meals were much simpler, per the master's request, and while tired, the girls were proud of their progress and satisfied in the way only a hard day's work can provide.

They were a very merry party and there was significantly less cringing than there had been before. The officers continued to call, but Mrs. Bennet planned no parties for them, and without Kitty and Lydia running into town and dragging home soldiers for tea, fewer of them ventured out of Meryton. Once it was made clear that Lydia would not be coming down at all and that Kitty was not formally out, the visits tapered down considerably.

There had been one officer, a Mr. Wickham, who had had a particular interest in Miss Elizabeth. He had shown her great attention and flirted and smiled with ease. She had received him with joy and had taken a certain feminine pleasure in being the object of such a man's attention. He was a great favorite among many in the area, especially among the Bennet women. He had favored Elizabeth enough to tell her about his past and about a particularly difficult experience with Mr. Darcy, Mr. Bingley's friend who had visited the area in the autumn.

Mr. Wickham told Elizabeth that he had been the son of the previous Mr. Darcy's steward and had grown up with Darcy, and that he was Mr. Darcy Sr.'s godson and had been that man's favorite. He and the younger Darcy had been friends, but Darcy had grown jealous of his father's affection for another and when his father passed and left a living for Mr.

Wickham, Darcy had prevented the disbursement of it on some sort of technicality, and poor Mr. Wickham was reduced to poverty and forced to eke out an existence in the militia.

Elizabeth was greatly touched by his tale of woe, being of tender heart and vain spirit. Mr. Darcy had insulted her before they were even introduced, and in a very humiliating way, though there may not be another way to be insulted. At the first assembly he and his party had attended in the neighborhood, Mr. Darcy's friend Mr. Bingley, an amiable and cheerful man, had suggested he dance with Elizabeth who was currently without a partner. Looking her over disdainfully, Mr. Darcy declared that she was not handsome enough to tempt him to dance. She! Elizabeth Bennet! Second of the Bennet sisters, famed as the most beautiful family in the county.

Elizabeth liked to think she was a fair lady, with good judgment and a kind disposition, but, oh, how she hated Mr. Darcy! She had laughed and told her friends the ridiculous story, for really she did not think he could have looked at her very closely, or perhaps there was something wrong with his eyes, or maybe he was accustomed to done-up women and did not appreciate simple beauty, and of course, she was not *so* vain, but it did sting. Yes, it did. She had decided then and there that though he may be rich, in her eyes, Mr. Darcy was most assuredly lacking.

Her subsequent encounters had been much of the same. He had not overtly insulted her, but he had been proud, arrogant, and dismissive. When Mr. Wickham told her of his mistreatment at the hands of the horrid Mr. Darcy, she readily believed him, for had she not been witness to his disdain herself, and in quite a personal matter? No, Mr. Darcy was not a good man—that, she was sure of. He was pompous and difficult and thought he was above everyone else. She disliked him heartily.

Mr. Wickham's constant attentions were a balm to her wounded pride and went some way to rebuilding her image of herself in her own mind. She was not undesirable; Mr. Wickham was clearly quite tempted by her beauty.

Alas, Mr. Wickham was poor and Elizabeth was not much better, having only a small dowry and not even receiving that until her mother passed on. There was no future for the two of them and she found that she did not really mind. He was charming, to be sure, and she was greatly flattered and appreciated his attention, but she knew her heart was not touched. Mr. Wickham was, well, she did not like to admit it because it made her sound terribly mean, but he was, quite simply, not enough. She was not sure what it was that he was lacking, or who *would* be enough, but she thought she would know it when she encountered it.

She discussed all of this in great detail with her Aunt Gardiner, a kind and understanding woman, and her aunt helped her to make sense of her convoluted feelings and congratulated her on not feeling anything very deep for Mr. Wickham, for he could not afford to marry her, and his prospects were severely lacking. In any case, by the next month he had moved on to another lady, a Miss Mary King who had recently inherited ten thousand pounds. She had not felt his defection keenly at all, confirming the untouched state of her heart, but Elizabeth did not like the words and looks of her neighbors who teased her for it. She reminded them that a man must have something to live on and that she and Wickham were only friends, no more.

One evening, after they had attended a party at Lucas Lodge, Jane and Elizabeth sat on Jane's bed, brushing out their hair and discussing the evening.

"What do you think will become of us, Jane?" Elizabeth asked.

"What do you mean?"

"I mean, do you think we will ever marry? Or will we live with uncle after father passes? Or worse, will we have to take employment?"

"Oh, surely not! We will not be as poor as that. And Papa is young still. He might live many more years. Surely we do not need to worry about that now," Jane soothed.

Elizabeth could not be so easily comforted. Her father was acting strangely, not just with his recent edicts about their comportment and education, but with his own activities as well. He no longer went for solitary rides—he had asked Jane to accompany him the last three times he'd ridden out. And he drank less wine at dinner, not that he had ever drunk much, and he often looked at her in a way that made her feel eerie, as if someone had stepped over her grave. Jane was not the person to discuss this with—she was determined to see the bright side on every matter and whatever evidence Elizabeth produced, Jane would find a way to explain it away. It was a maddening and endearing quality.

She wished she had someone to talk to, but Jane would not do and Charlotte would usually be her next choice, but she was marrying the ridiculous Mr. Collins soon and busy with preparations for the wedding and leaving her home. Besides that, she had changed, at least in Elizabeth's eyes. She had made a strange decision, to marry a man she neither respected nor held in any affection. Elizabeth supposed she must be looking at it as a sort of business arrangement—he would provide her a home and she would keep it for him, but she could not approve of so worthy a woman as Charlotte being wasted on so silly a man as Mr. Collins.

For now she would keep her thoughts to herself and hope that all was well with her father.

~

January brought with it a return of Mr. Collins, the heir apparent to Longbourn, for his wedding to Charlotte Lucas. Mrs. Bennet wanted to lament the loss of an eligible suitor, for after all, Mr. Collins had desired to marry a daughter of Longbourn to heal the breach in the family, and her home along with it, but did not. Her husband had commanded a peaceful house and as he was being so kind and attentive and taking such good care of their girls, she wanted to give him what he'd asked for. The three eldest Bennet daughters and their parents attended the very awkward wedding of their dear, sensible friend Charlotte and their annoying, but thankfully distant, bore of a cousin.

At the breakfast afterward, Charlotte asked Elizabeth, her particular friend, if she would come visit her at her new home in Hunsford Village in Kent when Charlotte's family made the journey in the spring.

Elizabeth couldn't help but imagine how awkward such a visit would be. After all, Mr. Collins had proposed to *her* a mere three days before proposing to, and being accepted by, her friend. Could there be a more awkward situation? She thought not. However, Charlotte was her very dear friend and had been for many years now and she didn't feel quite right saying no just because she didn't like her friend's husband— or her motives for marrying him.

So Elizabeth said she would ask her father and promised to write.

~

By early February, Mr. Bennet had secured a house on the seaside for the summer. It was in a quiet section of Margate, a seaside town in Kent not too popular with tourists. He agreed that Elizabeth could go visit her friend Charlotte at Easter, largely to keep peace with Mr. Collins They would collect her on their way to the seaside.

Jane had been invited to London after Christmas to stay with the Gardiners with the hope that she would see Mr. Bingley, the young man who'd stolen her heart and callously left the area last November. In the end, Mr. Bennet said no to the journey.

He didn't know how much longer he had left with his family, and he did not want to send off one of his favorite daughters when he knew his days were numbered and thought it was unlikely she would even see Mr. Bingley, making the entire journey an exercise in heartache. She was doing well at home, making progress in drawing and French especially, and her singing was improving. No, he would not send his sweet, beautiful daughter off to the wolves of London to have her heart broken. It would be much more prudent for her to continue her studies and find someone at the seaside. Perhaps he would send her to London for part of the season in the spring. For now, she would stay safe with him, where she belonged.

As the winter passed on, the girls at Longbourn continued their lessons and had two very proud parents to show for it. Having finally gotten tired of eating porridge, though it took over three weeks, Lydia agreed to participate and put forth effort in her lessons, which earned her regular meals that included meat and vegetables and the accompanying silver with which to eat them, but she still ate above stairs and was not permitted to sit with the family unless it was a holiday or she had been particularly well behaved. When they had guests, which wasn't terribly often but happened once or twice a fortnight, Kitty would eat upstairs with her and they would giggle and laugh like old times. When the family went out to neighborhood parties, the two youngest stayed home and read books or worked on their needlepoint.

The family soon learned why Lydia had been reluctant to sing or play for the master after she had performed tolerably well for the French tutor. She sang like a magpie. It would appear that the poor girl was positively tone deaf, which was very odd considering all her sisters had at least some sense of musicality and very disappointing to her mother's dream of having five daughters all singing like angels from heaven. No matter, she would learn to play tolerably well and leave the singing to someone else.

She looked quite different with her hair down in curls and her old dresses cut like a girl's instead of a woman's. She looked more like the girl she was and was subsequently treated like one by her sisters, but in the best possible way. She was read to by Jane when she complained her eyes hurt, and helped with her scales by Mary, who was the most disciplined of the Bennet sisters, and even snuck a sweet treat or two by her sister Elizabeth, who knew how much she liked raspberry biscuits. It took the length of a long cold winter, but Lydia eventually made peace with her place in the family as the doted on youngest sister and was pleased enough with that. Mr. Bennet was simply relieved that she had quit throwing fits, complaining incessantly, and flirting with everything in breeches. And, of course, he was proud of her French, which he was told by the tutor was quite good.

February brought with it Jane's twenty-second birthday which strengthened Mr. Bennet's resolve to find husbands for at least two of his daughters before his demise, preferably for his two eldest. Jane put up a brave front and never complained, but he could tell she was still saddened over Mr. Bingley's removal from the neighborhood. The cad had not even said goodbye. He had paid her an inordinate amount of attention, singled her out on every possible occasion, then hied off to London promising to be back within a few days but never actually returned. His sister had sent a letter, of course, but it was no substitute for his presence and it was not a kind note, deftly killing all of Jane's dreams with a swift stroke of the pen. But what else could be expected from Miss Bingley, a woman with such a spiteful tongue and prickly nature?

Mr. Bennet increased his time with Jane, hoping to make her just a bit more worldly-wise if he could, assigning her books with themes of betrayal and strategy in order to open her eyes to the darkness of the world. He feared for her tender heart when he was gone. She was still his first-born, his darling little girl handed to him by a midwife and held awkwardly in his shaking arms. He had never known love like he felt for the tiny little being that was his daughter, and he felt it still. The sense of responsibility and protection that he had felt so long ago was reasserting itself, and he vowed to put extra effort into Jane's preparation. She deserved it, for she was so sweet and kind, and more importantly, would be considered on the shelf in a few more years. Anything that was to be done had best be done now.

He spoke with Mrs. Bennet and she ordered new spring and summer gowns for the three eldest girls. For her birthday, he gifted Jane with a beautiful gold necklace on which a large, single white pearl suspended delicately. He knew it was extravagant, but he saw it as his final gift to his beloved daughter, a sort of token to remember him by. Already he was planning birthday gifts for each of his girls to be given throughout the next year.

Mrs. Bennet was not entirely in agreement with Mr. Bennet's plans and preferences. She still thought Mary had little chance of securing a husband, except for possibly a clerk or clergyman, and that it would be wiser to promote Kitty in her stead. And while she was happy with the attention being bestowed on Jane, she felt that so many dresses would be wasted on Elizabeth. In truth, it was only three day gowns, two morning dresses, and two ball gowns—one suitable for the theater—with matching pelisses and reticules. But Mrs. Bennet had always struggled to understand her second child. Elizabeth had always been more like her father and her mother didn't understand him either, despite twenty-three years of marriage.

Mr. Bennet was able to dissuade her from buying new things for Kitty and Lydia, which they could ill afford under his current scheme to save money and pay for masters and trips to the seaside, by encouraging her to focus on Jane.

"Just imagine how pretty Jane will be in her new gowns," he said convincingly.

And that did it. Jane was her prettiest daughter, even prettier than her mother, who had been a celebrated beauty in her time and was lovely still.

"How clever you are, Mr. Bennet! Yes, we will focus on Jane! Oh, how splendid she will be!"

"And you must find the most flattering things for Elizabeth," he continued.

"Oh, that girl! She will never find a husband with the way she goes on!"

"Elizabeth will have no problem finding a husband, and I'm sure he will be an exceedingly good one."

She gave him a look that showed how strongly she disagreed with him.

"Surely you know I understand men and what they want better than you, Mrs. Bennet, being one myself? Trust me, Elizabeth will be perfectly fine," assured Mr. Bennet.

Mrs. Bennet huffed and said no more about it, but smoothed her skirts and pursed her lips, swallowing her disagreement whole.

CHAPTER 4

Charlotte's father, Sir William Lucas, and her sister Maria, planned to visit her at her new home in Hunsford in early March. Sir William invited Elizabeth to ride with them, but Mr. Bennet did not like to lose her company so soon and convinced his old friend to delay several days by telling him that the roads would be in much better condition once winter was firmly behind them. It was decided that the carriage would drop Jane in London to spend some weeks with her Aunt and Uncle Gardiner and enjoy the season, and Mr. Bennet would collect both his daughters on the way to Margate.

Mr. Bennet made his daughters promise to keep up with their studies while they were away. Jane would continue with French and the pianoforte with the assistance of Mrs. Gardiner, and the drawing master had given her several tasks to complete. Elizabeth had no such resources at her disposal, not even a pianoforte, but she was sent with assignments nonetheless. Her music and French master gave her weeks' worth of daily assignments, and she was given a sketchbook by her drawing master that she was ordered to fill before her father collected her in five weeks' time. Her father sent her with two histories and a book of poetry; they would continue their discussions through correspondence. Elizabeth sighed but packed the books away with her belongings and promised she would do as she had been directed.

Mr. Bennet did not give Jane as many tasks as Elizabeth because he knew she would do them without being told, as she always had, and secondly because he wanted her to spend her time socializing and hopefully meeting a man she could respect and esteem. He had spoken at length with his brother Gardiner when they were in Hertfordshire over Christmas. He did not share his diagnosis—he had shared it with no one—but he was sure his brother suspected something by the way he looked at him so shrewdly.

Regardless of his suspicions, Gardiner had agreed to host Jane for a time during the season and to introduce her to as many eligible men as he could. Between the two of them, they decided a well-off tradesman might be best and most realistic. Jane was sensible, something a man of business would surely need in a wife, and very kind and gentle, qualities a man living near the warehouses could appreciate even more than the residents of Mayfair. And of course she was beautiful, easily the most beautiful woman of one's acquaintance. The fact that she was the daughter of a gentleman would bring a sense of prestige to whatever match she made. With his marching orders in hand, Gardiner was prepared to find his niece a husband.

~

Her second day in town, Jane attended a dinner party with her aunt and uncle. Her spirits were still low due to the absence of Mr. Bingley, the most amiable man she'd ever met, but she put forth a strong effort to be agreeable. She smiled and asked questions of the people she met before dinner and was very pleasant to her dinner partner, a Mr. Eastman. He was very kind, very handsome, and very recently married.

Mrs. Eastman shot interested glances at Jane throughout the meal and was overly inquisitive when the ladies withdrew, but Jane answered simply and discreetly, not giving the nosy woman any satisfaction. She was serene and agreeable, as she always was, but she was not blind to the looks she received from the women. At first, she told herself they were merely curious of a stranger to their circle, but eventually she began to recognize that the young unmarried women were not pleased by her presence, and neither were the older women with a daughter of marriageable age. The young married women, with the exception of Mrs. Eastman, were kind to her, though.

Jane stayed close to these women and hoped the night would end soon, wondering slightly when she had become so negative. Was this disillusionment?

The following weeks were much of the same. Dinner parties, balls both private and public, and outings to the museum and Hyde Park. Jane became friends with a Mrs. Caldwell who had recently married a merchant of no small means, and her cousin Mrs. Pearson, who was not much older than Jane herself, but had been married two years and had an infant son.

The three ladies went on outings together, took walks in the park, cooed over young Master Pearson when his nursemaid brought him in to see them, and took tea together several times a week. Mrs. Pearson was the second daughter of a wealthy ship magnate and had married into the gentry. Her large dowry had attracted Mr. Pearson and his failing estate. She was given entry to the quality through marriage; he was saved from destitution and humiliation. Mrs. Pearson had refused to give up her familial ties when she married, and so straddled the line between tradesman and gentry.

More importantly, Mrs. Pearson had an elder brother, Mr. Walker, who had been very attentive to Jane on the few occasions he had met her. The last time she took tea at Mrs. Pearson's, he had unexpectedly dropped by, just to say hello to his sister, and stayed for half an hour, talking almost exclusively to Jane.

Mr. Walker was pleasant and very gentlemanly in his address, always kind to Jane and to everyone she saw him interact with. After three weeks in town, Jane had danced with him twice at two balls, attended two dinners at his sister's—one only a small family party, and attended a musical soiree at his father's home. She found his family to be genteel and kind, and all seemed disposed to like her a great deal.

It was quite refreshing to be surrounded by genuine people, which she was shocked at herself for noticing, but after sending three letters unanswered to Caroline Bingley and calling on her only to be told the lady was not at home when Jane could clearly hear her talking to Mrs. Hurst in the drawing room, she was less sure of her friendship in that quarter. It seemed quite clear that Miss Bingley was ending the acquaintance and Jane could not think of why, unless it was that Miss Bingley simply did not like her.

Poor Jane felt very misused, after Miss Bingley had made such a fuss over her in Hertfordshire and gone on about what great friends they were. Why would she suddenly change her mind when Jane had done nothing at all? Or had Miss Bingley never truly been her friend and only acted as if she was? But if so, to what purpose?

Jane believed that all people were not only basically good, but *actually* good, and if their rude actions could not be easily explained, there must be some sort of great need that only they knew of that caused them to behave in such a way. She only ever had kind motives herself, and she simply could not comprehend how some people were vicious, or mean, or unkind on purpose; that some people actually *meant* to hurt others, or that they were unfeeling and selfish, doing what they wanted, when they wanted, without a thought about others affected by their actions. She was sure that they must simply have not realized what they were doing, that no one had ever taught them how to do right, that they were unaware of the consequences of their heedless decisions.

Her father had had many discussions with her over the past few months about the nature of people, using literature as a guide, impressing on her that not all could be trusted and that some were actually purposely dishonest while having all the appearance of goodness. Jane had not wanted to believe him, indeed had argued with him that there could be some sort of misunderstanding, but her father had been firm and without realizing it, Jane had learned something of the darker side of life. She was not at all pleased by it, and the disturbance of her mind was great.

If all in the world was not bright and clear, what was it?

So it was with great surprise and trepidation that she turned around at the small ball at Mrs. Pearson's only to come face to face with Mr. Bingley.

"Miss Bennet!" he cried, surprise all over his face.

"Mr. Bingley." Jane was no less shocked. She colored and looked to the floor.

"What brings you to London?" he asked.

"I am visiting my aunt and uncle." She glanced quickly behind her at the stylish looking couple talking to Mrs. Pearson's parents.

"Ah." Bingley seemed to run out of things to say and looked about awkwardly until Mr. Walker approached and reminded her that their set was next. She curtseyed to Mr. Bingley and left gratefully, her heart thudding in her chest.

Bingley walked the perimeter of the dance floor, not talking to anyone, simply watching Jane Bennet dance. She wondered what he was about, staring at her so. He had never looked at her like that in Hertfordshire. Would he ask her to dance? Would she accept?

Two sets later, Jane and Bingley stood across from each other. The dance was a sedate one, leaving plenty of time for conversation and cross examination. The first few minutes were spent in silence, each looking around them or at the floor, but never at each other.

"How do you know the Pearsons?" he finally asked.

"Mrs. Pearson has lately become a friend," she answered. "And you?"

"Pearson and I were in Cambridge together."

She nodded and they continued on in silence. Feeling all the awkwardness of quiet where there had once been no lack of conversation, Jane spoke.

"How are your sisters?"

"Well, thank you. And your family? Are they well?" he asked.

"Yes, they are, thank you."

The niceties were painful to both but Bingley seemed determined to go on. Jane was not sure how she felt about that.

"Are any of them here with you?" He gave a cursory glance around the ballroom.

"No, I am in London on my own. My younger sisters but one remain at Longbourn." At his questioning look, she added, "My sister Elizabeth has gone to Kent to visit our friend who has recently married and moved there."

"Oh? Anyone I know?"

"Yes. Miss Charlotte Lucas married my father's cousin Mr. Collins. They have settled in Kent where he has a living."

"Really!" He smiled brightly. "When you see her, please give Miss Lucas my heartfelt congratulations. She is such an amiable lady."

"Yes, she is. She is well missed in the neighborhood."

He squeezed her hand before releasing it to walk around her. "I am sorry you've lost a friend, Miss Bennet. But surely you can visit each other! Kent is not so great a distance."

"No, it is not, but I fear that her new responsibilities will not allow her to travel overmuch."

He nodded and they lapsed into silence again. When it was time to take her hand, he held it a little too tightly and kept it a little too long. They soon overcame their shyness of looking at each other and once he had caught her gaze, he stared at her, his grey-green eyes never leaving hers, and thus they finished the dance without looking at anyone else.

That night as she lay in bed, Jane was in turmoil. What could he mean by holding her hand in such a way? She had convinced herself that she had been wrong about him, that he had only meant to offer her friendship and that her desire for more had colored her impressions. But he had been quite unmistakable tonight. Her friends and her aunt had all remarked on it after their dance. How he had stared at her, how he had ignored everyone else around them. Mrs. Pearson informed Jane that Mr. Bingley had asked after her.

What was she to think? Oh, teasing, teasing man! It would be so much easier if he could simply tell her what he meant by all his confusing actions. And so she had another shock: Jane Bennet was *irritated* with Mr. Bingley.

CHAPTER 5

On Thursday the nineteenth of March, Elizabeth Bennet, Sir William, and Maria Lucas arrived at Hunsford parsonage in Kent, the new home of her friend Charlotte Collins. The first few days were as expected. Charlotte showed them all around her little home: the gardens, the small orchard, her chicken coop (of which Charlotte was exceedingly proud), the kitchen garden, and, of course, the house. The friends drank tea and caught up, sharing all their news and laughing together.

On Monday, they were invited to take tea at Rosings Park, home of Lady Catherine De Bourgh, personal advisor to Mr. Collins and benefactress of his small living. After bowing deeply and reciting a small monologue on how charming Miss De Bourgh looked and how fine her mother's dress was, Mr. Collins introduced his new family, Sir William and Maria Lucas, and his distant cousin, who would sadly be without a home when he inherited her father's estate in Hertfordshire, Miss Elizabeth Bennet.

Lady Catherine looked them all over and nodded, and directed them each to seats around hers, placed in such a way that she could see everyone with only a tiny turn of her head. After questioning Sir William for a few moments and finding herself bored, she moved on to Elizabeth.

"Miss Bennet, you come from Hertfordshire?" she called in strident tones.

"Yes, ma'am. Near a town called Meryton," answered Elizabeth.

"You live on your father's estate?"

"Yes, ma'am."

"It is entailed on Mr. Collins. It is fortunate for my rector but quite disconcerting for you," continued Lady Catherine. "You have no brothers?"

"No, ma'am."

She tsked. "A pity. Whenever there is an entailment, sons should always be born. Rosings has no such encroachment. Anne will inherit everything." She smiled at her pale daughter sitting to her left. Anne smiled weakly back and wrapped her shawl more tightly around her shoulders.

Elizabeth only nodded and sipped her tea.

Several minutes went by with nothing heard but the tinkling of china as cups were placed on saucers. The lone bird chirping outside the window seemed uncommonly loud.

"You are the eldest, Miss Bennet?" asked Lady Catherine.

"No, I am the second."

"And how many of you are there?" she asked with a suspicious look, as if she expected additional Bennet sisters to leap out from behind the tapestry.

"We are five sisters, ma'am," replied Elizabeth.

"Five!" Lady Catherine clutched her chest as if she couldn't breathe. "And you only the second?"

"Yes."

"And you are out."

"Yes."

"Is your elder sister married?"

"No, ma'am."

"Are your younger sisters out?"

"One, ma'am."

"Well, three daughters out, and none married! Your mother should take you to town for a season. Surely at least one of you could find a husband," Lady Catherine advised.

"My eldest sister is currently having a season in London," said Elizabeth.

"Oh! Oh, well that is good. Very good, as she should do." Lady Catherine smiled as if her advice had just been taken and continued her inquisition.

"Do you play, Miss Bennet?" Lady Catherine continued her questioning.

"Yes, ma'am, but not very well," answered Elizabeth.

"She has a lovely singing voice," Charlotte added, but was ignored completely.

"You should practice! That is the only way to become truly

proficient. You must play for us while you are here. Mrs. Collins always hits the keys too hard. I have told her she must practice to achieve true proficiency." She glared at Charlotte. "Do your sisters play?"

"Yes, ma'am, all," Elizabeth replied. Jane had only mastered simple tunes, Kitty was little better, and Lydia could hardly make it through her scales, but they *were* playing. Besides, she and Mary had improved markedly; that had to count for something.

Lady Catherine nodded approvingly. "And do you all sing?"

"All but one, ma'am."

"Do you draw?"

"Yes, ma'am, but I am not very talented. My sisters fare much better than I."

"Do they all draw?"

"Yes, all."

"Which languages do you speak?"

"Only French and English, ma'am."

"Well, that is something at least." She glared at Charlotte again. "I don't know why anyone wants to learn that dreadful German. All that spitting and hacking. It makes one sound positively ill!"

Elizabeth smiled. "I agree, Lady Catherine."

The great lady nodded again. "And that Italian! Entirely too much enthusiasm. It isn't good for one's health."

Elizabeth hid her smile behind her teacup.

"Miss Lucas," called Lady Catherine. At this, Maria's head shot up and her eyes went wide as saucers, "do you play and sing? Perhaps you and Miss Bennet could perform a duet for us."

"Oh! I, well, I…" she stammered, looking helplessly from Elizabeth to her sister and back to Lady Catherine.

Finally, Elizabeth rose and spoke. "What a wonderful idea, Lady Catherine. Come, Miss Lucas. I will play and we shall sing together."

Maria smiled gratefully and quickly followed Elizabeth through a set of open doors to the pianoforte. It was in a small room connected to the drawing room, able to be closed off but appearing as if it were open most of the time.

Elizabeth looked through the music and chose a simple country song, not too vigorous, and gave Maria the alto part while she took the soprano. Maria had a full, soft voice, but not having had any formal training, she didn't really know how to use it to her advantage. Elizabeth had previously been a moderately good singer and middling player, but nearly four months of daily lessons can improve one rather quickly, and she could now play significantly more difficult pieces than she could prior to her lessons, with fewer mistakes and better timing. Her voice had also become more confident and with the frequent exercise, she had expanded her range, allowing her to sing a wider variety of songs.

When they were through, the gentlemen clapped and complimented the ladies.

"That was nicely done, Miss Bennet. Play us another. Miss Lucas, you may turn her pages," Lady Catherine declared.

Elizabeth stifled her laugh and winked at Maria, who gladly turned the pages while she sang. After half an hour, Elizabeth rose from the bench and rejoined the group in the drawing room.

"Miss Bennet, if you want to maintain your voice and your skills, you must practice. Mrs. Collins has no instrument, but I have told her that she may play in Mrs. Jenkinson's room. She would be in nobody's way, in that part of the house. I now extend the same invitation to you." She smiled beneficently, as if she were bestowing a great treat.

"Thank you, ma'am. I would love to be able to practice, but I do not want to disturb Mrs. Jenkinson's private quarters," said Elizabeth.

"Nonsense! She wouldn't be disturbed at all. I insist," declared Lady Catherine.

Knowing her father would want her to take every opportunity to practice, and remembering her promise to him, Elizabeth nodded and agreed.

~

Midday Tuesday, after taking a walk in a very pretty grove and helping Charlotte with some cooking, Elizabeth gathered her sheet music and went to Rosings. She asked the butler to direct her to Mrs. Jenkinson's room where she was to practice her music. He made no expression, but Elizabeth thought he must feel how irregular this was. After all, she was the daughter of a gentleman and this was the companion's private room. She could not help but feel she was both invading another's privacy and disturbing the delicate balance that existed between servant and served, or in this case, almost servant. But she had made a promise to practice and practice she would.

He led her downstairs to an apartment not far from the servant's hall. She could hear the noise of the kitchen in the distance. The room was neat and tidy and furnished comfortably but sparsely. Elizabeth thanked the butler and closed the door behind her, quickly setting out her music and glancing at the clock. One hour; she would practice for one hour and then she would go.

Reading through the new sheet music her father had bought for her, Elizabeth set herself to working on the first movement. She picked her way through the opening chords and carefully began to play. She sincerely hoped few of the staff were around, for she knew her playing did her no credit. After fifty long, tedious minutes of working on Mozart, she stretched her cramped back and flexed her fingers.

Just for fun, she began a lively jig she had often played at home for dances and that she knew from memory. The piece brought a smile to her face, especially since it was so much easier for her to play it now than it had been before, and she laughed freely and moved on to another, a lively Scottish air that she sang along with, attempting the brogue passably and cheering herself considerably in the process. After playing and singing two more songs, she realized she had gone over her self-imposed time limit and quickly jumped up, gathering her music together and dashing out of the room.

She nearly ran into two maids in the hall who seemed to have been listening near the door. Elizabeth excused herself and hurried upstairs.

Unbeknownst to Elizabeth, she had created quite a stir below stairs. The housekeeper had been angry to have the room used for such a purpose. Angry at the mistress for suggesting it and angry at the young lady for accepting. It would disrupt her staff and upset Mrs. Jenkinson, whom she would have to soothe later. But she eventually decided not to be upset about something she could not change and made herself scarce for the duration of the young lady's visit.

Once Elizabeth had begun, the kitchen staff, busy preparing dinner, smiled to each other to hear the instrument being played. Of course, the practice was not very enjoyable to listen to. It wasn't bad exactly, but neither was it pleasant, so they tried to ignore it and went on about their business. But once she got going and began playing jigs, two scullery maids grabbed each other by the arms and danced through the kitchen, Cook hollering at them to stay out of the way. One of the footmen came out of the silver room and danced a quick jig with the undercook, and for a good fifteen minutes, the kitchen of Rosings Park was a very happy place.

And so a new routine was set. Elizabeth began every morning with a walk through the park, then helped Charlotte in the kitchen, improving her own cooking skills in the process. She answered her letters and had tea with her friends, then went to Rosings for an hour of practice. She went over her time on several occasions, but not terribly, and she always ended every practice session with a few songs she knew, unknowingly creating regular afternoon dances for the servants.

She did her singing practice on her daily walk. She would wander through manicured gardens and wild groves, singing scales and simple tunes to warm up her voice, then practicing the newer pieces that tested her range. On more than one occasion she was joined in song by the local birds, an experience that never failed to make her laugh.

When she returned from her morning walk Thursday, Charlotte informed Elizabeth of the impending arrival of Lady Catherine's nephews.

"Her nephews? As in more than one?" Elizabeth asked.

Charlotte nodded.

"Did she say which ones?"

"I'm afraid not, but I think Mr. Darcy is one of them. She spoke of him quite a bit before you arrived and mentioned an impending visit," replied Charlotte.

"Oh! I wish it were any nephew but him! Why is he tormenting me? Does he not know how I loath to see him?"

"I'll be sure to tell him to consult your feelings on all future familial visits when I next see him, Miss Bennet," Charlotte teased.

"Thank you, Charlotte. You are a dear."

Charlotte laughed and left the room, leaving Elizabeth alone.

"Of all the estates in England, his aunt must live in the one my cousin is vicar to. Of course!"

She blew out her candle and went to sleep, making plans to avoid Mr. Darcy as much as possible. Hopefully the second nephew wouldn't be so bad, but judging by the rest of the family, she wouldn't hold out *too* much hope.

CHAPTER 6

Jane had never had so many social engagements in her life. Nearly every day there was something. A musical evening with friends of her aunt, a dinner party with her uncle's business acquaintances, a ball, a tea, a night at the theater. After a fortnight in town, she was exhausted!

Her friendship with Mrs. Caldwell and Mrs. Pearson grew stronger daily. The ladies were very kind and seemed genuine to Jane, though her newfound doubt in people made her question her own abilities to discern character. She was not at all happy about that development.

At least she was being given ample opportunity to meet and converse with men who had no connection to Hertfordshire. She had come to London before, of course, but her schedule had never been quite this active. Now, her aunt and uncle seemed to be eagerly pushing her towards courtship. They introduced her to several very eligible men, some with as good an income as Mr. Bingley, and gave her every encouragement. It was all very odd, but Jane took it in stride as she always did.

Perhaps the oddest thing of all was Mr. Bingley.

His behavior toward her at the Pearsons' ball had left her in a muddle, but it had been several days since she had seen him. Now, at a musical performance at a public room, whom should she see trying to catch her attention across the room? Mr. Bingley, in a very handsome blue coat, with his sister Miss Bingley. He had seen Jane and quickly made his way to her while Caroline glared at her. Was Miss Bingley truly a bad egg, then?

How disappointing.

And an alarming confirmation of her father's advice regarding human nature.

Setting aside her disenchantment with the human race, Jane smiled and held her hand out to Mr. Bingley. He bowed over it and smiled at her joyfully; her heart stumbled a bit before breaking out into a run. She registered that he was looking at her expectantly. His lips had moved. What had he said?

"Good evening, Mr. Bingley," she managed.

"Are you here with your aunt and uncle?" he asked.

"Yes. They are just there." She pointed to the same couple she had indicated at the ball.

"Might you introduce me?"

"Of course." She led him toward her relations just as they finished conversing with another couple. "Aunt, Uncle, this is Mr. Bingley. I met him in Hertfordshire last autumn. This is my Uncle and Aunt Gardiner."

Bingley bowed gallantly and smiled, happy to be meeting Miss Bennet's relatives and oblivious to the wariness in their gazes. They continued on in simple conversation, Bingley being as charming as he ever was, and the Gardiners eventually thawing to him. Finally, he asked where they were sitting and Mrs. Gardiner, being a genial hostess, asked if he would like to join them. He said he would just tell his party and hastened off like an excited boy granted a treat.

Even as she shook her head, Jane couldn't help but smile.

Bingley approached his sister and her friends with less bounce in his step than he had left them with. He had not wanted to come tonight, preferring to stay in his rooms and think. But Caroline had whined and wheedled and finally told him something about there being a man she thought was showing interest in her and wanting her brother to examine the situation for her. He should have known she was lying to get her way, but he was so anxious to marry her off that he came along. Of course there was no such man. Caroline said something must have come up that caused him to cancel, but Bingley knew she was lying.

However, there was a *lady* that would like to marry into the Bingley family. Caroline introduced her old school friend with a sickly sweet smile and a look in her eyes he remembered from childhood. It often preceded the breaking of his favorite toy. He had accepted the introduction to the blonde beauty, who was remarkably similar to Jane Bennet in stature and coloring, and then made his way to the outskirts of the group, feeling put out with Caroline's manipulations and angry at himself for falling for it once again. Would he never learn with her?

He so sincerely wanted her to be nice, *wanted* her to have good motives, *wanted* her to actually care about his happiness and be kind to those around her. Was that so ridiculous? He was beginning to think it was. It might be a nice imagining, having kind sisters instead of catty ones, but it wasn't reality, and perhaps it was time to let the dream die. He felt an ache at the thought of it, but also relief. Did not hope deferred make the heart sick?

And then, just as he was deciding he had had enough of his pernicious sister, the crowd parted and he saw an angel. Or rather he saw Jane Bennet. But was it any wonder he thought her an angel considering the harridan he had grown up with? Without a moment's delay and not a word to his sister, he made his way to her. Perhaps this night would not be a waste, after all.

~

Poor Jane. Just as she was accepting that she would have to choose a man to marry, and that said man would *not* be Mr. Bingley, who should sit next to her at a concert? Who should be so alarmingly close that his coat sleeve would brush against her arm so many times? Who would look at her with the sweetest, most guileless look in his eyes when the music was particularly pleasing? How was her heart to stand it?

She was so tired of the confusion, of the people who said one thing while meaning another, and the relatives trying to make her see the world as she sincerely hoped it wasn't. Mr. Bingley's artlessness was a relief and made her heart soften. But before she could allow the sweet softness to take over, she remembered her anticipation at seeing him after the ball in Hertfordshire, and how she had waited for him to come and then received his sister's horrid letter, destroying all her hopes. He had left her, heartbroken and humiliated in front of her neighbors, whispered about behind fans and sniggered at when she left the room.

Mr. Bingley's candor was as false as his sister's, only he was much better at it. Perhaps he really did like her. Perhaps he was simply oblivious to how his actions affected her, in which case he was an inconsiderate man with little honor, playing with women's hearts as he did. She pulled her arm in tight to her body and scooted to the far edge of her seat. She would not be anyone's play thing. She may be good, but she was not stupid, and she would not be played a fool. Again.

~

Bingley called on Jane at the Gardiners' home in a few days. He was as attentive as ever, but she was more reserved. She was polite and kind, according to her nature, but she offered him no encouragement. He could not really blame her. His actions had certainly been confusing.

And he would have been discouraged if it weren't for the telltale blush that rushed onto her cheeks when he kissed her hand after their first meeting. Or the way she stammered when he helped her with her shawl before a walk in the park at his second call, or the gooseflesh that had leapt onto her bare arms when he danced with her at a ball. So he continued to call, hoping to soften her regard.

Meanwhile, Caroline was being insufferable, as she nearly always was. They could be pleasant together, but there was a reason he kept his own rooms instead of living with his siblings. He had a meeting with his solicitor to assess the state of Caroline's dowry and go over the conditions in his father's will. The only stipulation for its release seemed to be Charles's approval of the husband. If he were not available, it fell to an uncle.

This knowledge in mind, he decided to begin his own search for Caroline's husband. She was a year older than him, making her nearly four and twenty. He thought it wasn't presumptuous of him to think she had better get to it quickly before she was considered on the shelf. He also thought his chances were better at getting a certain woman to want to marry him if he could promise his sister would not be living with them.

This decisiveness was a bit new for him; he usually talked everything over with a trusted friend like Darcy before making any decisions— he was more like a big brother, really. But Darcy had been preoccupied of late. They had spent little time together before Darcy was due to leave for Kent and instead of waiting around, Bingley thought he would try his hand at figuring out what to do with his sister. He would consult with others before making any drastic decisions, probably Darcy and his uncle in Scarborough, but he had just turned twenty-three; surely it was time to do some things on his own?

He would begin by dealing with his sister. *Heaven help me.*

CHAPTER 7

Saturday morning, after a hearty breakfast and a swiftly written letter to her mother, Elizabeth went for a walk in the park. As had become her habit, she sang as she walked through the grove, a secluded and pretty part of the park that had escaped Lady Catherine's fastidious manicuring.

There was a little stream meandering alongside her and she stood on its banks and threw petals of the cherry blossom she was holding into the water as she sang a country song about a shepherd who'd fallen in love with an unattainable maiden.

"Pardon me. I didn't mean to disturb you."

Elizabeth jumped and pressed her hand to her heart. Standing not ten feet away was a tall man, with broad shoulders and blond hair, a smile on his face as he looked directly at her. She quickly deduced by his clothes that he was a gentleman and assumed he was one of the mysterious nephews, though he was certainly not Mr. Darcy. The man rapidly approaching them, however, was.

"Ah, Darcy, there you are!" cried the blond man. "I was walking along and stumbled across this lovely creature. Shall we introduce ourselves?"

"That is hardly necessary, Fitzwilliam," said Mr. Darcy. "Miss Bennet, it is a pleasure to see you." He bowed and she curtseyed, saying nothing. "May I introduce my cousin, Colonel Fitzwilliam? This is Miss Elizabeth Bennet of Longbourn in Hertfordshire."

Another round of bows and curtseys ensued. "I am pleased to meet you, Colonel Fitzwilliam. Mr. Darcy." She bobbed again. "Good day." She walked away from them, leaving the men to look at each other quizzically before following after her.

"You are staying at the parsonage, are you not? Please, allow us to escort you," Colonel Fitzwilliam said quickly. She stopped and looked at him and then at his cousin before nodding.

"Very well." She began walking again, now flanked on either side by Lady Catherine's nephews.

"How do you find Kent, Miss Bennet?" Mr. Darcy asked quietly from her right.

"It is very beautiful," she answered.

He nodded.

They fell silent.

Elizabeth felt all the awkwardness of having been caught in so indecorous a pursuit by a stranger, and then forced to keep company with Mr. Darcy. Of all people! She had hoped to avoid him as long as possible, and here she was, a foot away from him, walking down the lane like old friends, only they had nothing to say to each other.

Colonel Fitzwilliam, never one to be silent when he could be speaking to a pretty lady, began asking her about her home. At first, his questions were simple and her answers even simpler, but they persevered, and before they reached the garden gate, the colonel and Elizabeth had laughed twice and shared innumerable smiles about the vagaries of village life and market towns. Elizabeth invited them in for tea and they were quickly introduced to Charlotte and Maria and conversation continued much like it had outside. Mr. Darcy sat quietly, speaking only when necessary, Colonel Fitzwilliam had enough to say for both of them, and Maria was so nervous she said nothing at all. Charlotte and Elizabeth kept the colonel well entertained between the two of them and Mr. Darcy seemed happy to simply observe. After half an hour, the gentlemen left, the colonel all smiles and Mr. Darcy wearing his usual haughty expression.

That afternoon, as was now her habit, Elizabeth went to Rosings to practice her music. The butler greeted her as he usually did and a footman guided her downstairs. She practiced for an hour, ended with a song she knew by memory and enjoyed playing, and went upstairs and let herself out a side door near the stairwell.

What she didn't know was that Mr. Darcy was in the room just above, standing at the window looking out at the estate.

"What is Miss Bennet doing here?" he asked.

"Sir?"

"Nothing, Timms. I just saw Miss Bennet leaving and wondered if she was visiting my aunt," Darcy mused as his valet continued laying out his riding clothes.

"As I understand it, she visits around this time every day to practice the pianoforte."

"Practice? Where?"

"In the companion's room. Will there be anything else, sir?"

"No, that will be all. Thank you, Timms."

~

The Monday following Easter (and a long and tedious Easter sermon followed by an even longer holiday dinner), Darcy and Colonel Fitzwilliam spent the morning reviewing estate accounts. After tea, Darcy took a turn in the garden and when Miss Bennet exited the house after her usual pianoforte practice, he offered to escort her home. She deferred at first, saying it wasn't necessary and she was perfectly fine on her own, but he insisted.

They did not speak for the first five minutes, until they were out of sight of the house and walking through a sunny grove.

"How long will you stay in Kent, Miss Bennet?" he asked.

"My father will collect me at the end of the month," she answered.

"Does he have business in Kent?"

"I believe he means to speak to Mr. Collins about the estate, but otherwise it is a pleasure trip." At Mr. Darcy's confused look, and indeed, who could blame him, for speaking with Mr. Collins could never be termed a pleasure trip by any sensible person, she explained. "My father has taken a house in Margate for the summer. He and my mother and sisters will stop here for me, after collecting my eldest sister in London."

He nodded. "How is Miss Bennet enjoying London?"

"She likes it well enough. She has made many new acquaintances there."

"It is a busy season in town," he said.

They walked on in silence until they reached the parsonage gate.

"Thank you, Mr. Darcy." She curtseyed. He bowed and wished her good day, then left.

Elizabeth entered the parlor where Charlotte sat near the window, sewing something white and lacy.

"Was that Mr. Darcy walking with you?"

"Yes, he escorted me from the main house." She sighed and dropped into a chair.

"What did you talk about?" Charlotte asked.

"Nothing, it would seem. I told him we were going to Margate after leaving here and that Jane was in London. That was all. Hardly a riveting conversation," she replied with a bored expression.

"We can't all be as bright and sparkling as you, Eliza," Charlotte teased.

"I would settle for tolerably interesting at this point," Elizabeth retorted.

Both women laughed and the topic changed to other things.

~

The next day, Mr. Darcy once again met Elizabeth when she left the house. He walked her home, they spoke a mere five sentences between them, and he left her at the parsonage gate. She thought fate was terribly perverse to have him around just when she would be leaving Rosings and not the amiable Colonel Fitzwilliam, but thought no more of it. He was absent the remainder of the week.

The following Monday, it happened again. He even ran into her twice on her morning walks and joined her. He was always civil and acted somewhat happy to see her, even though she knew he was only being polite. She dearly wished he would simply greet her and move on, but it was not to be.

The parsonage was invited to Rosings for tea and cards on Wednesday and Friday for dinner. She enjoyed her conversations with Colonel Fitzwilliam very much. He was similar to herself; at ease in company, good at discourse, and quick to laugh. Mr. Darcy sat near them and tried to join the conversation occasionally, but he often commented on a topic just after they had moved on to a new one, and after a few attempts, he sat close but remained silent except for the odd sound of agreement.

Colonel Fitzwilliam was fond of hearing Elizabeth play and often asked her to favor them with a song. He turned her pages and laughed with her behind the pianoforte while Darcy suffered his aunt and cousin on the other side of the room, a distracted look on his face. Elizabeth wondered what he was about, frowning so at everything that was said and glaring in her direction every few minutes. She knew her playing wasn't perfect, but it was much improved and Colonel Fitzwilliam seemed to find her perfectly entertaining. She told herself to put Mr. Darcy out of her mind and focused on charming and being charmed by the good colonel.

Darcy and Colonel Fitzwilliam called again Saturday morning. Darcy often sat slightly back from the group and Elizabeth wondered why he bothered coming if he wasn't going to speak to anyone. They were in company often enough; surely he was accustomed to their presence by now? She thought his lack of conversation was indicative of his belief in his own superiority and it confirmed that her assessment of him in Hertfordshire had been correct. She had seen him nearly every day that week, but she doubted he'd spoken more than a dozen sentences altogether. *Insufferable man.*

Monday, he was in the garden when she left Rosings and he fell into step beside her, alternately making dull conversation and watching her in a way that made her feel inadequate somehow. She raised her chin in defiance and walked on, hurrying her pace. He was there again the day after that, and the day after that. Thursday, Mr. Darcy was not waiting when she stepped out of the house, and Elizabeth breathed a sigh of relief and walked on her own.

Friday, he was awaiting her outside Rosings' side door, and she thought she saw him jump a little when she arrived, as if he had been leaning against the wall *waiting* for her. For the first time, and perhaps belatedly, she wondered if he was meeting her on purpose. She had thought he simply liked to walk in the garden on a sunny afternoon before tea, a perfectly normal habit, and eventually their paths would stop crossing, but now she wondered if that wasn't the case. She couldn't really blame him. Three weeks at Rosings could make anyone long for escape.

"If I didn't know better, Mr. Darcy, I would guess you were hoping to spot me," she teased. Elizabeth was never one to hold in her thoughts when Mr. Darcy was involved.

He looked away for a moment, before giving her a small smile.

"Did you enjoy your music today, Miss Bennet?"

"Yes, I did. I have almost mastered this piece." She gestured to the music sheets she was carrying. "And how did you spend your morning?"

It was the first time she had asked him anything beyond the weather and he seemed pleased by her interest.

"I have been reviewing the crops in the home farm and discussed some possible alterations for the next season with my aunt's steward. And you?"

"Oh, the usual. I took a walk, wrote a letter to my mother and my sister, helped Charlotte in the kitchen, and then I came here."

"The kitchen? I didn't know you were adept at the art of cookery, Miss Bennet," he said.

"Adept is not the appropriate word, Mr. Darcy. Stumbling or awkward might be better," she noticed he smiled slightly, "but it is enjoyable and I want to spend time with and be of use to my friend. My father thinks it is a useful skill to learn, and I am inclined to agree with him."

"Did you cook at Longbourn, then?" he asked.

"Only recently." She did not want to tell him about her father's recent about-face in parenting and expose her family more than they already were, but she also wanted to discuss her suspicions with someone sensible. Regardless of her opinion on his personality, she had never thought Mr. Darcy *silly*. Charlotte could not be trusted not to say anything to Mr. Collins, and that would only be humiliating and possibly disastrous if it was what she suspected. She also admitted to herself that a man's perspective, and that of someone older than her twenty years, might be helpful, though she could hardly expect Mr. Darcy to be that person. Perhaps Colonel Fitzwilliam would be a good confidante?

After another moment's hesitation, she noticed Mr. Darcy was looking at her expectantly. "Forgive me, Mr. Darcy, my mind wandered. I meant only that my father has recently added to his daughters' usual education and cookery is one of those additions."

"Oh? What sort of additions?" He looked curious now, and she realized she must answer something.

"He has engaged masters for us," she said simply.

"What sort of masters?" Mr. Darcy seemed determined to continue this conversation.

"Music, drawing, and French." He nodded his head in approval and she couldn't resist adding, "And he is tutoring us in literature himself, to improve our minds with extensive reading." She had meant to tease him about his ideal of the accomplished woman, but her words provoked an unexpected response. Mr. Darcy laughed. Not a loud guffaw and she never saw more than his front teeth, but he most certainly chuckled and shook his head.

"And what sort of books are Mr. Bennet's daughters reading?" he asked. She couldn't help but notice that his eyes looked happy, and she wondered at their semi-pleasant conversation.

"Each of us is different. My two youngest sisters are focusing primarily on history, though different periods. My sister Mary is currently reading poetry, and Jane is reading Hamlet."

"And you?"

"Nothing at the moment, though I just finished a book on war strategies."

He chuckled again and she smiled in response. Looking up, she saw they had reached the parsonage.

"Good day, Mr. Darcy."

"Good day, Miss Bennet." He bowed over her hand and left, his countenance still looking happier than she had ever seen it before. *How odd*.

Monday he walked her home while she discussed the weather and a little of the book she was translating. Tuesday he was absent.

Wednesday, he was there again. She did not stop to greet him but merely nodded in his direction and carried on, knowing he would step beside her.

"Are you always so diligent in your music practice, Miss Bennet?" he asked.

"No, quite the opposite, actually. I promised my father that I would practice when I could on this trip. When Lady Catherine offered the opportunity, I couldn't say no."

He nodded. "Are you also practicing your drawing and French while you are here?"

"Yes, to an extent. I draw most days on my own, and I have a French book my tutor sent with me to translate."

"I speak French. I would be happy to assist you if you'd like," he offered.

"Thank you, Mr. Darcy, that is very kind of you, but I'm satisfied with my progress at present." He nodded and they walked on silently a few minutes more. She felt relieved he had accepted her refusal so graciously. She was half afraid he would be like Lady Catherine and insist she practice French daily in the butler's office. She could not fathom spending an hour alone with Mr. Darcy, studying or not.

"What has brought about the change in your family?"

"Excuse me?"

"Pardon me. You said your father has changed his parenting habits and that things were now being done differently. I merely wondered what the cause was."

"In truth, I do not know." She hesitated, not sure what to say and uncertain if she should confide in Mr. Darcy, but knowing she desperately needed to talk to someone. "Mr. Darcy, might I ask you something? I mean, your opinion on something?"

"Yes, of course."

"I will have to ask you to keep this in strict confidence, for it is only my own conjecture and I have no facts to corroborate my thoughts."

"You have my word, Miss Bennet."

She nodded. "You see, my father has never taken much interest in his children before now. He has always been kind to me and those of us that wanted to learn never lacked for instruction, but one could certainly

41

be indolent if one wished." Darcy nodded again, saying nothing. "But last winter, just before Christmas, everything changed.

"Suddenly there were masters in the house and he was assigning books to read and actually discussing them. He insisted we help my mother with the household accounts, though only Jane and I had done so previously, and he took a house by the seaside for the summer, when he never travels. My sisters Catherine and Lydia are no longer out, and he even moved Lydia back to the nursery!"

At this Mr. Darcy looked thoughtful and nodded his head slightly.

"Do you suppose… oh, I am being silly, never mind," she closed her mouth and walked swiftly ahead.

"Miss Bennet!" He quickly caught up to her and said, "Please, continue. This is quite intriguing."

She paused, took a deep breath and looked around before speaking quietly. "Do you suppose it's possible that something is wrong with him?" At Mr. Darcy's raised brow, she hastily continued, "Not with his mind, I do not mean that what he is doing is silly. On the contrary, I have wished he would do exactly this for some time, but it is so out of the ordinary, and so unlike him, I cannot help but think that something must have brought it on. Surely he did not wake up one day and suddenly think his daughters needed to learn French and that the youngest should go back to the nursery?"

"No, it does not sound likely. You think there is something amiss with his health?"

She licked her lips and nodded, looking around her worriedly. "It is as if he is trying to give us everything he can, before he can give us no more," she said softly.

She looked to the ground and her expression was hidden by her bonnet, but Mr. Darcy was sure she was upset. "It does not sound implausible. My father did something similar in his last days."

"He did?" She looked up in surprise.

"Yes. He knew for some months that his end was near. He had already been training me to take over the estate, but he had a new vigor. Even at mealtimes, he spoke to me of investments and tenants and road projects. It was as if he wanted to impart all his knowledge while he had the time."

Elizabeth nodded, feeling dangerously close to losing her composure. "He has never taken us to the seaside before." Mr. Darcy only nodded and walked alongside her slowly, while she hid behind her bonnet. "He gave Jane a beautiful necklace for her birthday. He has given us gifts before, but something about this one…" She trailed off, despising herself for exposing so much to Mr. Darcy of all people, but also feeling immense relief at having unburdened herself. "I am sorry, Mr. Darcy. I am afraid I'm not good company today," she said.

He handed her his handkerchief and she dabbed at her eyes before handing it back to him. "It is no trouble at all, Miss Bennet. I am honored to share your confidence."

They had reached the parsonage by now and he bowed deeply. She gave him a weak smile and a curtsey, then went silently into the house.

Elizabeth went straight to her room where she thoroughly berated herself for talking to Mr. Darcy. *Mr. Darcy* of all people! She had grown accustomed to his presence and his quiet questions on all their walks. She had forgotten herself and let her worry for her father overtake her good sense. She had asked him to keep a confidence of hers! He was not even a friend! How could she have done such a thing? She burned with embarrassment—she had just spilled her heart to a man with little compassion and even less respect for those beneath him, as he most certainly viewed her to be.

If he walked with her again tomorrow, she would apologize for overstepping and speaking of things she should not have and hope that would put an end to it. Her family would arrive in two days' time and shortly after that, they would be on their way to Margate and her first glimpse of the sea. She could survive a few more days in Mr. Darcy's company, but she must be careful not to be alone with him. After she apologized, that is.

.

CHAPTER 8

The following day was rainy and muddy and Elizabeth stayed in the parsonage, much to Mr. Darcy's disappointment and his valet's displeasure when he cleaned his employer's boots.

Friday, Mr. Darcy spent the morning riding over the estate with his aunt's steward and was so late getting back that Elizabeth had come and gone from her regular music practice. He sighed and was disappointed, but told himself there was still tomorrow. Her family was arriving, so he planned to meet her in the grove on her morning walk if he could, or perhaps her family would arrive late in the day and she would come to practice her music at her usual time.

He had spent the morning thinking of her as he rode across the Kent countryside. He was decided. He would offer for her. He really had no other choice, as he had come to love her so dearly he was sure he would go mad without her. He had surprised himself when, several days ago, his cousin Fitzwilliam had commented on how well Miss Bennet had looked at dinner. Something in Fitzwilliam's expression, in the way he waggled his eyebrows and smiled at Miss Bennet when they rejoined the ladies, had set Darcy on edge. He was jealous! He, Fitzwilliam Alexander Darcy, was jealous of his verbose cousin and the many smiles he cajoled from his beloved.

He was decided to ask, and now had only to find the right words to say and an opportune time. It was great luck that her father was visiting Hunsford on his way to Margate. It would save him a trip to Hertfordshire, which would have been impossible anyway since the family was not in residence, and allow him to avoid visiting Margate and spending time with Elizabeth's family, an exercise he would like to avoid if possible.

The following morning, Darcy was disappointed not to find Elizabeth in the grove. She had walked into the village on an errand for Charlotte and hurried home to prepare for her family's arrival, but of course Darcy did not know that, and he returned to Rosings disappointed.

The Bennets arrived midday at Hunsford with all the fanfare that could be expected of a carriage filled with five ladies and one man. There were hugs and kisses all around and a proud Charlotte showed them to their rooms. Jane was sharing with Elizabeth, Kitty with Maria, and Lydia with Mary. Mr. and Mrs. Bennet were given the grandest guest room (the younger girls' rooms were family apartments not yet taken with tiny Collinses), and Mr. Collins happily droned on about the changes and improvements Lady Catherine had made to the house when he accepted the living.

Dinner was a lively affair and Mrs. Bennet complimented Charlotte on her table, which made Charlotte beam and Mrs. Bennet say marriage became her so much so that she was almost pretty. Elizabeth apologized quietly to her friend while Jane hung her head in mortification. Everyone retired early after such a full day, and Jane and Elizabeth eagerly curled up in their bed to share their experiences of the last week.

"Do you think Mr. Bingley will return to Netherfield?" Elizabeth asked after Jane told her that she had seen Mr. Bingley and that he had called on her after the ball and had been present at several other dinners and events. He had even invited her to dine with his family.

"I do not know." Jane twisted her hands and looked uncharacteristically conflicted.

"Has your heart healed, then?" Elizabeth asked gently.

"Yes and no. I still ache from the way he left so unexpectedly, and I will always think him the most amiable man of my acquaintance, but I have come to wonder if that is the best kind of husband."

"What do you mean, Jane?"

"My friend in London, Mrs. Caldwell, I wrote you about her, is recently married to a friend of uncle's. He runs a business and manages his income, and yet he had time to court his wife and he courts her still. He is attentive and thoughtful and very kind."

"But is he handsome?" Elizabeth teased.

Jane laughed and tried to glare at her sister. "Actually, no, but that is not the point! Mr. Bingley, who has no business to run and no family to look after, or even a home or estate to take care of, could not be bothered to say goodbye to the neighborhood, not even his closest acquaintance." Jane looked down and fiddled with a thread on the bedclothes. "Not even me."

"Oh, Janie!" Elizabeth put her arm round her sister and hugged her close.

"I simply wonder if a man who is so easily swayed and convinced is the best sort of husband. Mr. Pearson, Mr. Bingley's friend, came with his wife to see me off. They were all so considerate and kind. It was a stark contrast to Mr. and Miss Bingley's behavior."

"Yes, it would be," agreed Elizabeth.

"Lizzy, I have never felt myself as confused as I am now. My heart wants Mr. Bingley still, but my reason tells me that life with a sister who dislikes and disdains me as much as Miss Bingley clearly does would be unpleasant at best. And would I really like being married to a man who cannot even maintain his own schedule? Does that not sound like folly to you?"

Elizabeth had never heard her sister speak in such a way before. Jane was usually so docile, so serene and peaceful. But Elizabeth could remember a few occasions when Jane had been stubborn when she felt she was right. Those who did not know her well would be surprised to believe Jane Bennet could ever disagree with anyone, but they did not know Jane.

"Did Mr. Bingley give any reason for not returning to Hertfordshire?"

"No, he did not. He merely said something had come up in town that prevented his return and vaguely mentioned his sisters. He said Miss Bingley had written to inform us of his plans."

"Did you tell him you'd received naught but the first letter from Netherfield?"

"No. I did not want to be petty. Miss Bingley has made it clear she does not want me matched with her brother. And again, that makes me think perhaps encouraging Mr. Bingley is not a good idea if it will bring disharmony to the family."

"Do you believe he wants you to encourage him?" asked Elizabeth.

"Perhaps," replied Jane.

"Is he behaving as he did in Hertfordshire?"

"In some ways. He is as charming and as amiable, but he seems both more sure and more frightened than before."

"Perhaps he is sure that he wants you and frightened he has lost you," suggested Elizabeth.

Jane tilted her head as she thought about the prospect.

"Did he meet Mr. Walker in London?" Elizabeth asked eagerly.

Jane had written often of Mr. Walker, Mrs. Pearson's older brother, and she had been much in company with him in London.

"Yes, they met. They were cordial to each other, but I do not believe they are friends," said Jane.

"Do you have romantic feelings for Mr. Walker? Do you think he has those feelings for you?"

"I don't think so. Mr. Walker is a kind and intelligent man. I enjoy conversing with him and benefiting from his greater information, but my heart is not touched as yet. I do esteem him and respect him as a friend, and given time, perhaps I could feel more, but I'm afraid I am not capable of it at the moment." She sighed and laid her head on the pillow. "As for Mr. Walker's feelings for me, I hardly know. He has said nothing and neither has his sister. I believe he likes me and he frequently asks me to dance, but beyond that, I know nothing."

"Oh, dear Jane!" Elizabeth stroked her sister's hair and lay down beside her. "I am so sorry your heart is going through this. It could not happen to a less deserving person. You have always been so good. It is not fair!"

"Would you wish heartache on someone else then? No, I will manage. As Papa says, it is the way of the world and unfortunately, cannot be avoided. I will be fine."

Elizabeth nodded and kissed her sister's cheek, then blew out the candle and went to sleep.

~

While the women were preparing for bed above stairs, Mr. Bennet asked Mr. Collins to speak with him in the study. After listening to Mr. Collins drone on for a quarter hour, Bennet finally interrupted.

"Mr. Collins, I'd like to go over some estate papers with you, since you are to inherit."

"Oh! Of course!" Collins put his brandy glass on the side table and leaned forward. "I would be only too happy to discuss the great estate of Longbourn with you, though it can be nothing to Rosings Park. Lady Catherine says that a gentleman must have an estate and a proud one, of which I am sure —"

"Yes, I'm sure," Mr. Bennet interrupted. "Now, here is the map of the home farm. You see in these fields we plant barley, and this is where the cows graze." He continued on in a quiet voice, pointing to the diagram he'd brought and explaining what went where and who was responsible for what. He was describing the fifth tenant family when he noticed Mr. Collins's eyes glazing over and his head beginning to tip.

"These are the entail documents, and this describes what is left with the estate and what is my wife's personal property. Of course she has a year to leave Longbourn for Dunley Cottage. You remember that one—it is the land at the back of the property nearest to Netherfield. It is currently let by the Jones family, but they will be given ample time to remove themselves, and I imagine Mr. Carter's cottage will be empty by then and would be an ideal location." Mr. Bennet tapped Collins' boot with his own and the younger man jolted upright.

"Yes, of course, Mr. Carter, the um, the one in, hmm."

"The man in Mulberry Farm. You must remember, Mr. Collins! I was just speaking of him. He is getting on in years and his wife died last spring. His three daughters have all married and he is working the land alone with a hired boy." Mr. Bennet had in fact not told Mr. Collins that, but that was a technicality.

"Oh, yes! The widower Mr. Carter. I remember, of course."

Bennet nodded. "Now, as I was saying, Mrs. Bennet and our daughters will remove to Dunley, the Jones family will go to Mulberry Farm, and Mr. Carter will likely move to one of his daughters. Sign here, please."

"Oh, right, yes. Mr. Carter will be most happy with his daughters." Mr. Collins scratched his name next to Mr. Bennet's on the paper.

"Yes, I'm sure he will." Bennet quickly folded the paper and placed it in the packet he'd brought with him, then poured Collins another glass of the ill-tasting brandy.

By the end of the conversation, Bennet was able to secure Mr. Collins' signature on documents stating that all the Bennet family jewels would stay with the Bennet daughters, on account of Mr. Collins not really being a Bennet. He'd convinced his younger cousin that it would be the perfect olive branch and would right any wrongs perceived in the entailment and ensure his welcome in the community. Mrs. Bennet and any unmarried daughters had lifetime rights to live in Dunley Cottage rent free, and Mrs. Bennet herself would receive four-hundred pounds per annum from the estate, plus an additional fifty pounds for any unmarried daughters.

He knew it was a lot, and if his daughters were not to marry it would deprive Collins of over a quarter of the estate's annual income, but his first loyalty was to his wife and children, not to his buffoon of a cousin. Besides, the daughters were nearly all of a marriageable age. Surely some of them would marry soon, hopefully at least one (though preferably two) before he died. He could not, would not, feel guilty about providing for his family.

CHAPTER 9

The next morning was Sunday and everyone was up and dressing for church to hear Mr. Collins give his sermon. He was excessively nervous about it and ran about the house, telling everyone to hurry and rushing through his own preparations so that his appearance was not what it could have been. Thankfully, Charlotte pulled him aside and quickly set him to rights as the entire family assembled at the door and prepared to walk to church.

Their small processional was quite a sight. Mr. Collins walked with Charlotte and Maria on either arm, Mr. Bennet with Mrs. Bennet and Jane, Elizabeth next to Mary, and Kitty and Lydia followed. Kitty was in more grown-up clothes, but wore her hair down as a sign that she was not yet out, while Lydia was dressed as the girl she was, with long strawberry blonde curls cascading down her back and a braid wrapped round her crown. She was on her best behavior, speaking only when spoken to and doing nothing to usurp her older sisters. Her father had threatened her seriously that any rudeness or soldier chasing or sister teasing would be rewarded with a lonely trip back to Longbourn and the watchful eye of Mrs. Hill while her family enjoyed the seaside without her.

Lady Catherine did not particularly like what she saw, but she did feel a certain perverse fascination to see the Bennets up close. Miss Elizabeth Bennet was a pretty little thing, and certainly very lively, especially when near Anne, who was so very dull in comparison. Unfortunately.

The eldest Bennet daughter was quite easily the prettiest woman she had ever seen, except for herself when she was younger, of course. The next sister was fairly unremarkable but not unpleasant to look at, and the two children in the back seemed like nice enough girls. The service was predictably dull and drawn out and afterward, Lady Catherine issued an invitation for dinner to the Hunsford party. They had previously been invited to tea, but Lady Catherine found she wanted to learn more about these Bennets before they departed on the morrow.

Mr. Collins thanked her profusely for such an undeserved honor and the attention bestowed on his humble family. Mr. Bennet merely smiled and thanked her, as did Mrs. Bennet, who was too much in awe to say anything else.

~

Darcy had a plan. Since he had been unable to speak to or see Elizabeth the day before, he planned to offer for her before dinner. He would ask her to take a quick turn in the gardens, or if the weather changed, he would speak to her in a corner. The pianoforte would also be a likely location. He could suggest she play and offer to turn the pages for her. Under the cover of music and with the privacy afforded by the instrument's location, he would pour out his heart and ask for her hand. He dressed with particular care and waited in the drawing room with his heart pounding.

The Bennets arrived in good time. The two youngest, Kitty and Lydia, had stayed at the parsonage, and Maria, feeling odd arriving without them and outshone by the eldest and prettiest Bennet sisters, stayed with them.

Mr. and Mrs. Collins entered with Mr. and Mrs. Bennet directly behind them. Jane, Elizabeth, and Mary followed. Everyone was introduced to Miss Anne De Bourgh and her companion, Mrs. Jenkinson, and asked to sit. Lady Catherine quickly began quizzing the elder Bennets and found an eager recipient for her advice in Mrs. Bennet, who was only too happy to hear what the great lady had to say.

Colonel Fitzwilliam was quite enchanted with two pretty women and another who would have been more attractive had she not been next to her sisters. He quickly engaged all three women in conversation, including Charlotte and Darcy occasionally, and enjoyed his role of storyteller and center of attention immensely.

After a polite amount of time had passed, Darcy suggested Miss Elizabeth play as Lady Catherine did so love her music. Before he could offer to turn her pages, Elizabeth and Mary had looked at each other and nodded, silently agreeing on something, before they both made their way to the pianoforte.

"Shall we move closer to the instrument?" Jane suggested. "I believe this will be a charming performance."

The gentlemen gladly moved with her, though Darcy wondered how it would be a charming performance with Mary Bennet playing. He had heard her more than once in Hertfordshire and he sometimes thought his ears were still ringing.

He was in for a surprise.

Elizabeth and Mary played a duet, both playing on the instrument, and eventually Elizabeth began singing in her high, clear voice. He had only heard her sing once since coming to Rosings and that had been a simple tune, not a song like this that was designed to challenge the performer and impress the audience. Before he knew what had happened, Mary Bennet had joined in with a soft alto, all the more surprising because she had sung the soprano part in Hertfordshire. Of course, her being a natural alto explained why her attempts had always gone awry.

The song ended with applause all around and then Mr. Bennet made a request. Next he knew, Mary was playing a lively air and Jane had joined her sisters behind the pianoforte. The two eldest sang while Mary's hands flew across the keys, invigorating the air around them and filling the room with an almost palpable joy. Then the most extraordinary thing happened. When the song came to the part that was usually sung by a man, and in this case would have been sung by Mary's low voice, Colonel Fitzwilliam began singing!

He had a pleasing baritone and sang with aplomb, to the great delight of the ladies who could not stop smiling at him. The next verse Elizabeth sang directly to the colonel, as the song dictated, and he actually sang back to her! Then Jane took a turn and before they were done, his sneaky cousin had sung with every Bennet sister in the place! They finished to a hearty round of applause and before they could begin another song, dinner was announced.

Darcy cursed his ill luck and the rain that kept them from walking out and his fool cousin for stealing the smiles that should have been his. Elizabeth was leaving tomorrow! He had to ask her tonight; it was his last chance! And he must speak to Mr. Bennet before they left, if only to give him permission to write to her while she was at the seaside. They were to be there above three months. He could not become engaged and then go an entire three months without seeing or even hearing from his beloved. It was not to be borne!

Dinner was no better. He was seated two places away from Elizabeth, her sister Jane between them. They participated in conversations together and he was able to talk to her, but there was no opportunity for private discourse. After an interminable meal, during which his aunt continued to heap advice upon her newest supplicant while Mr. Collins commended everything she said, the ladies finally departed for the drawing room and the men remained behind. Darcy quickly pulled aside his cousin and asked him to leave him alone with Mr. Bennet to discuss some private business. Fitzwilliam merely winked and poured himself and Mr. Collins a drink while Darcy asked Mr. Bennet to join him in the library for a moment.

"Mr. Bennet, would you like a brandy?" Darcy asked as he closed the door behind them.

"No, thank you." Mr. Bennet seemed greatly distracted by the shelves of books he was surrounded by and he walked along slowly, reading the titles and occasionally touching a spine.

"I understand from your daughter that you are a great reader," Darcy said, more from the need to do something than an actual interest in the conversation.

"Yes. There is nothing so good on a cold day as a good book and a warm fire."

Darcy agreed. Then, swallowing his nervousness, for he had wanted to talk to Elizabeth before talking to her father, but there was no opportunity—well, no opportunity lately—and here he had the perfect opportunity with Mr. Bennet, he began.

"Mr. Bennet, there is something I would like to speak to you about."

"Ah, yes, of course. What do you wish to speak of?" Bennet continued to peruse the shelves, unconcerned about the impending conversation.

Darcy had planned to have this conversation face to face, but how could he do that when the man refused to turn around? Could nothing go to plan?

"Sir, I would like permission, and your blessing, to marry Miss Elizabeth," Darcy stated formally.

Mr. Bennet stopped where he was, his hand reaching toward a volume, and slowly turned to look at Mr. Darcy. "You want to marry my daughter Elizabeth?"

"Yes."

Mr. Bennet stared at him. "Has she accepted you?"

Darcy breathed deeply and worked his jaw. "I have not had a chance to ask her. That is, I have not had a moment alone to offer my hand."

Mr. Bennet nodded slowly, then walked to a chair near the window and eased himself into it. "Why?" he asked.

"Why?" repeated Darcy.

"Yes, why do you want to marry Elizabeth?"

Darcy looked surprised for a moment, then opened and closed his mouth twice before speaking. "I love her, sir. I do not believe I could lead a complete life without her. I am sure we are well matched in mind and character, and I can assure you that I will always treat her with respect and kindness. I am prepared to be very generous with her settlement and with any children we may have." He sat in the chair opposite Bennet's.

Mr. Bennet nodded again, his hands steepled in front of his mouth and his eyes looking into the distance. "You love my Lizzy," he said quietly.

"Yes, I do. Very much," Mr. Darcy said, just as quietly.

"Mr. Darcy, I will have to ask you some questions that I know you will not like, but before I can agree to this in good conscience, I must ask them for my daughter's sake."

Darcy sat up straight and squared his shoulders. "Go ahead, sir. I would do the same for my own sister and cannot fault your desire to see your daughter safe and happy."

"Very good. Do you drink to excess, Mr. Darcy?"

Darcy was somewhat surprised. He had thought the questions would be more about his income than his behavior, but he supposed it was a reasonable question, so he answered. "Not often. I have, upon occasion, over imbibed. Usually at a holiday or when something unexpected has occurred, but I do not make a habit of it."

"And when you have, have you done anything you might regret? Have you gambled unwisely? Do you become violent? Are your morals left behind with your sobriety?"

Darcy looked mildly appalled, but thinking he would want to know the same thing about a man who wanted to marry Georgiana, he answered, "No, sir. I do not gamble as a general rule, beyond a drawing room game, and I have never forgotten myself. I believe the worst instance was on the eve of my cousin's wedding and I sang a very bad rendition of an Italian love song and was put to bed by my valet."

Mr. Bennet stifled a laugh. "Very well. Is your estate mortgaged or entailed?"

Darcy was more prepared for this question and relaxed significantly. No one could find fault with Pemberley. "No and somewhat. The estate is not mortgaged and there is an entailment on the original portion of the land and the house, but it is not entailed away from the female line and should I not have any children, my sister's child would inherit. The remaining property is mine to do with as I please."

Mr. Bennet nodded. "And your sister, would she live with you and my daughter?"

"I hope she would, after a period of adjustment for us to become accustomed to each other." Mr. Bennet smiled slightly and Darcy shifted in his seat. "Georgiana is only sixteen and a sweet, unassuming girl. I believe she and Miss Elizabeth would get along well."

"Where would you live?" Mr. Bennet sat back in his chair as if he were just relaxing on a Sunday evening, which, once Darcy thought of it, he supposed he was.

"I currently spend roughly half the year at Pemberley. Once I marry, I hope to increase my time there. I also have a house in town and spend the season there."

"Would Elizabeth be permitted to visit her family?" he asked quietly. Bennet's eyes were on the floor.

Darcy paused. He had hoped, originally, to minimize her contact with her family and see them only when necessary, but after speaking to Elizabeth about her father and hearing about the changes made in their household, he wondered if Mr. Bennet was coming to the end of his life. And the youngest two girls, who had always been the biggest problem besides the mother—who had been remarkably well-mannered on this visit—were no longer out and seemed to have been taken in hand by their father. He could not know if it would continue, but he could hope.

"Yes, sir, I would ensure she had the means to travel to Hertfordshire whenever she wanted, and it would be no hardship to visit on the way to and from London. You would always be welcome at Pemberley, sir." Darcy almost hadn't said the last, but seeing the old man already missing his daughter made him think about Georgiana and how, some day soon, he would have to give her up to a man he would hope loved her as much as he.

"You should know that her dowry is only a thousand pounds when her mother passes."

"That is not a concern, sir. Please, distribute her portion among your other daughters."

Mr. Bennet nodded. "Very well. I give you my permission and my blessing. Take good care of my girl."

Darcy smiled the widest smile Mr. Bennet had ever seen him don and shook the older man's hand vigorously. "Thank you, sir. I'll take excellent care of her and will treasure her always. You have my word."

"One more thing, Mr. Darcy."

The younger man looked at him expectantly.

"Allow me to talk to Elizabeth first. I will speak with her tonight, and you may speak with her in the morning before we depart. I assume you would want to correspond while we are in Margate?"

"Yes, of course. Do I have your permission to write to her, then?" asked Darcy.

"Yes, yes, of course. Have you thought about a wedding date?"

"I have, but I was unsure of your family's plans."

"If I may make a suggestion?"

Darcy nodded.

"I would like to see her wed before the summer ends. Not so soon that she has no time to prepare, but not so far out that you despair of the day ever coming," said Mr. Bennet.

"Why do we not marry in London? It would be an easy distance from Margate and your family could stay in my home," suggested Darcy.

"We will have been in Margate long enough to have the banns read there, if you'd rather. London will be frightfully hot in midsummer. Or you could purchase a special license and residency would not apply," supplied Mr. Bennet.

Darcy did not want to tell him why he wished to avoid the Bennet family and Margate, where he had no control over anything that was happening and would be forced into unpleasant company, but it was becoming more difficult not to say something of the matter. "I will be very busy in town, making sure everything is ready for Miss Elizabeth's arrival and getting my affairs in order so that I may be at leisure after we are wed."

Mr. Bennet nodded. "Very well. I will plan on London in midsummer. Shall we say the first of July? A little more than two months' time?"

"I was hoping for closer to six weeks, sir. I wanted to take Miss Elizabeth on a wedding trip and it would be best to travel in summer," said Darcy.

"Where did you have in mind?"

"I had thought The Lakes. She mentioned once that she hoped to see them one day and I thought it would be an ideal destination. We could easily go to Pemberley afterward and stay through the autumn and winter if we did not want to return to town for the little season."

"Would one of her sisters accompany her, or would you prefer your sister do the job?"

Darcy shifted uncomfortably. "I had hoped we would travel alone. Once we are returned to Pemberley, her sisters, indeed all your family, would be welcome to visit."

"I see." Mr. Bennet nodded. "I will have to discuss this with Mrs. Bennet and Elizabeth, of course, but I believe a wedding in mid-June and a trip to The Lakes after will be acceptable. Is there a place I can tell

Elizabeth to meet you in the morning?"

Darcy was taken aback that a father would suggest an assignation so blatantly, but he quickly answered, "There is a grove she favors. I will meet her there before breakfast."

"Very good. Do not worry, Mr. Darcy, I trust you." Mr. Bennet chuckled. "I would not agree to let you marry my daughter if I did not."

Darcy looked ashamed of his earlier thoughts and nodded.

"If I may give you a piece of advice," Mr. Bennet said. "Go slowly with Elizabeth. My daughter does not tell me everything, but I believe I am correct when I say her feelings are not equal to yours."

Darcy nodded once in response, trying to keep the surprise from his eyes. Mr. Bennet turned to walk out the door and Darcy followed slowly. Truly, he did not know if he had ever given her feelings much thought before, but if he had been forced to guess, he would have said she felt similarly to him. They were much of a mind and he felt she understood him and he her, and that was why they would do so well together.

He took a deep breath. It was no matter. Of course his feelings were stronger, as they should be. He was to be the leader of their household, after all; it would not do for him to feel less than she did. And she was a lady. She would have kept her feelings in check until she was sure of his. Poor dear, she likely wondered why he had not spoken up. He had walked with her almost daily but spoken nothing of love or marriage. How could he have let her suffer so?

When they returned to the drawing room, both men's eyes were drawn to Elizabeth where she sat at the pianoforte, playing and singing with her sisters and Colonel Fitzwilliam who had rejoined the ladies. Darcy sat down and enjoyed the show, gazing upon her with a soft expression on his face. When she looked his direction, he smiled so brightly at her that she lost her place in the music and wondered what he was about.

CHAPTER 10

After they arrived at the parsonage, Mr. Bennet asked Elizabeth to join him in the garden. It was newly dark and she slipped out behind her father and joined him on a stone bench near the far wall, well away from the house.

"Lizzy, I must speak to you." He took her hand and looked at her face, shadowed in the evening light.

"Yes, Papa?" Elizabeth was nervous. What would he tell her? Would her fears be confirmed?

"I need to tell you something, but I must ask you not to react until I am finished, and you must not run off, but stay here and speak with me when I am through, for I have not the energy to chase you down." He smiled at the last and she returned it.

"Very well, Papa. I am listening and I will not run away."

"I spoke with Mr. Darcy this evening. He is an intelligent man, well regarded, respectable."

"He is. And rude, proud, and thoughtless," she added lightly. She looked to her father to join in her joke, but he was serious. "What is it, Papa?"

"Do you really find him thoughtless?" He also found Mr. Darcy proud, but perhaps not overly so, and while he could be rude, Mr. Bennet wondered if he could actually be very thoughtful. After all, he had remembered Elizabeth's desire to see The Lake District.

Elizabeth thought on her father's question for a moment, and remembered Mr. Darcy listening to her confession a few days ago, and how he had handed her his handkerchief and been kind while she was in distress.

"No, I suppose he is not," she said slowly.

"And is he always rude? Has he never been polite or civil to you?"

Again she thought for a moment before answering her father. "No, he is not *always* rude, but when he is, it is quite memorable."

They shared a smile and Mr. Bennet took her hand in his and looked at her seriously. "My dear Elizabeth, Mr. Darcy is in love with you."

She looked at him for a moment and then laughed. "Papa! I don't think Mr. Darcy would appreciate you making such distasteful jokes. Although it is very funny." She laughed and looked at her father who was not laughing with her. "Papa?"

"My little Lizzy, this is not a joke."

She stared at him. "Mr. Darcy? In love with me?"

He nodded.

"With *me*?"

He nodded again and squeezed her hand.

"But I am not tolerable enough to tempt him to dance!"

"He danced with you at Netherfield," said Mr. Bennet.

She looked at him, her face confused and reflecting a dawning horror.

"He is intelligent and well read. He is respectable and not ridiculous. Capable of holding a decent conversation and I imagine he argues and debates intelligently. He is thoughtful, Lizzy, at least where you are concerned."

She began to shake her head and lean away from her father, too afraid to speak the thoughts that were swirling through her mind faster than she could sort them.

"He is not an unattractive man," Mr. Bennet's expression showed his distaste for this particular topic, but he would not have his daughter believe him unfeeling or unaware of the difficulties a woman faced in her marriage and the intimacy that came with it. "He does not smell of cabbage or sweat profusely," he tried to tease. Deciding he should be more practical, he added, "He is a very busy man, I doubt he would want to be entertained all day. He will have his own activities to keep him occupied."

"Papa," she whispered, on the verge of tears.

"My sweet Lizzy, he loves you, very dearly. He will take good care of you, and when I am gone, your mother and sisters."

She cried in earnest now.

"Please, my darling girl, you will be all right. He will be good to you, I know it. I trust him. Please don't cry, my dear."

"But, but, it's Mr. *Darcy*! He does not like me! How can he, how can we, I cannot! I simply cannot! Please do not ask it of me, Papa!"

Mr. Bennet was feeling nearly as distraught as his daughter at the sight of her tears. "Lizzy, you must listen to me."

She sniffled and looked toward him.

"Mr. Darcy is an honest man."

She interrupted him. "Honest! What of his behavior towards Mr. Wickham? And I strongly suspect he had something to do with Mr. Bingley never coming back to Netherfield."

Mr. Bennet shook his head. "You are too much like me sometimes, Lizzy. Think! Use the cleverness you are so known for! Mr. Bingley is his own man. No matter what anyone tells him, he has the right to come and go as he pleases. If he was persuaded to stay away by Mr. Darcy, and we do not know that he was, is that truly the kind of man you wish your sister to marry? She who is not forceful herself? All their decisions would be made by others! And has not Jane seen Mr. Bingley again in town, several times? Has she not met other men, other suitors, perhaps more worthy than Mr. Bingley?"

She watched him with wide eyes and he shook his head. "Lizzy, you must not lay the problems of the world on Mr. Darcy's doorstep. Jane has seen Mr. Bingley's true character and it is now for her to decide what she will do. She is the one who will have to live with him, after all."

"And would I not have to live with Mr. Darcy?" she asked sharply.

"Yes, but you see, Jane is in a hypothetical situation. Pretty and sweet as she is, she has not had a single proposal, while you are in possession of two. You must open your eyes to Mr. Darcy's good qualities, Lizzy. It is the only way you will be happy and respectable. And he is a respectable man. I do not know the particulars of what happened with Mr. Wickham, but I do know that he is always at the gaming tables when they are available, and I also know that he was very quick to tell you his tale of woe, and very keen to avoid Mr. Darcy." He saw his daughter was about to protest and held up his hand. "You have a clever mind, Lizzy. Tell me, why did he speak to you as he did? Why did he not come to the Netherfield ball when he said he would? And why, I might ask, is a man his age only beginning in the militia? Do not let your mind be carried away by your vanity, Elizabeth. He complimented you while Mr. Darcy insulted you; yes, I see that. And he is handsome and amiable and very charming. But do not lose your head over it! You do not know the grief from choosing for the wrong reasons, Elizabeth, and I pray you never do."

"Is marrying for nothing but material gain not also a wrong reason?"

she cried.

"You are determined to be against him! Are you truly so stubborn? It must be my fault for not having taught you better. Ask yourself this: would you be as inclined to believe everything Mr. Wickham said, after an acquaintance of days, if it came from Mr. Collins? Do not speak, just think on it." He was silent and getting angry himself, and so let his daughter stew on what he had said.

Long used to obeying her father, Elizabeth did as he asked. She imagined Mr. Collins speaking to her so intimately on so short an acquaintance and felt nothing but revulsion and disbelief. Swallowing her pride, she spoke slowly.

"I may have been hasty in my judgment of the situation between Mr. Darcy and Mr. Wickham. But Mr. Darcy has said nothing to refute Mr. Wickham's claims," she said.

"Have you asked him?"

She looked at him with surprise.

"Of course not, it would be improper," he said, dripping with sarcasm. "Mr. Darcy is not one to bandy his personal business about the neighborhood. Neither am I, I might add."

She looked at him worriedly for a moment before hanging her head. "You have given Mr. Darcy your consent?"

"And my blessing, yes. He did want to speak to you first, but he said he hasn't had a chance."

"Not had a chance! He has walked with me almost daily –" She stopped herself as realization dawned on her. "Was he courting me? All those times he walked me back to the parsonage, I thought it was just perverse fate," she said quietly, confused wonder in her voice. "How could I have missed it?"

"We often do not see that which we do not wish to see," he said.

Elizabeth laid her head on her father's shoulder, exhaustion overcoming her. Disbelief coloring her voice, she asked, "Father, do you actually think I could be happy with Mr. Darcy?"

"Yes, I think you could. You are not built for low spirits. Your liveliness will brighten his disposition and his greater information and position in the world will feed your mind in ways you never imagined. Picture it, Lizzy, quiet evenings spent in front of the fire with a good book, the man beside you would be quiet and reading his own tome, not blathering on about insipid topics," he chuckled while Elizabeth smiled weakly. "Intelligent discourse, travel, elegant company. Mr. Darcy will make a good companion in time, I think. You may have to train him a bit, but if anyone can do it, it is you."

Silent tears tracked down her cheeks as she realized her father was deadly serious and would not support her refusal. But still, she had to ask.

"What will happen if I refuse him?" She felt her father stiffen. "Will you throw me from Longbourn? Will I be forced to find employment or take refuge with whatever relatives will take me in? Will Mr. Darcy seek revenge for his humiliation?"

"I would never throw you out, my dearest daughter, and I do not believe Mr. Darcy is the kind to seek revenge on a lady for nothing but refusing his suit. However, he is a powerful man and I would not actively seek to anger him."

"Do I have a choice?" she asked in a small voice.

"There is always a choice, Elizabeth. But I beseech you to listen to your father. I know what's best, and I have lived longer in this world than you. A woman without protection is in a precarious position. I would not like to see it happen to you, my most beloved child. Please, accept Mr. Darcy when he asks you in the morning. Write to him while you are away and come to know him without prejudice. Open yourself to the possibility of caring for him and respect the man that he is. He will take good care of you and look after your mother and sisters. That is not to be taken lightly."

"Why will we need protection, Papa?" she asked so quietly he almost didn't hear her.

He stroked her hair and said quietly, "No one knows what the future holds, my dear." He kissed the top of her head and asked, "Will you marry Mr. Darcy?"

She took a deep breath and shuddered against him. "It is one of the only things you have ever asked of me, Papa. I could not do it for someone I loved less."

"Very good, my dear. In time, I hope you will come to see you do this for yourself as well."

Feeling all the weight of the promise she'd just made, she leaned on her father and wept bitter, heart-rending tears.

~

Elizabeth slept fitfully and when she set out to meet Mr. Darcy, she looked wan and tired. She pinched her cheeks and reminded herself to be polite, then headed towards the grove. Mr. Darcy was already there, pacing near the stream.

"Miss Elizabeth!" He smiled and approached her quickly, taking both her hands in his and squeezing them tightly. "I am so glad to see you."

"Did you think I wouldn't come?"

He only smiled in response and looped her arm in his. They walked in silence a few minutes before he said, "I gather you spoke with your father?"

"Yes, we spoke last night," she answered, her eyes on the ground.

He stopped and faced her, causing her to do the same. "Miss Elizabeth, you must allow me to tell you how ardently I admire and love you." She blushed and looked down, not knowing what to say. He needed no encouragement to continue. "I am sorry I spoke to your father before you. It had not been my intention." She nodded. He took a deep breath and straightened his tall frame fully. "Miss Elizabeth, would you do me the very great honor of accepting my hand in marriage?"

She took a breath, rose her face to his long enough to see his eyes shining in expectation, looked back to the ground and said, "Yes, Mr. Darcy. I accept."

He smiled radiantly and raised one hand to his lips and then the other, pressing fervent kisses on her gloved hands.

"Thank you, Elizabeth." She startled and looked up at the familiar address and he smiled to see her surprise. He caressed her cheek with one hand, slowly and deliberately, and she grew so flustered she looked all around, not knowing where to rest her eyes, and finally settled on the buttons of his waistcoat.

He took her arm and began walking again, this time pulling her as close as possible and resting his hand over her smaller one on his arm. His thumb rubbed lazy circles on the back of her hand, giving her the strangest urge to swat him away.

"Are you looking forward to the seaside?" he inquired.

"Yes, I am. It will be my first trip and I am quite eager to see the shore," she said, grateful to speak of something other than their engagement.

"May I write to you there?"

"You may," she answered quietly.

"And will you write to me?"

She flushed. "If you wish it."

"I do. Has your father spoken to you of a wedding date?"

"No, there has not been time," she replied.

"We had discussed the middle of June. It would give you enough time to prepare but still leave plenty of time for us to travel on a wedding trip."

"June?"

"Do you object?"

She did, most strenuously, but if her father wished it, she saw no other way. She was not ready to openly defy him and run away. What better circumstances could she possibly hope to find through that method?

"It is a bit sudden, but I believe I could be prepared by then."

He squeezed her hand in sympathy. "I know it is a great many changes at once, more so for you than for me. I shall live in the same house and have largely the same activities with the lovely addition of your presence. You will have a new home, a new role within that home, and only my presence to comfort you when you have long had a house full of family. Georgiana will eventually join us, but I understand that you do not know her as yet."

She understood that he meant well, but his speech had the unwanted effect of making her want to burst into tears. How would she do it? Leave her sisters and her parents and her beloved Hertfordshire and go live with a man she hardly knew? She looked away and blinked rapidly, not wanting him to see her tears. They would do her no good now.

Darcy walked her back to the parsonage and stepped inside to have a word with her father while she joined her sisters Mary, Kitty, and Jane at breakfast. Thankfully, Mr. Collins had been called to the sickbed of an elderly parishioner early that morning, so the Bennet family was left in relative peace. Her mother was still preparing for the journey and she gratefully sat at the quiet table and ate, looking around her and glumly wondering how many more meals like this she would have. It was likely Jane would be married soon, too, hopefully to a man she esteemed and could love one day if she did not already. Jane had always been the lucky sister.

Before her mother came down, Elizabeth finished her meal and went to the parlor to meet with Mr. Darcy and her father. Mr. Bennet smiled when she came in and pressed her arm as he walked past her out of the room.

"You may have a few moments to say goodbye," he said, and closed the door behind him.

Her eyes widened at the sight of the closed door and she turned back to Mr. Darcy, her shock still evident on her face.

"Your father seems to trust me a great deal," he said, a bit bashfully she thought. But that must have been her imagination, for surely Mr. Darcy was never bashful or nervous.

"I'm sure he would not have given his consent if he did not," she said noncommittally.

He nodded and came toward her, taking both her hands in his and bringing them to his chest.

"My dearest, loveliest, Elizabeth. I shall miss you while you are away."

She looked at him in wonder.

"Surely that does not surprise you?" he said with a smile.

She startled and looked away. "Yes, sir, I'm afraid it does."

"Elizabeth, when a man loves a woman as I love you, separations are not desirable occurrences," he explained in a soft voice.

She wasn't sure if he was reprimanding her or flirting. He lifted one hand and kissed the inside of her wrist delicately. *Definitely flirting.*

"Promise you will write to me, dearest," he requested in a low voice.

Without thinking, she found herself responding with a soft, "Of course."

He kissed her bare hand and she felt a strange warm sensation where his lips met her skin. "Safe travels, Elizabeth."

"You as well, Mr. Darcy."

He gave her one last look, then escorted her outside where her father was overseeing the luggage being loaded onto the carriage.

"When will I see you again?" she asked. She was curious about the plans he had made with her father and wanted to prepare herself, but he smiled at the question.

"Your father said he will bring you to London a few days before the ceremony."

She wanted to ask why they were marrying in London and not from Longbourn or Pemberley or even Margate, but she didn't have a chance. Her father interrupted and then Mr. Darcy was walking up the lane to Rosings.

CHAPTER 11

The house in Margate was a small blue cottage surrounded by a flower garden just beginning to bloom. It was close enough to the sea that waves could be heard in the background, but the water could not be seen. The Bennet family poured into the home, quickly exploring and deciding who would get each room. There were three bedrooms to be distributed among five girls. Before their father's changes, they would have split into pairs: the two eldest and the two youngest, leaving Mary at odds. But now, they were all conscious of a new order and unsure how to proceed.

Lydia had originally declared loudly that she and Kitty would take the large room with the pink paper and the soft green linens, but when she heard her father's footsteps, she remembered she was the youngest and, therefore, least entitled sister and that she was to be on her best behavior or risk being sent home.

When Mr. Bennet entered the hall, he found five pairs of eyes looking at him expectantly. He chuckled and asked what they were about.

"How would you like the rooms arranged, Papa?" Mary asked softly.

"I believe that is your mother's purview," he responded. The shrill sounds of Mrs. Bennet ordering the housekeeper about and giving instructions to the maids rang through the house. "Jane, as your mother is otherwise occupied, I will entrust you with this most important task. You have precedence, after all." He smiled at his eldest and stood back next to his daughters.

"You want me to choose all the rooms?" He nodded. Jane looked uncertain. "Including yours?"

"It is not far from what you would be doing as mistress of your own home one day. Surely it is a manageable task."

Jane proceeded to walk into the bedrooms, mentally calculating their size and how many people each room could comfortably hold and the size of the accompanying dressing room or if there even was one. Her sisters watched her curiously from the hall, feeling an odd sense of suspense with this simple task.

Mr. Bennet, as usual, had an ulterior motive in asking his daughter to choose for him. He had no doubt that she would give her mother and father the grandest of the rooms. But as the eldest, she should be the one to receive her own room while her younger sisters shared. It was her right, but she had never been one to put herself forward other than walking at the head of the line when going in to dinner. She knew her place, but she had never been one to exercise it when it could possibly put someone else out. She reprimanded her younger sisters when it was called for, but they rarely listened for more than a moment. In contrast, Elizabeth had once famously dragged Lydia inside by her ear when her younger sister would not heed her command.

Jane had made significant strides in her studies and in her evaluation of human character. She could see more of a person's true nature than she could before, and she seemed wiser, but she was not any happier. Mr. Bennet knew that she was Jane still. She preferred to see the best in people and would always want things to be simple and clear cut, without mystery or falseness. He only hoped he could guide her long enough for her to see the world as it was, or at least more realistically than she usually did, but also be able to maintain her joy in life. He did want to leave her when he had begun the play but not completed the final act.

In the end, Jane made her father proud. She assigned her father and mother the two largest apartments with ample dressing rooms. She gave Kitty and Lydia a moderate sized room with a view of the street, and Elizabeth and Mary the slightly nicer room with a view of the garden, in respect to their ages. She gave herself a small bedroom overlooking the back garden. It was smaller than the others, but no less grand in its decoration, and it featured a lovely balcony through a set of glass doors. She had felt a tiny twinge at giving such a decadent feature to herself and not to her sisters who would have also enjoyed it, but she judged that the room was not large enough for two comfortably, and that as the eldest, she ought to have her own chamber. She also did not think it wise to constantly leave Mary on her own as had been their pattern in the past.

Decisions made, the girls quickly set to unpacking and within an hour, they were setting off for their first glimpse of the sea.

~

After seeing Elizabeth off, Darcy left for London with his cousin. He wasn't at his townhouse an hour before he had dispatched a letter to his solicitor requesting an appointment. He then busied himself planning Elizabeth's settlement. He felt almost giddy with excitement over what he could give her and the lifestyle she would be able to lead as his wife, so much better than the one she had been living as a Miss Bennet. After he'd made all the necessary notes, he toured the mistress's chambers.

He hadn't been in them for some time and most of the furniture was covered in sheets. He carefully lifted the white cloth from a chair near the fireplace and sat down, imagining what this room would look like with Elizabeth in it. He didn't know how she would like to decorate it, but he could not wait to see her installed so close to him. Their chambers were across the hall from one another, and there was a sitting room at the end of the corridor, with an adjoining door to his bedchamber. The mistress's sitting room was in another location. He wished there was an adjoining door to her rooms, like he'd seen in other homes, so the couple could traverse between rooms without everyone in the house being aware of their comings and goings. Perhaps he could create a door? The eastern wall of her chamber bordered his sitting room. In fact, he rarely used his sitting room, having a library, private study, and other rooms in this enormous house at his disposal. If he was going to sit and read, he did so by the fire in his own chamber. He used his private sitting room at Pemberley most often when they had guests or when he wished to lounge about in his robe, but that, too, was infrequent.

Perhaps he and Elizabeth could share this sitting room together and have their own bedchambers? The sofa in the sitting room might be more conducive to a couple relaxing in the evening than the chair next to the fire in his bedchamber. Though sharing a chair with Elizabeth was not an unappealing prospect. He felt odd making these sorts of decisions at all, let alone without Elizabeth, but he could not help the eager smile that formed when he thought of bringing her here as his wife.

He summoned the housekeeper and informed her of the work he wished done and asked her to select a suitable workman to complete the job. She almost raised a brow at his words, but quickly schooled her features.

Once these tasks were completed, he did the only logical thing he could think to do. He sat down and wrote a letter to Elizabeth.

~

Returning from a walk on their third day in Margate, Elizabeth was greeted by her father with a letter for her. The handwriting was distinctly masculine and she took it carefully and carried it to her room, grateful that Mary was practicing her music downstairs. She sank into the chair next to the window and broke the seal, taking a deep breath of salty air before reading.

My Dear Elizabeth,

You cannot imagine my joy at being able to address you as such. My time in town has been spent preparing for our impending marriage. The mistress' suite is being aired and the settlement papers should be prepared by the end of the week.

Georgiana is beside herself with excitement. She has told me no fewer than five times how she has always longed for a sister. I am glad I may oblige her with such a charming one as you.

How do you find the seaside? I wish I could have been with you when you saw it for the first time and thus been part of what must remain an indelible memory in your mind. It comforts me to know that your first sight of The Lakes will be at my side and will be the first of many memories we make together.

I do not know if you will have decided any of this yet, but Georgiana wishes to know what color your wedding gown will be. She will begin shopping soon and she would like to wear something complementary but does not wish to insult you by wearing the same color. There, my promise is now discharged and I may continue on topics more interesting to the male sex, or at least to me.

Have I told you how completely I adore you and with what anticipation I look forward to our union? I am sure that we will be very happy together. Six weeks has never seemed so long.

Think of me while you are walking in the sand and remember how dearly I miss your smile.

Yours,
F. Darcy

How was she to respond to such a letter? What could she possibly say in reply? "It's all very well that you adore me and cannot wait to be married to me, but I look on the event as one would a trip to the guillotine." No! She could not! It would be completely inappropriate and likely quite cruel. He seemed to be rather in love with her, though how true his feelings were she could not say. He barely knew her! How could a deep and abiding love come from so slight an acquaintance between such disparate characters?

Deciding it was best to get the unpleasant task dealt with and out of the way, she sat at the writing desk and began a reply. She only left off twice and spent the better part of two days working on it in some form or another before she finally finished and gave it to her father to post.

~

In London, Darcy had just finished his final meeting with the solicitor and walked into his home with a spring in his step. Tomorrow, the final copy of the settlement would be prepared and he could send it to Mr. Bennet. Once the articles were signed, he would announce it to his family and they would know he was a claimed man.

His mood further increased when he saw a letter from Elizabeth on his desk. He ran his finger over the 'B' stamped into the wax before opening it and beginning to read. He read it once through, his brow furrowing deeper the further he read, before reading the entire thing again.

Her first lines were about the sea and what she had seen so far. However, when he got towards the middle, he saw this.

I must speak of something difficult, but I fear my justice cannot allow it to go unsaid. I must tell you that I have doubts of our conjugal felicity. You speak of love and adoration, but I cannot help but feel that you do not know me well at all, and therefore I question your feelings. Rather, I question the longevity and depth of those feelings, and if they are strong enough to overcome our differences. Will they wane when the bloom has gone from the rose? Will you eventually cease to think me charming and merely find me impertinent? Will you resent and hate me for not being suited to you and your position in the world? I could not bear to live with a husband who despises me.

I do not mean to be insulting and please take these words with the honest intention with which they were written. I mean this as no slight on your character whatsoever, only that we may not be suited.

I have no desire to injure you or embarrass you. As yet, the engagement has not been announced to my family, and unless you have announced it, you may withdraw without consequence. I certainly would not hold it against you. However, if you wish to continue as planned, you have my word that I will say no more about the topic and I will endeavor to be a good wife to you.

Sincerely,
Elizabeth Bennet

After the third reading, Darcy was incensed. He quickly dashed off a reply and sent it immediately.

~

Two days later, Elizabeth received a letter. She recognized Darcy's neat hand and quickly broke the seal.

Elizabeth,

We will proceed as planned.

Darcy

CHAPTER 12

In London, Darcy was in a fine state. What had she been thinking? Not suited? They were perfectly suited! Why did she think he had chosen her? Because she had a fine figure and a pretty face? Surely she must know he had seen many pretty faces but had never been tempted to propose marriage before. He knew she was sheltered and young, but surely she knew she wasn't the only pretty girl of his acquaintance?

After two days of ranting and silently questioning his own sanity—who desires to marry a penniless woman that does not desire to marry him?—Darcy decided to give her questions the benefit of rational thought. She had said her justice could not allow her doubts to go unspoken. Well, his justice could not allow her questions to go unexamined. After careful thought and deliberation, he came to the same conclusion he had all the other times he had thought about marrying Elizabeth Bennet. The advantages far outweighed any negatives. Yes, they were unfamiliar with each other, but that would change with time. He believed they truly were suited and he knew his feelings would not fade. They had only grown stronger since he'd met her last autumn and that was without being in her presence.

Once he had seen her in Kent, his feelings had grown enormously, to the point he could hardly think of anything else. He knew this part of it all, this fever of the heart, would not, could not, last forever, but he also knew that the abiding care he felt for her was long lasting and that his enjoyment of her presence was unlikely to diminish with time. He could only imagine how much more he would come to enjoy her when they were permitted to spend unlimited amounts of time together, undisturbed and unchaperoned. He imagined that once they were fully intimate with one another, there would be an unshakeable bond between them, in addition to the increase of feelings and pleasure in her company such closeness would necessarily bring.

Still, she should not have tried to cry off. Or to convince him to do it for her. It was cowardly of her. His pride told him to let her worry about it for a while and hopefully that would teach her not to try to break a promise, especially with him. A smaller, quieter part of him was very worried about her actions and the thoughts that must have led to them. Her obvious lack of attachment to him was surprisingly disturbing. What would it mean for their future together? Her father had told him she did not love him as he loved her, as was only right, but her lack of devotion was worrying.

Alas, his pride won out and he did not send her another letter for nearly a fortnight, letting her bask in the uncertainty she was sure to be feeling.

~

Elizabeth spent the next few days in constant fear of the repercussions of her actions. What had she been thinking? Why did she write that letter? She simply hadn't been able to resist an opportunity to escape what she saw as an untenable situation. She had promised her father she would accept him, but if Mr. Darcy wanted to be released, she would not hold him. Truly, she was terrified of the future and angry over being forced into such a situation. Of course she would try to change her circumstances! Mr. Darcy was not the sort of man she had thought to marry, and she was terribly afraid her future would hold very little in the way of joy.

She had to admit to also feeling guilty about receiving his letter and affections. Mr. Darcy clearly felt strongly for her. And she was angry at him for feeling that way. What right did he have to come into her peaceful world and fall in love with her? To force her hand by speaking to her father before herself? To be so rich her father couldn't refuse?

She had no way of knowing if his feelings were lasting or not, but *he* certainly believed they were. She read his letter with some measure of repulsion and increasing embarrassment, as if it was written for someone else and she was trespassing in a most intimate way. She couldn't allow him to humiliate himself by continuing to speak and write to her in such a way, believing that she at least welcomed his affections even if she didn't return them. It was all too much!

And now she had angered him. She had angered the man who would have ultimate power over her in a matter of weeks. The settlement had arrived shortly before Darcy's letter and her father had happily signed it.

It was done. Her mother and sisters had been told and she had an appointment with a dressmaker that afternoon. There was no turning back now.

But instead of marrying a man who loved her and wished to please her, she would marry a man who was angry at her and likely had no desire to please her at all; a man whom she had humiliated and attempted to jilt. What had she been thinking? Stupid, stupid, girl. Wretched, wretched mistake!

~

After a week had passed, and he had calmed enough to think about it clearly, Darcy wondered that she just didn't break the engagement herself. He thought she either wasn't brave enough to do it herself and wanted the decision taken away from her, though he doubted that was likely, or she feared her family, namely her father, would not support her if she did. He thought the latter was more probable until he was at a dinner with his Fitzwilliam cousins and, quite by accident, heard a lady sharing her concerns about marriage with a group of women and how little a lady knew a man before being completely in his power. The lady had expressed her fears about accepting a proposal on short acquaintance and before he heard more, he'd walked away, but it did make him think that a large part of Elizabeth's reasoning might have been based in fear. Of the unknown, and chiefly of him, and what life with him would be like.

She did not know him. She had said in her letter that he did not know her well, and perhaps he didn't know her in the way she thought he should, but he had spent countless hours observing her in a variety of situations and felt he really did know her. Not as well as he would once they had lived together for a time, but well enough. And that was when he realized she did not feel the same about him.

She had not spent hours observing him. It was not in her nature to observe without engaging and she was much younger than he. She likely did not know what to look for. She had not spent endless evenings in drawing rooms with desperate would-be husbands fawning for her attention. She did not have his experience with society or with the world at large. She would not know how he compared to other men. The only men she knew were in Hertfordshire's limited society. She could not help but think his feelings similar to her own. She did not know him well or feel secure in her choice, so she assumed he must feel the same.

Well, he did not.

After a few more days had passed, his anger with her had faded and he found compassion for her. She would be thrust into a new role and a new place with a man she felt was nearly a stranger. She could not know the depth of his feelings—he had not told her. She could not know his reputation for kindness and integrity—they were not from the same circles. She could not know he intended to support her in whatever way she needed and to do his utmost to be an exemplary husband. She had seen poor examples and could not know her future was much brighter than her mother's.

She would see. He would show her.

~

Twelve days. Elizabeth had received Mr. Darcy's brief reply to her letter twelve days ago, but he had yet to send a longer missive. She assumed he had been in contact with her father, at least in regard to signing the settlement, but for whatever reason, though she likely knew the reason perfectly well, he was not communicating with her. Elizabeth was in a state of anxiety beyond anything she had experienced before. The documents were signed, the date was set, the announcement had been sent to all her family. It was done—she was as good as married now. Breaking an official engagement was nearly impossible and would be humiliating in the extreme. She couldn't think of doing such a thing, even if she thought her father would support her, and she was sure he would not.

After another restless night and no word from her betrothed, she concluded he was not going to send her a lengthier letter. The questions she'd dreaded were clearly not coming. Deciding she had to do something, she sat down to write a letter to Mr. Darcy. She had said she would say nothing more about their lack of suitability and endeavor to be a good wife to him, and so she would. Starting now.

Dear Mr. Darcy,

How is London? I hope your business is being seen to satisfactorily. (This is ridiculous, but what else can I start with?) How is your sister? I cannot wait to meet her. I hope we shall be good friends. (And I dearly hope she is not as proud and awful as Mr. Wickham said she is. I could not bear two Darcys staring at me all day long.)

Margate is just as pleasant as I hoped it would be. I walk along the shore daily. (Really, Elizabeth, could you be more dull?) I'm afraid I have become quite tan! I hope you will not mind a brown bride overmuch. Mama is constantly telling me to carry a parasol and stay out of the sun, but when the light is dancing on the water so prettily, I cannot be bothered with such mundane details as parasols.

My sister Catherine has become quite enamored of the birds near a small pier. She feeds them old bread and some of them have come close enough to actually eat out of her hand! I have never seen the like of it. I tried the same myself, but the birds would not come so close to me. Perhaps they know that I would reach out to pet them would they venture so near. Catherine has always had a way with animals. She has been sketching them ceaselessly since we arrived. I have included her drawing of the marmalade cat that sits in our back garden. I have taken to calling him Felix and sneak him fish scraps after dinner. He is a delightfully fat thing and makes the sweetest purring sound when I scratch behind his ears. I haven't enjoyed such simple pleasures since I was a child. I am very glad my father has taken this house for the summer. Everyone is so much more relaxed than they usually are—the sea air appears to be working its magic on the Bennet family.

Have you ever been to the sea? What a question! I'm sure a man such as you, who has lived in the world, has seen a great many things. (This may be the most boring letter ever written. Think of something interesting to say or quit torturing the poor man!) Do you want to know something scandalous? You must promise not to tell my mother, for she would never let me hear the end of it. Yesterday, while out walking, I removed my shoes and stockings and walked barefoot in the sand. It felt delightful under my feet! I even picked up my skirt and walked into the water. It was like nothing I've ever felt before. It was soft and foaming and cool all at the same time. I laughed in sheer delight. I'm sure the children playing nearby thought I had lost my senses. But, oh! It was so lovely!

I am wanted by my mother so I must close now. (She spent a good three minutes thinking of how to end her letter.) Give my best to your sister.

E. B.

P. S. You mentioned The Lakes in a previous letter. Are you planning a journey thither? Might I know when? I have always longed to see The Lakes!

It was not the most riveting letter she'd ever written, but she supposed it would have to do. She sanded and blotted it, pressed her seal into the wax, and sent it on its way. Hopefully it would buy her some measure of good will with her future husband.

~

Darcy received Elizabeth's letter with a mixture of confusion and trepidation. He had been working on his own letter to her, wondering what he should say and how they should proceed. He was even considering a trip to Margate to spend time with her. Slightly appalled at how desperately he wanted to know what was written, and more importantly the tone of her letter and whether or not she was jilting him, he broke the seal and began to read. He scanned through it quickly, looking for words like "break," "engagement," and "sorry." Happily, he found none and leaned back to read it more slowly.

It was obvious that she was unsure what she should say to him, but she did seem to be keeping her word in regards to not talking about her attempt to end their betrothal. He was pleased and happy she was enjoying a season of relaxation with her family before he carried her off to Derbyshire. He recognized a bit of her liveliness in her words and thought she simply needed to accustom herself to the idea of their being wed. It probably hadn't helped that immediately following their engagement they'd separated. If they had been able to stay together, even for just a few days, she probably would have felt less odd about it all.

He picked up his pen to reply to her.

Dearest Elizabeth,
Dear Elizabeth,

I am pleased to hear you are enjoying the seaside. I have many fond memories of visiting the shore with my family as a lad. (Great, Darcy, bore her to tears why don't you?) *~~I am glad you have this time with your family prior to the wedding. Derbyshire is a great distance from Hertfordshire and you aren't likely to see them often.~~* (Seriously, old man? Are you trying to frighten her? "Come away to my dungeon in the north. You'll never see anyone you love again." Stupid man!)

As regards the Lake District, I thought we might take our wedding trip there. I remember you saying you'd always wanted to see the area and thought it would be an ideal location. We can spend the first few days in London, then begin the journey north. We can return to Pemberley afterward and remain there until the spring. I spoke of it to your father and he thought it a good plan. Mayhap your family will join us in the autumn or perhaps for the festive season. I shall leave that to you and your father to decide.

Georgiana was asking about you again—you are one of her favorite topics of conversation—and I realized I do not know when your birthday is. Nor do I know precisely how old you are. Please oblige me with these details as well as what sort of gifts you prefer and whether you favor Mozart over Saleiri.

I hope to complete my business in town within the next fortnight, and then perhaps I will join you in Margate. Until then, I remain,

Yours,

F. Darcy

Darcy satisfied himself that it was a passable effort and that it would have to do. He made a fair copy, put the old one in the drawer of his desk, and put it on the pile of outgoing mail.

~

Elizabeth opened Darcy's letter with more than a little nervousness. She had no idea how he would receive her letter, or if he was even willing to be civil with her after what she had suggested. It was with great relief that she read his lines and noticed he seemed to be putting it behind him, just as she had. It would seem they were going to pretend it had never happened. Only, she did notice there were no endearments in this letter. Of course, she hadn't really expected them. What man makes love to a woman who has just asked to be released from their engagement? But still, she wondered if she had damaged something irreparably and what the consequences would be. She was no expert on marriage, but she did think a husband who loved his wife was likely to be much kinder than one who did not.

Deciding there was nothing she could do about it at present, she set to writing her reply.

Dear Mr. Darcy,

The Lakes sound like a wonderful idea for a wedding trip! I long to see them! Thank you for arranging it—it is very thoughtful of you. As for answers to your questions, my birthdate is the fourteenth of July. Mayhap I will celebrate this year in the Lake District? That sounds like a charming gift to me. My exact age should remain a mystery, as no woman likes such information spread abroad, but if you can keep it to yourself I will tell you. This summer I shall attain my majority. There. Now you know I am but twenty years of age to your—well, isn't this odd? It would seem I do not know how old you are, either. Now, sir, I do think it only fair that you tell me forthwith since I was gracious enough to provide you with the same information about myself. Men are never so secretive about their ages, anyway.

While you are divulging personal information, would you be so kind as to tell me your favorite color and scent and your favorite dishes? My mother would like to know. Not that I am uninterested, but if I am going to ask questions, I would prefer to know your favorite book and which pastimes you prefer. Do you favor riding over shooting? Do you like to fish? My uncle is very fond of it, but it has always seemed frightfully dull to me, though perhaps I am missing something of import.

Papa has sent for more music from town and I am learning a new Mozart concerto. I prefer him to most composers, though if I am being honest I must admit to dearly loving Scotch airs. They always feel light and happy and never fail to leave me smiling. In answer to your other question, I do not know what sort of gifts I prefer—the thoughtful kind, I suppose. I do not need expensive jewels or extravagant parties—though a room full of friends is always enjoyable. My favorite gift to date is a necklace from my uncle. He was on a business trip to Spain, many years ago, and he saw an intricately carved locket in a small shop in some out of the way place. He said it immediately made him think of me and as the next day was my birthday, he bought it. I hung it on a ribbon and wore it daily for years until the hinge broke. I'm sure it was not too expensive, though it was beautifully done, but my uncle was right—it was ideally suited to me. Perhaps that is one of the reasons I loved it so much. It proved to me just how well he knew me. I'd suspected and I knew we shared a special bond—he is my godfather as well as my uncle—but this added proof was very welcome.

I am wanted by my mother so I must close.

Faithfully,
Elizabeth Bennet

She questioned somewhat her closing, but she thought it a measure of goodwill and decided to leave it. Before she posted it, she went to her father in the parlor and asked if he would like to add a note to her letter.

"No, I sent Mr. Darcy a letter two days ago. I am not so forlorn for correspondence that I already feel the need to write again."

Elizabeth smiled and sat next to him on the settee. "Father, has Mr. Darcy spoken to you about the wedding trip?"

"Yes, he has. He wishes to take you to The Lakes; he remembered you'd mentioned wanting to see them."

"Yes, that part I know and it is very kind of him." She ignored the very pointed look her father was giving her. "I was wondering who is to accompany us? Did you discuss it?"

At this Mr. Bennet lost his teasing smile and looked grave for a moment. "We did. I asked him if his own sister would perform the job or one of your own. He said he would rather you go just the two of you," her brows raised to her hairline, "and I said we could discuss it later. Shall I take it from your expression that you do not favor the idea of a month long tête–à–tête?"

She chose her words carefully. "I have done as you asked and tried to see Mr. Darcy through new eyes, and I admit that he is a great deal more amiable than I would have thought, at least in his letters, but I am not comfortable with spending such prolonged time in each other's sole company, with nothing to keep us occupied." Mr. Bennet raised his brows and Elizabeth felt herself blushing to the roots of her hair. "I mean, no estate business or calls to make. We will be quite at our leisure and I fear the proximity will do more harm than good."

"You may be correct, though of course there is no way to know for certain. It is possible the lack of other companions will force you to converse in ways and on topics you might otherwise not, creating a greater closeness significantly sooner than would otherwise be expected. And of course it is entirely possible that you will meet some of Mr. Darcy's acquaintance whilst there; he does have a much broader circle than we do. And you can always make friends anywhere."

Elizabeth nodded. "True, but is it not also likely the added intimacy will prove overwhelming and lead to a heightened sense of anxiety, making it difficult to become truly friends and leave us on edge and snapping at each other? We barely know one another!"

"True, all true, but we cannot know for certain. If you could, who would you like to accompany you? A sister usually does the job, and you have plenty to choose from, though I'm sure your mother would perform the service if you asked." He laughed aloud at the look on his daughter's face.

"I would prefer to take Jane. If anyone could provide comfort and sensible advice during this time, it is she, but I do not know if it is a wise idea."

He nodded. "In what way, exactly?"

"In every way! Jane is having such a lovely time here at the shore, I would hate to pull her away."

"Would she not have a lovely time at The Lakes?"

"And she was getting along so well with Mr. Parker and had seen Mr. Bingley," Elizabeth continued. "As it stands, she will be back in London the week of the wedding. Who knows what will happen then? What if Mr. Bingley renews his courtship and aunt and uncle invite her to stay again, or he decides to follow her here? Margate is a much easier distance."

"Do we even know if either gentleman will be in town? Mr. Parker is likely to be there, due to his business, but do you know Mr. Bingley's plans?"

Her shoulders slumped. "No."

"Is Mr. Bingley not Mr. Darcy's closest friend? Might endearing your sister to her new brother reap greater rewards in that quarter?"

"I suppose it could. So you believe Jane should accompany me?"

"No! Of course not!"

Elizabeth looked surprised at his vehement response, then smiled when she saw the gleam in his eyes.

"Who will I converse with if my two eldest abandon me to run away to The Lakes?"

Elizabeth laughed aloud. "Oh, Father! We would never abandon you. Mr. Darcy said I could have the family to visit in the autumn, or perhaps over Christmas. What do you think of that? Jane and I could go to The Lakes, then on to Pemberley. In October, you could all join us there?" She grew excited at the prospect and he almost couldn't resist her broad smile.

"I do not know, child. I must speak to your mother. We will have already been from home quite some time. I will need to wait until after the harvest." Mr. Bennet was not insensible to the benefits to be reaped from spending a month or more at his wealthy son-in-law's home. The money they would save on food alone would be impressive, not to mention the reduced staff.

"Please come, father, at least for a little while. I will be so far from home and everything will be so new."

Her voice was small and Mr. Bennet felt deeply for his daughter. She would be facing so many new challenges, and all because he had asked her to, because he had failed to plan appropriately and allow his daughter to marry a man she cared for, or at least one with whom she was comfortable. Her distress was a sharp point in his otherwise happy manner and he readily agreed.

"Of course, my dear. We will come to you in your new home. Your papa will not abandon you." He looked at her seriously for a moment and furrowed his brow. "I know you will rise to the occasion, no matter the situation. I have the utmost faith in you."

Her smile was a little wobbly as she thanked him and reached to give him a hug before saying she needed to see the sea one more time before sundown and practically ran down to the beach in an effort to forget the tumult of her present life.

CHAPTER 13

Darcy read Elizabeth's letter with an increasingly growing smile. She was sounding more like her old self. All would be well. Elizabeth had said nothing about a traveling companion. Perhaps she was warming to the idea of being alone together; or her father had spoken to her. Either way, he was closer than ever to bringing home his bride, and he couldn't remember the last time he'd felt so happy.

On his way home from the club that afternoon, Darcy stopped into a small jewelry store. He wandered around, looking from display to display, hoping something would jump out at him. After Elizabeth's tale of her favorite gift from the uncle who knew her so well, he'd been able to think of little else but doing the same. He would buy her a gift that would suit her perfectly and she would realize how well he knew her, how well-matched they were, and it would have the added bonus of increasing her affection for him. This was a great responsibility to place on one tiny gift, and just when he thought he'd found the right thing, something else would catch his eye. In the end, the pressure of choosing something so perfect proved to be too much and he left the store in a frustrated huff.

He walked along Bond Street and made a stop at his tailor, as had been arranged, for a final fitting of his wedding coat. He was wearing blue. His sister had assured him that it was fashionable but he wouldn't look like a dandy and the color was very complementary to his complexion. He'd agreed and wondered what Elizabeth was wearing. She hadn't mentioned it in her letters. He hoped they would look well together, then immediately chastised himself for such a dandified thought.

As he was walking to his carriage, he passed a small hat shop that had a display of hair combs in the window. A pair caught his eye and he stepped closer. They had a cluster of small blue flowers—he didn't know what kind, and he thought them very pretty and very like Elizabeth. Simple, beautiful, sweet, not seeking attention but sparkling just the same. He quickly stepped inside and bought the combs and had them wrapped and was on his way home in five minutes, a curious smile on his face.

Before he could become distracted, he closed himself in his study to write a letter to his betrothed.

Dearest Elizabeth,

I hope you are well. I'm so glad you are pleased with going to The Lakes. I think you will enjoy them immensely. I have borrowed a house from a friend of mine, John Lansdowne. He has an ideal place just off the shore of Lake Windermere and has agreed to allow us the use of it for a month. I have visited it twice before—it is a comfortable house and has a sweeping view of the lake as it is settled on a bit of a rise. There is a small boat that we can use to go out on the water. There is also an island not too far off shore that we could picnic on if you'd like.

In answer to your question, I do enjoy fishing. I'm sure someone as lively as yourself would find it incredibly dull, but I have always found it relaxing. There are no pressing matters needing my attention, no disputes for me to settle or stewards to discuss business with. It is best early in the morning when the day is still and I can watch the forest around the stream awaken. There is a particularly good fishing spot about one and one half miles from the house. It is in a small glade where the water swells. Many of the animals come there for a drink and if you sit very still, the deer will approach the stream without a look in your direction. My father took me there as a boy; I cannot wait to show it to you. I am sure you would find it a peaceful place to escape with a good book.

I cannot wait to show you Pemberley. I know you will love it. There are paths and trails abounding—I'm sure even you will be satisfied with them. We should arrive there in August and you will be able to see it in all its summer glory.

I know it is dull, but there is some business that must be settled. I was speaking with my housekeeper about your imminent arrival and she wished to know if you will be bringing your maid with you. Also, will you be bringing a horse? I shall alert the stables if you intend to. If you do not, I will have to find you a suitable mount. Do you have any preferences? I believe there is a horse in Pemberley's stables that will suit until a new one can be procured, but I should like you to have a new mount if you do not wish to bring your own.

I still do not know the color of your gown. I am choosing to see it as a small oversight and not a deliberate attempt to be mysterious, though I am sure you will be lovely whatever you wear. Georgiana insisted I wear blue, and so a new coat has been made in that color. I hope it will suit—G is desperately worried that we will clash.

Yours,
F. Darcy

~

Elizabeth had mixed emotions on reading his latest. She seemed back in his good graces, which was of course a good thing, and though he was a touch high handed, he wasn't too offensive. She decided being her usual lively, impertinent self was the right thing to do. After all, if he had fallen in love with her, it was not because she flattered and flirted with him. He must have seen something he liked and she saw no reason to alter what was clearly working in her favor.

Dear Mr. Darcy,

I can assure you I would never attempt to be mysterious, and if I were, I would probably not be very successful at it! I did not tell you the color of my dress because in my usual fashion, I waited until the absolute last moment to choose the fabric. The style came easily enough, but the color was very contentious. My mother and I could not agree, not a terribly unusual occurrence, and I was being stubborn as I often am. Please consider yourself duly warned, sir! I can be terribly mule-like when it comes to the color of my gowns! You should be pleased to hear that we finally settled on a light blue, so I am sure we shall look fine together. Mother says it matches my eyes and refuses to believe me when I tell her they are more green than blue. She has her heart set on five blue eyed daughters and will not hear a word otherwise.

Though Mary's have been positively hazel since she was three, but you did not hear that from me.

Now, about this horse business. I am happy that you wish me to begin my new life with a new horse, but I must tell you that I am no horsewoman and beg you not to go to any expense on that front. I'm sure whatever docile creature you have in the stables will do. I am really not very skilled and a fine animal would be wasted on me.

I do not intend to bring my maid. I share her with my sisters Jane and Mary, and I am sure they would not appreciate me taking her from them. Perhaps your housekeeper has a suggestion? Maybe one of the housemaids can be trained up for the position? Forgive me if I am overstepping, but I have noticed that promoting from within has always done well for the spirits and loyalty of the staff.

Now, for my favorite topic: The Lakes! I cannot tell you how I look forward to it. I'm sure your friend's house will be lovely and a picnic on an island sounds like perfection. I have been meaning to ask you whom you intend to accompany us. I had thought to ask my sister Jane, but she is needed by our parents here. My sister Mary would possibly like to go, but I wanted to speak with you before I invited her. Had you intended to invite your sister? I do not know if she is yet out. How old is she?

And might I remind you, sir, you never told me your age! I do not like to be kept in ignorance on such a subject. And I still do not know your favorite meals. And, most grievous of all, I do not know your given name. I am embarrassed to admit it, but I do not, and I would be mortified to ask my father and admit to my ignorance. If it was ever mentioned in Hertfordshire I have forgotten, and your aunt and cousin always called you 'Darcy'. I know it begins with an 'F', but that is the extent of my knowledge. So in two weeks' time, I am to marry a man whose name and age I do not know, and whom I shall likely feed inedible meals because he will not tell me if he prefers venison to mutton. For shame! I must insist you rectify these mistakes, at once, sir!

Impertinently Yours,
Elizabeth Bennet

~

My Dear Elizabeth,

I will wait upon you as soon as possible and answer all your questions. We cannot have you walking down the aisle in ignorance, now can we? I shall be right behind this letter.

F.D.

Elizabeth looked up from reading this latest to see her father entering the room, followed by Mr. Darcy.

"Mr. Darcy!" She stood hastily and his letter dropped from her hand. He quickly stepped in front of her and picked it up while she gave a hasty curtsey.

"Hello, Elizabeth," he said warmly.

She felt her cheeks flush. Smiling nervously, she said, "Hello, Mr. Darcy."

"Fitzwilliam."

"Hmm?"

"Please, call me Fitzwilliam. It is my given name."

"Oh! Oh, of course, Fitzwilliam," she said shyly.

He smiled. "Would you care to take a walk?"

"My father…," she looked around, suddenly realizing her father had left them alone. Again. "Yes, a walk would be nice."

She led him out of the house and down to the shore. They walked along silently for a few minutes before he spoke.

"How are you?"

"I am well. And you? Was your journey pleasant?"

"Yes, perfectly uneventful. We made excellent time," he replied.

She nodded and continued looking at the ground.

"Is there nothing you wish to say? No questions for me?"

She could tell by the look on his face what sort of questions he had in mind. Would that dratted letter follow her forever? "No sir, I said I would say no more about it, and I shan't."

"Truly?"

"A lady keeps her word, sir," she said, slightly offended.

"Very well, then. But please allow me to say, Elizabeth, I have the greatest faith in our felicity. We are well suited, truly, and I can assure you I will be the best of husbands to you. You will have no cause to repine."

She blushed at the ardent look on his face. "Neither shall you."

He smiled, nodded, and tucked her arm into his.

"Do you have many engagements this week?" he asked.

"Not many, no. We are due at a neighbor's for tea and cards this evening, and there is an assembly Thursday. I am sure you will not be expected to attend. Where are you staying?"

"At the Dorcester."

"I've heard it's beautiful inside."

"Yes, it is." He paused and looked down at her. "I have something for you." He reached into his pocket and pulled out a small box.

She took it awkwardly and thanked him.

"Aren't you going to open it?" he asked.

She smiled uneasily and pulled the top off the small box. Inside were two shining blue hair combs. They were very pretty and not gaudy, thankfully, but neither were they a style she favored.

"Thank you, it's very kind of you. It really isn't necessary to buy me gifts."

"I enjoy giving them to you." He waited for her to extol the virtues of the gift and by extension, himself, but the words never came. She slid the small box into the pocket of her dress and continued walking as if nothing had just occurred between them.

Darcy was confused.

"I made the mistake of bringing bread for the birds once," she said. "I was completely surrounded. I had to hurry back to the house." She laughed as she told the story and he smiled tightly.

Is she really not going to say anything at all?

They continued on in silence, him deciding not to think about the gift anymore and her looking towards the water with a distant look on her face. After a lengthy silence, Darcy spoke.

"Would your mother allow you to stay behind this evening? I assume your younger sisters will remain?"

"I do not know. Kitty was going to accompany us this evening to visit with the daughter of the house. Lydia is not much of a chaperone," she said awkwardly.

"Your father will not mind. I shall speak to him when we return," he said decidedly.

She was shocked by his presumption, but quickly dismissed the feeling. Why should she be shocked? Had he not always done what pleased him exactly when it pleased him and expected everyone to go along with his plan? Even his own cousin had been at Mr. Darcy's mercy. If a colonel in His Majesty's army and the son of an earl was no proof against his high-handedness, what chance had she? She, merely a Miss Bennet of Longbourn, a small estate in the country. How could she expect him to consider her in his plans? How could she expect him to allow her to make decisions as simple as whether she would stay home or go out?

She took a deep breath and said, "I do not know if my mother can spare me this evening, though I'm sure you would be welcome to join us if you'd like." *Though they are likely too low for you to suffer their company.*

"I do not desire company after a journey, but I thank you for the invitation."

Then why do you not stay alone? Why insist on my company? Oh, that's right! I am no longer 'company', but will soon be simply an extension of yourself. Of course! How could I have been so silly!

She nodded and walked on, stopping to pick up a smooth stone and hurl it into the water. Darcy watched her silently for several minutes, an odd feeling intruding on his notice. He could not place what it was exactly, but Elizabeth seemed unhappy. Why? They had been getting along so well in their letters. He'd convinced himself her attempt to cry off had simply been bridal jitters and maidenly fears. Clearly she was growing more accustomed to him, or so she seemed in her letters. In person, she was still a bit uneasy, but was that not to be expected after a month's separation and the eventful time they were in? She would grow used to his presence in time, just like she had grown used to him in their correspondence. He just needed to continue to show her affection and kindness and she would grow in ease and affection for him.

By now they had turned back and were nearing the path to the Bennet cottage. He caught her hand as she turned away to go up the stone steps leading away from the shore.

"Elizabeth?"

"Yes?"

He squeezed her hand. "Know that I will do anything within my power to make you comfortable—I will do anything for your happiness. You must know this."

She nodded and smiled just a little, then looked ahead and quickened her pace.

After speaking briefly with her father, Darcy went to his hotel and Elizabeth sat down with a book before preparing for dinner. Mrs. Bennet had invited Darcy to join them, of course, and he had readily agreed. He had spoken with her father. After dinner, the remainder of her family would go to the neighbors for cards while she and Mr. Darcy stayed behind with Lydia. The latter was not in any way a deterrent to the couple spending time alone together, and Mr. Darcy seemed very pleased with his achievement while Elizabeth felt mildly queasy.

She did not know that her father could hardly say no to Mr. Darcy, knowing that his family would be entirely in the young man's power in a matter of months. Mr. Bennet wished for Mr. Darcy to think of his family with affection and ease, as accommodating and kind people, not as cantankerous fathers and difficult relations. Darcy was exactly what he had been looking for. A trifle serious perhaps, but that was not necessarily a bad thing. He had enough money to take care of his favorite well and to take care of his widow if it came to it. He would expose the family to a wider circle of acquaintance and the connection would ensure better marriages for the other girls.

Darcy was measured, intelligent, and not afraid of difficult tasks, something that would serve him well in his marriage and in raising his own children. Bennet also thought it would be very useful once he was gone, since he did not trust Mrs. Bennet to keep Lydia in line. The young girl had improved immensely, but she was still wild at heart, and he knew as soon as the firm hand was removed, she would revert to her previous ways. He hoped the impression was lasting and that it would not change easily, but he was too realistic to believe that would come to pass.

Mr. Darcy was an answer to a most fervent prayer. He could be nothing but grateful. He hoped his daughter would realize it in time.

~

Darcy headed to the Bennet cottage shortly after changing for dinner. His plan was to help Elizabeth to know him better and thereby set her at ease about their impending marriage. He was sure that once she felt more comfortable with him, the idea of sharing his life would be one that made her happy instead of trepidatious. He was still insulted she had tried to end the engagement—what man wouldn't be? But he was wise enough to know that what he loved about her was her energy and liveliness and that if she was frightened of him, or of the idea of marriage with him, those qualities would diminish.

So he set about making her easy with him.

~

Dinner came before Elizabeth was prepared to face her betrothed, but she had no choice in the matter. Time marched on, and so did Mrs. Bennet. She made Elizabeth try on no fewer than three dresses before settling on the first that Elizabeth had chosen before her mother's intrusion. Her hair was curled, plaited, and woven into an intricate style that was much too fancy for a family dinner at home. After her mother left the room, having given her daughter extensive instructions on how to behave when Mr. Darcy arrived and all the things she *must not* say, Elizabeth accidentally pulled several of the pins out of her hair and Jane had to help her put it back up in a much simpler style.

The two eldest Bennet sisters stepped into the drawing room just as Mr. Darcy's carriage pulled into the drive, leaving Mrs. Bennet only a few moments to glare at and berate her second daughter, though it must be said that she was significantly less strident than she had been in the past.

Mr. Darcy entered the room to curtseys from the five Bennet women present and a shallow bow from Mr. Bennet.

Mrs. Bennet stepped forward to greet him. "Welcome, Mr. Darcy. Please, sit here next to Elizabeth. She looks charming tonight, does she not?"

"Yes, she does." He smiled and sat between Elizabeth and her mother.

"That dress is particularly becoming, don't you think? Elizabeth has excellent taste in colors. She always chooses just the right one to flatter her complexion."

Darcy caught Elizabeth's eye for a moment and she had to bite her cheek to stifle a smirk. Darcy winked at her and turned to her mother. "A talent she gets from her mother, no doubt."

"Oh, Mr. Darcy, you are too kind." She tittered and began a conversation with Jane, her motherly duties complete for the moment.

Darcy faced Elizabeth and smiled. "How are you this evening, Elizabeth?"

She was still a little startled from his having winked at her. Mr. Darcy, *winking*! "I am well, Mr. Darcy." He raised a brow. "Fitzwilliam," she added quietly.

They spoke of inconsequential things; music, the weather, an opera

Darcy had seen while in town, until they were called in to dinner and the conversation continued and included her father and Jane. The two men carried on a lively conversation of books, each a little surprised that they had several favorites in common. Elizabeth watched her betrothed speaking to her father comfortably, a look of ease on both their faces. Her father's expression was missing its usual wry humor and she knew he was genuinely enjoying conversing with Darcy and was not silently laughing behind his eyes. In that moment, she felt a greater hope than she had felt throughout her engagement. It was not happiness, not exactly, but a feeling that she *might* be happy in the future, that there was at least a chance it might happen.

She felt lighter than she had in weeks and laughed with her sisters, occasionally chiming in on the men's conversation. When she made intelligent comments, Darcy would look at her with a certain light in his eyes and smile, and she felt a warmth towards him she had hitherto never felt before.

Soon enough dinner was over and the Bennets left for their card party. Elizabeth led Darcy to the parlor where she sat on a settee near the window. He sat next to her, not too close, and laid his hand beside hers on the seat.

"I enjoyed dinner very much," he said.

"I am glad. My mother will be pleased. She enjoys hosting."

"She was a very able hostess and the meal was quite fine, but I enjoyed the company more."

She smiled warmly at him and he could not resist placing his hand over hers on the cushion.

"Elizabeth, you are lovely," he said softly, his body turned in her direction.

She blushed and looked down. "You flatter me, Mr. Darcy."

"I speak the truth. And my name is Fitzwilliam."

She laughed. "Yes, I've noticed you've wasted no time at all calling me Elizabeth."

"What do you mean?"

"Simply that as soon as I accepted your proposal, I was Elizabeth to you. You have not called me Miss Bennet or Miss Elizabeth once. You are very good at the proprieties, Mr. Darcy," she said teasingly.

"Not all the proprieties, Miss Bennet." She raised a brow in question and he looked around the empty room, raising his own brow in response.

She flushed again, annoyed at herself for this ridiculous tendency, and answered, "Touché, Fitzwilliam."

He smiled when she said his name and scooted a little closer, moving their joined hands to his knee. "Propriety has its place, but there are times when it should be set aside."

"Really? Like when?"

"When a man desperately wishes to kiss his betrothed."

Her mouth formed a silent 'O' and she looked at him wide-eyed, her mouth going just a little dry.

"Elizabeth," he whispered, leaning closer and closer until looking at him made her eyes cross. She closed her eyes and the next thing she knew there was a warm, soft sensation on her lips, and then it was over.

"Oh," she said after opening her eyes.

He smiled and squeezed her hand. "I am pleased to be your first kiss."

"How do you know you are my first kiss?"

"Some things are evident, my dear."

She flushed in embarrassment and looked away, saying indignantly, "Would you prefer a woman who kissed every man she came across?" He laughed. A deep, happy sound that echoed across the empty room. She stood to leave. "I am glad you are amused, Mr. Darcy. Excuse me." But was stopped by his hand grasping hers.

"Don't be angry, darling. Come here." He pulled her down next to him on the sofa and she went grudgingly, her body small and stiff next to his. He couldn't help chuckling again and turned her chin gently towards him. He stroked her cheek softly as his laughter faded and she eventually raised her eyes to his. He traced his fingers over her lips and looked at her questioningly. "May I?"

She nodded reluctantly and he leaned in, pressing a kiss to the corner of her mouth, first one and then the other, before kissing her more fully. She stayed stiff and immobile, refusing to give him the satisfaction of returning his kiss if he was only going to make fun of her.

He chuckled again and said quietly, "My beautiful, stubborn little woman. You are right." Her eyes snapped to his. "I would not like a woman who kissed every man she came across, but I would like a woman who kissed the one she was engaged to."

He kissed her again, swiftly, and pulled back to smile at her charmingly, as if he knew a great joke that she couldn't possibly understand.

"I am not stubborn," she said, crossing her arms over her chest. He laughed again.

"Whatever you say, my love." He leaned back and crossed one leg over his knee, the very picture of relaxation and comfort, which only vexed Elizabeth more, as she was feeling decidedly tense and uncomfortable.

Taking advantage of his repose, she rose swiftly and crossed the room to the instrument.

"I shall play for you," she said simply.

"Very well," he replied.

"Thank you for the permission," she said sarcastically.

He laughed again, his chest rumbling. Elizabeth began pounding the keys at an awkward volume and kept her eyes on the music. She would not give him the satisfaction of looking at him. Teasing man!

She spent a full forty minutes at the pianoforte, playing songs from memory and eventually taking out the piece she had recently learned and playing it to perfection. She ended with a gentle flourish and leaned back, much calmer and pleased with her efforts.

"That was beautiful," Mr. Darcy said from his place across the room.

His voice was sincere and his smile genuine, so she responded in kind, "Thank you."

He rose suddenly and came toward her. "It's a pleasant evening. Shall we take a turn in the garden?"

She nodded and took his hand to rise, and he placed it on his arm. They walked slowly on the paths near the house, neither saying anything for several minutes.

"What is the schedule for our journey, or is it not yet fixed?" she asked.

"Do you mean the wedding tour itself or the events leading up to it?" he clarified.

"The latter," she replied.

"Well, as I understand it, you will leave for London in six days. Your father says you will stay with a relative in town, though I did offer my home to your family." She nodded. He continued, "I believe the week before the wedding will be largely comprised of shopping to complete your trousseau, though that is your mother's purview. Then we will be wed on the seventeenth at church and there will be a breakfast following." He spoke clearly in a crisp tone, as if reciting his lessons for his tutor. If he had not stroked the back of her hand and pulled her a little closer, she would not have known he had any affection for her at all.

"And after that?" she asked. Her voice sounded thick and choked to her own ears, but he did not seem to notice.

"We shall remain at Darcy House six days and then begin our journey to The Lakes."

She could hear the excitement in his voice, though it was subtle, and a small amount of it transferred to her. She had always wanted to see The Lakes; they would be beautiful regardless of who she was seeing them with. Travel was its own reward and she was sure this would only be the first of many trips. She reminded herself that he was a busy man with a wide acquaintance and she would not be required to be at his beck and call. Surely he would have things to do, letters to write, hopefully friends to visit. And her sister coming with her would make it more bearable. But then, he had requested they travel alone.

"Fitzwilliam?"

"Yes, dear?" He smiled at her warmly.

"I shall have to get used to that."

"Used to what? Being called dear?"

"Well, yes, but I was referring to your smile."

"Pardon me?" he said, clearly confused.

"I have not seen you smile above ten times in all of our acquaintance."

"Truly?"

She nodded. "But today alone you have smiled, or at least looked moderately pleased, nearly your entire visit."

"Shall I flatter you and say it is all down to your enchanting presence?"

"Flattery has its place, but right now I think I'd prefer to hear the truth."

He sighed. "The truth is that when I met you in Hertfordshire, I had just come away from a difficult family situation that had left me frustrated and angry and a great many other things I shouldn't say to a lady." Her face showed surprise and then sympathy, and he gave her a tired smile. "And I'm sure this will not surprise you, but Rosings is not the most relaxing place to visit."

"I don't know what you mean. I found it delightful."

He laughed aloud. "I take it all back. It is absolutely down to you and your lively presence. You make me laugh when I would otherwise brood, and I find you so wholly delightful I cannot help but smile when I see you, nor be anything but pleased when I recall we are to spend the rest of our lives together."

He raised her hand to his lips for a kiss and she blushed, then looked away annoyed. "Fitzwilliam, you are making me blush."

"I know. That is half the fun of complimenting you."

She tried to glare at him but a hint of a smile came through. "What is the other half?"

"Saying it aloud. It is so strong a feeling in me that if I do not say it, it will surely do me harm."

She blushed again, but was not annoyed this time. He led her to a small bench under an arbor and they sat together, their legs touching lightly due to the size of the seat.

"What were you going to ask me?" asked Darcy.

"Hmm?"

"Before we got distracted, you sounded as if you had a question for me."

"Oh, yes, I wanted to talk to you about who would accompany us on our wedding trip. My father said you had mentioned wanting to go alone, but it seemed undecided."

"And you want to know…?" he asked.

"Do you? Wish to go alone? And why?"

"Yes, I do wish to go alone. Because I would like to be with you without anyone else getting in the way."

"In the way? How could my sister be in the way? She is the least obtrusive person I know."

"In the carriage there would be all three of us if your sister came along, but if we went alone, we would have time to talk or rest peacefully. I might take your hand or kiss you without an audience." He took her hand and kissed it as if to show her what the trip would be like.

She was terrified. Did he wish to kiss her the entire journey? It would take days! Surely that wasn't normal. They would get tired, would they not?

"What are you thinking, my love?" he asked.

"Fitzwilliam, surely you do not intend to kiss me for five whole days!"

He laughed at the look of shock on her face. "This may surprise you, dearest, but I intend to kiss you every day of our wedding trip, and every day after we return to Pemberley, and likely every day after that until I am too old to do the job properly, though do not be surprised if I try anyway."

She looked at him in astonishment, wondering who this man in front of her was. He was being charming and funny, and completely unlike the Mr. Darcy she knew. Wickham had said he could be agreeable in company, and she had heard him make witty remarks in Hertfordshire in the autumn, but this blatant merry making, this *happy* man was not one she recognized.

"I am sorry to shock you, my dear. I should not jest about such things. Forgive me," he apologized, looking genuinely sorry and a bit concerned by her lack of response.

"I am not offended, but I thank you for the apology. I am merely surprised, that is all. The Mr. Darcy I knew did not speak with such levity. Nor did he flirt so blatantly."

He smiled. "Perhaps that is because I am Fitzwilliam to you now."

CHAPTER 14

Mrs. Bennet was in a predicament. Her husband had been lovely of late. Indeed, since the winter, he had been kinder and more solicitous of her needs. She found that she enjoyed his quiet company in the evening when he would sit near the fire with a book while she embroidered. He had ceased mocking her with his high-minded jokes that she did not understand. Even Mrs. Bennet knew when she was being mocked, regardless of whether or not she understood the joke itself. His company had been pleasant, his behavior had been amenable, and they had taken several ambling walks along the shore, often at sundown in what she believed was her most flattering light.

Just two nights ago, she was sure he had looked at her with the same softness in his eyes he had used when they were young and newly married. At the time, she was flustered and blushed and continued on with the conversation they were having about their daughters, but it had unnerved her. That night, she had waited for her husband in her chambers, sure he would come to her. She had worn her most flattering nightgown and left her nightcap off, her still bright hair cascading over one shoulder and curling at the ends. But he had not come. Her candle had burned low and she had eventually realized that the door between their chambers was to remain closed. With a sadness she had not expected, she put out her light and went to sleep.

No one could blame her for being a trifle aloof the next day, nor for refusing her husband when he asked her to accompany him on a walk. She avoided him the whole of the day and the following one as well, until she found herself, quite to her surprise, missing his company. And so she joined him for a walk along the beach after dinner, as she had prior to her upset.

Now here she was, brushing her hair out and wishing her husband would come to her but surprised at wishing it. It had been years since they had engaged in such activities, but it was not as if they were in their dotage. She would not be forty until October and she fancied herself still an attractive woman.

He should be happy to be received by her! Mrs. Goulding wasn't half as pretty and a good five years older, and Mrs. Bennet knew for a fact that her husband still visited her regularly. And her sister Phillips, two years her senior, received her husband almost nightly, if her complaints were to be believed. Surely she was a great deal more attractive than either of them! And Mrs. Long! She was over fifty if she was a day! Mrs. Bennet still had beautiful hair and color in her cheeks. Mr. Bennet should appreciate what he had and show his wife the respect she deserved, or at least her beauty deserved.

And so Mrs. Bennet went back and forth between indignation and attraction, wishing her husband would arrive and berating him for not coming. At one point she talked herself into believing that he was showing her respect by not coming to her. After all, everyone knew it was dreadfully unpleasant and only something to be put up with by a dutiful wife. But, after she had decided he was being most kind in not importuning her, she felt a niggling doubt in her mind, in the place she tried to ignore as much as possible, telling her that she really *did* want him to come, at least for a little while.

Deciding it was better to feel flattered by his respect for her in not coming, and knowing she would be equally flattered by his unconquerable desire if he did, she climbed into bed but left her hair down, just in case.

~

Mr. Bennet was in a quandary. His wife had been looking very fetching of late. The sea air brightened her complexion and her eyes were almost always soft and happy now, not frantic and angry like they so often were at Longbourn. She had been less shrill and more patient. She had been a good listener and a fine companion. When he had suffered a headache several days before, she read to him in a soothing voice and placed a cool cloth on his brow. It was quite endearing.

He looked toward the door between their chambers with longing. It had been longer than he could remember since he had lain with his wife, and he was very sorely tempted now. But the physician had explicitly told him to not overexcite himself or put undue strain on his heart. He had felt winded after a long walk the first week they had been at

Margate, and so every day he had added a few steps to his stroll until he was feeling quite healthy. Now, after a full month by the seaside, he felt stronger and more relaxed than ever.

But he knew that nothing compared to loving his wife. It was like a hundred walks along the shore, like climbing a thousand steps. He was not sure his heart could take the exertion and he was not willing to take the risk. But, oh! How he was tempted!

Out of a feeling he was certain was sheer lunacy, he wrote a quick letter to his friend Dr. Withers and asked him explicitly which activities were allowed and which were not. He posted it immediately.

~

Mr. Bennet had never awaited a letter as eagerly as he did the one from his friend Dr. Withers. The first few lines were notes about his general health, what he should be eating and reminding him to avoid spirits. Then, his old friend emerged. He teased Bennet mercilessly about his predicament and how desperately miserable he must be to have such an attractive wife and be frightened to lie with her. Of course, he ended all of this with the advice that if Bennet felt he could traverse a decent distance without becoming winded, if stairs were not an issue for him, and if the lying itself were not too vigorous, he could proceed without undue fear.

Bennet stood at the bottom of the stairs with a look of determination on his face. He had been traversing the steps daily since their arrival, but never with such a goal in mind. He placed one foot on the riser and drew himself up. He felt nothing. He did another, then another, and still nothing. Finally, he took the remainder of the steps in rapid succession, only to arrive at the top slightly winded but not unduly out of breath.

Pleased by his efforts, he promised himself he would try again after tea.

Finally, after three long days of walking greater distances and surreptitiously sneaking off to the stairs, Mr. Bennet was ready. Gathering his nerve, he knocked on the door to his wife's room.

Mrs. Bennet was sitting up in bed, her cap securely in place. She had been just about to turn down the lamp when she heard a knock. A knock from the inner door that led to her husband's room. Startled, she called for her visitor to enter, surprised, yet not, to see her husband coming into her room. For who else could it have been? But she had grown so used to his not coming, she was unprepared for his entrance.

"Mrs. Bennet, Agnes, may I come in?" he asked, feeling foolish over his own nervousness and oddly intimidated by the woman before him. She really was very beautiful. When had he stopped seeing her as such and begun viewing her as merely an amusement to be made sport of? His body deftly reminded him that there were much better things to do with such a woman than laugh at her.

She nodded silently, wondering what he was about and wishing she hadn't put her cap on. She looked so much younger without it. She still had her glorious color, a bright honey shade that reflected light and had started more than one argument amongst her sister and friends on whether it was in fact blonde or a very light brown. Either way, it was much envied and she knew she looked most attractive with it tumbling about her shoulders, her large natural curls winding enticingly down her figure.

He approached the bed slowly, and when he looked down, she quickly snatched the cap off her head.

He smiled at the braid over her shoulder and took her hand in his. "Agnes, may I join you tonight?"

Her eyes widened and she nodded silently, her heart suddenly pounding and nervous flutterings swimming through her middle. She scooted over to make room for him and he climbed in next to her. He extinguished the light, but the curtains were not drawn—Mrs. Bennet liked the sea breeze and the sound of the sea; it soothed her nerves (and she had heard made one look younger), so she had slept with an open window throughout their visit.

Thomas Bennet was thoroughly entranced, and felt himself fully twenty-seven and in bed with his young new wife. The moonlight gave her skin a pleasant glow and the smell of her, so familiar and yet so long forgotten, was soothing and enticing all at once.

He loved her with a dedication to thoroughness she hadn't felt since they were newly wed, and his own desire to not overtax his heart caused him to move slowly, much to his wife's approval. Everything he did was deliberate. He would not waste time on fripperies. He was determined to make every moment count and Agnes Bennet was the lucky beneficiary of his efforts.

When he rose to leave some hours later, Agnes impulsively grabbed his arm and said one word.

"Stay."

He turned around and lay by his wife, sleeping next to her for the first time in over fifteen years."

CHAPTER 15

Elizabeth was vexed when she realized she had spoken to Mr. Darcy about a companion for their journey but that nothing had been settled. She had thought to speak with Jane and ask her what she would wish to do. She did not want to deprive her father of all good company, but Jane might like to go. Of course, she might also say yes only because Elizabeth asked her, so she would have to be careful to make it clear she would be happy to take Mary in her place if Jane would rather stay at the shore.

Of course, Mary had never really traveled anywhere, and she did not have Jane's beauty or sweet spirit. It was possible she would never marry, or not for some time. This might be her only chance for such an experience. Of course, she might attend Jane on her wedding trip, but Elizabeth thought it likely that Jane would love her new husband, or at least like him, and a companion might not be as important to her. At least she had two sisters to choose from. She should speak to Jane and ask her opinion about it all. Her sister's level-headedness would be helpful in her decision.

But what if Mr. Darcy said no? It was the custom for the bride to take a companion on the wedding tour, but he would technically be in control of said tour and her sister would be under his protection for the duration. He could decline if he wished. It would be strange and impolite, certainly, and would look very odd, but he did have the right.

Oh! Why had she not secured an answer the night before?

"Mr. Darcy, Miss."

Elizabeth looked up from her embroidery as the maid announced her betrothed's presence. She smiled and stood to greet him.

"Fitzwilliam, I'm glad you're here. There's something we must speak of."

His heart sped up just a tiny bit at her welcoming smile and he felt a little like a green schoolboy as he nodded to her sister and went to Elizabeth. He kissed her hand and sat beside her. "What is it, my dear?"

"The wedding trip! We discussed it yesterday but we came to no conclusions."

"Ah, yes. I believe you know my sentiments. What do you wish to do?" he asked neutrally.

"I believe I would like my sister to accompany us," she said quietly, looking at her embroidery. She looked up in time to see his face twitch slightly, his mouth turning down in a frown.

Darcy quickly schooled his features and sighed. "Very well. If that is your wish, I cannot deny you. I will make the necessary arrangements."

He rose and she impulsively grabbed his sleeve.

He looked down at her and smiled tightly. "I must speak with your father about something. I will return shortly."

She hated that she felt as if she were hurting him by her answer, even though she knew it was a perfectly acceptable custom for the bride's sister to accompany the couple. She smiled uneasily as Darcy nodded to Mary and went to her father.

Elizabeth felt unsettled. Guilt and anger fought equally for her attention and she took a deep breath to calm herself. How dare he make her feel guilty for wanting only what every other woman she knew required? Well, not every woman. Charlotte had gone directly to Kent following her wedding breakfast with no one to accompany her to her new home. And when Miss Goulding wed two years prior, she had not taken a companion on their trip to Ireland. Her own Aunt and Uncle Gardiner had travelled alone following their wedding, but they had been deeply in love. *As Mr. Darcy is in love with you,* she told herself.

Oh, dear! Why could she not be selfish and mercenary, caring for no one but herself? If she were, she would be happy to marry a rich man and not care that he was made *un*happy by her decision to bring a companion on their journey. But no, by some perverse fate, she had to be unhappy she was marrying a man she did not love, and yet still be troubled by the idea of injuring him with her decisions. She was sure it was a curious error in her own nature that caused her to feel such disparate emotions. What kind of woman cares for the feelings of a man she is unhappy to be marrying? *A Bennet woman, that's who.*

Perhaps she could talk to him. Mayhap they could work something out that would suit them both. Much to her chagrin, she felt a sick feeling in her stomach at the thought of his expression when she had told him she essentially did not want to be alone with him. The way he had sighed and squared his shoulders, as if she were thrusting burdens upon him that he must bear alone. No, she could not live with this uneasiness. She must speak with him.

Her father and Mr. Darcy entered the sitting room together and Darcy resumed his seat next to her. She put her hand on his sleeve and spoke quietly, "Would you walk with me? I need some air."

"Yes, of course."

They walked along the shore, Kitty and Mary walking arm in arm ahead of them. He had not offered his arm and she had not taken it. She looked at him from the corner of her eye, wondering if it had been a simple misstep, or if he had deliberately withheld.

"Fitzwilliam," she said, looping her arm through his. "We must have an awkward conversation."

He looked at her with a mixture of wariness and surprise. "Very well. I am listening."

"I hope you will speak as well. Otherwise it will be less a conversation and more an oration." She smiled and he returned it slightly.

"You have secured my participation. Now what do you wish to speak of?"

"Our wedding journey. And our impending marriage." She stumbled slightly over the last word but hoped he hadn't noticed. "I am from a family of women, sir. I cannot remember a time when I have not had another female near me. Even when I have visited my relations in town, I have been with my aunt or my cousins or accompanied by Jane. The idea of being… alone, with a man, well, it is so very strange. And a bit frightening. I am not saying I am frightened of you, you have been very kind," she hurriedly added, "but as you said in Kent, it will be a very great adjustment for me. A new name and position, a whole new life, and yours will stay mainly the same, which is why I suppose you never hear of the groom's brother attending a wedding trip." She smiled at her joke and he joined her.

"Elizabeth, you do not have to convince me. It is perfectly normal to wish your sister with you at such a time. It is well within your rights to request it."

"Yes, but it has made you unhappy," she looked up at him and he looked away, toward the water.

"I thought I was less obvious than that," he said after some moments had passed.

"Perhaps not to everyone. Mayhap I am coming to know you better." She smiled again and pulled him along. "Sir, I do not wish discord between us. I am not built for unhappiness. I wished to suggest that perhaps we find a way that will make us both happy."

"What do you suggest?"

"Well, perhaps you could tell me how you envision our trip progressing, how we would spend our time, and that might help me to feel less anxious about it all."

"Very well. At first, we shall be in London. Once we have begun our journey, we will progress in the normal way. Coaching inns, stops to change the horses. The inns have already been notified and we shall have satisfactory accommodations. Our servants will travel ahead with the luggage. I had thought that we might like to take the smaller carriage. It is not as spacious, but the windows open more fully when the weather is fine. I had thought you might like that," he said self-consciously.

She squeezed his arm. "I would. And what about when we arrive. We are staying in your friend's house?"

"Yes, he has a rather spacious cottage on the southern side of the lake. There is a cook, housekeeper, and under maids, but no butler. I will bring two of my own footmen in addition to the coachman and groom. Of course, your maid and my valet will be there when we arrive. If you wish, you can write to the housekeeper and tell her your meal preferences before we depart."

"Thank you, I shall."

He nodded. "We will likely be tired from our journey, so I thought the first few days we might do nothing other than relax. There is a path leading down to the lake's edge and another wrapping partially around the shore. I thought we could sleep as late as we want, take a walk before breakfast, read on the benches in the garden before dressing for dinner, and walk again as the sun sets. It is a spectacular view from the top of the hill. There is a small boat we could take out onto the water and have picnics on the shore. I hoped you might consent to play for me after dinner some evenings, and perhaps sing."

He smiled at her as he said it and she unexpectedly colored.

"There is some society, of course, and after a few days of rest we could venture into town and see who is about. There is a concert hall and an assembly room. There will be a calendar of sorts at the cottage when we arrive. You know I am not fond of balls, but if you wished to attend an assembly, I could be convinced."

She smiled at his flirtation and was happy to see him returned to good spirits. "And how would I do that, sir, for you know I am very fond of dancing?"

His eyes darkened for a moment and he leaned down until his lips nearly touched her ear. "Elizabeth, one kiss from your lips, and I will give you anything you ask of me."

"Oh." She blushed and looked down, suddenly discomposed and the skin of her neck tingling where his hot breath had touched it. "I will have to remember that, sir. If there is ever a time when we disagree, I shall know how to carry the day."

He smiled. "You do that."

They walked in comfortable silence for several minutes before Elizabeth spoke again.

"Well, that settles it. I cannot take Jane. She would be frightfully bored. And Mary would likely not mind spending the time reading on her own, but I cannot think that would be good for her. And of course she would be made uncomfortable by sitting every evening in the drawing room while you watch me play and make that face you make when you are being so frightfully serious." She sighed and looked about casually. "No, I cannot subject my poor sisters to such treatment. We shall have to go alone."

He suddenly gripped her arm and turned her to him a little too strongly. "Are you sure, Elizabeth? You are not teasing or making one of your jokes?"

She shook her head while smiling coyly.

"It is cruel to toy with a man in such a way. Now tell me clearly. Are you saying you will go The Lakes with me alone? No companions, no sisters, just the two of us?"

"And a small army of servants, yes," she replied.

He pulled her to him and planted a swift kiss to her lips, then just as quickly pulled back and placed her hand on his arm and continued walking as if nothing had happened. She smiled and saw his mouth tick out of the corner of her eye.

"You have made me very happy, Elizabeth," he said quietly, squeezing her hand on his arm.

She placed her other hand on his arm in response, bringing her closer to him. "I would like to make a request."

"Anything, my love."

"I would like for Jane and possibly Mary to come to Pemberley when we return. My family will just be returning from the seaside and father must stay at Longbourn through the harvest and mother with him, but he said they might come in the autumn. I propose that my sisters come in August, then return with my family."

He raised her hand to his mouth and kissed it gently, holding it to his lips for several moments. "Consider it done."

~

Though Elizabeth felt apprehensive about having agreed to the unaccompanied wedding tour, she felt a sweet, warm sensation at Fitzwilliam's happiness in the scheme. She was not blind to the affection of such a man. His was not the calculated flattery or imagined attachment of Mr. Collins. He was a man of sense and education, who had lived in the world. He was intelligent and, as far as she could see, a decent man. She was beginning to think she had a chance at happiness, and she sat at the pianoforte the next morning feeling more hopeful than ever.

"Lizzy! I've a letter from Maria! Would you like to read it?" Lydia bounded into the room, waving the paper in the air.

"Read it to me, dear. I must continue my practice."

Lydia settled herself on the chair next to her sister and read over Elizabeth's playing as her fingers moved up and down the scales. There was news of Meryton and all its goings-on. Who had hosted a dinner party, who had worn an ugly dress to the party, who had flirted with whom at the party. The milliner had gotten in some particularly ugly bonnets and the pig had escaped into the rose garden again.

Then Maria described in minute detail every moment of the assembly where she had danced every dance and several of them with officers, including Mr. Wickham. He had been engaged briefly to Miss Mary King, an orphan living with an uncle. Miss King had come into an inheritance of ten thousand pounds, become engaged to Mr. Wickham, and then whisked away to Liverpool by yet another uncle, the engagement broken. Wickham had seemingly moved on without any signs of heartbreak or disappointment. No one was terribly surprised; Mary King was a freckled little thing and while Elizabeth and Jane had often said they thought her face fresh and youthful, they knew such was not the fashion.

Maria's letter told of her dance with Mr. Wickham and how gentlemanly he had been. How he had smiled and complimented and charmed her thoroughly and how everyone would miss him now that the militia had gone to Brighton.

Elizabeth felt decidedly unsettled. Mr. Wickham had been her friend. They were not family and she had not seen him overmuch since his engagement to Miss King, but still, he had been a friend. She knew her father's points had merit and that was why she had listened to him.

She had been willing to give her betrothed the benefit of the doubt, but now, realizing how neatly she had put Mr. Wickham out of her mind while being courted by the man who had taken away his living, she felt slightly disgusted with herself. It was one thing to give Mr. Darcy the benefit of the doubt, it was another to turn her back on a friend.

When Mr. Darcy arrived a half hour later, she was just finishing up a song. She relinquished the instrument to her sister and joined Mr. Darcy and her family outside. They sat in the shade, Mr. Bennet reading a book while his wife and eldest daughter embroidered handkerchiefs. Darcy and Elizabeth sat some distance from them. Far enough for private conversation, but close enough to be properly chaperoned.

"How are you today, my dear?" he asked.

"I am well. And you?"

"Very well."

He looked at her in that dark way he had looked at her in Hunsford, only now she knew finding fault was the last thing on his mind. She did not know how to respond and looked away. He took her hand where it lay on the bench between them and stroked his thumb over her bare knuckles.

He seemed content to sit and watch the flowers bloom while Elizabeth was growing more anxious by the minute. She was dreading the questions she had to ask but knew it must be done. They had been getting along so well the last two days and she was fairly certain what she wished to ask would make him angry. Why was he not speaking! *This is Mr. Darcy. Of course he will not begin the conversation.*

She was debating whether it was better to have the conversation here where there was a quick retreat inside, or if they should go for a walk where they would have more privacy should things become heated. Before she could decide, Mr. Darcy rose and asked her parents if they would mind if they went for a stroll along the water. Mrs. Bennet smiled and agreed happily while her father nodded absently, clearly engrossed in his book.

They had been along the shore some minutes before Elizabeth spoke.

"Mr. Darcy, may I ask you a question?"

"Of course, Miss Bennet," he said her name pointedly and she smiled.

"*Fitzwilliam*, there is something I wish to ask you about." He nodded and she continued nervously. "When we were in Hertfordshire, we met on the street in Meryton once. Do you remember?" He nodded, his brow lowered and his eyes suspicious. She swallowed and continued on. "I had just met a new officer in the militia. The two of you had a strong reaction to each other and, well, I'm ashamed to admit it, but Mr. Wickham told me about it later, and I encouraged him. At my aunt's card party, he related a history to me, involving you, and, well, much of it seemed rather, ahem, rather audacious, and I wondered if you might tell me your side of the story?" She finished rapidly, her stunted question leaving her embarrassed and awkward. She snuck a glance at Darcy, but he was looking directly ahead, his profile impossibly straight and perfect.

"What did Mr. Wickham tell you?" he bit out, his tone barely civil.

She looked around nervously, then said in a quiet but steady voice, "He said that he had been a favorite of your father's and that the two of you had been childhood friends. You had gone to school together and your father had promised him a living. He said it was done in such an informal way so that when your father passed, you were able to deny him the living and leave him penniless."

They walked on in tense silence for some time until Darcy spoke. "Did you believe him?"

Elizabeth chastised herself. She was well and truly trapped now and could not avoid an answer to the question she had most wished not to discuss. "At first, I found it hard to believe," she said hesitantly, "I had not thought you would do such a thing, but then he had such information and was so vehement." She trailed off, her eyes on the sand.

"So you believed him."

Feeling utterly wretched and not entirely sure why, she nodded.

Darcy sighed. She felt his whole body tighten through her hand on his arm.

"Will I never be free of that man!" he finally exclaimed quietly.

Stealing a glance at his face, Elizabeth was alarmed by what she saw. He was red and tense, his brows low over his eyes and his mouth set tightly. His jaw clenched so hard she could see it flexing. She had the sudden urge to touch his face, to relieve him of whatever pain he was in and offer what comfort she could. Before she knew what she was about, she had stepped halfway in front of him and her hand was caressing his jaw. His eyes opened wide in surprise and then softened as he looked upon her.

"Tell me what troubles you, Fitzwilliam. Do not carry this burden alone."

He sighed again, resumed their walk, now with her hand clasped tightly under his on his arm, and began. "Wickham was the son of my father's steward, an excellent man. He and my father had grown up together, his father had been steward before him, and their relationship was a steady one. My father was Wickham's godfather. George was always getting into scrapes but when we were children, it was harmless. As we got older, he became more and more unruly, less scrupulous. My father refused to see him for what he was. Old Mr. Wickham had died and my father promised to care for George. He felt loyal to his friend and he was fond of young Wickham.

"Father wished for him to join the church and had planned for him to take on the living at Kympton, a village near Pemberley. Being of an age with him, I knew Wickham ought not be a clergyman. He performed poorly at university and when my father passed, he left all charade of goodness behind. Not a week later, he swaggered into my father's study and asked what the old man had left for him." Darcy clenched his hand and Elizabeth gasped at the callousness of such behavior.

"My father had left him a thousand pounds and if Wickham took orders, he would receive the living at Kympton when it became available. George scoffed at this, not wanting to be a clergyman any more than I wanted him to be. He said he wished to study the law and asked for the value of the living, which he was given. I sent him on his way with three thousand pounds in addition to the legacy. I know not how he lived, but I can imagine."

Elizabeth shook her head, shocked at Wickham's behavior and at her own stupidity for believing him. Had she always been so gullible? Out of a sense of solidarity and overwhelmed by her own confusion, she briefly laid her head on Darcy's shoulder. She had stood upright again before he could react, but he was touched by the gesture.

"A few years later, the incumbent at Kympton died and Wickham wrote asking for the living, stating that my father had wished it expressly and he knew I would not want to deny his wishes. I reminded him of our agreement and that he had already received his payment, and he returned with such language as I cannot repeat to a lady, but I am sure his anger was in direct relation to his distressed circumstances."

"Four thousand pounds! How could he have gone through such a sum on his own? No family to care for, no house to maintain. It is so hard to believe," Elizabeth said.

"Wickham has never had trouble spending funds, and rarely on anything useful. He has left debt and ruin everywhere he has ever been."

Elizabeth stared wide-eyed as Darcy continued. "I thought our paths would never cross again until last summer when he intruded upon my notice in a most grievous way. I had sent my sister to Ramsgate with her companion, a Mrs. Younge. We were sorely deceived in her character and while she had charge of my fifteen-year-old sister, she allowed Wickham access to her. He visited Ramsgate and came upon Georgiana supposedly by chance, but he and Mrs. Younge had conspired all along. He courted her, lied to her, made her believe he was in love with her and she with him, and planned to elope with her. If I had not arrived unexpectedly and surprised them, they would have succeeded with their plan. My sister would be bound for life to that blackguard and he would have her dowry of thirty thousand pounds." He stopped talking but his body was rigid and his jaw worked, grinding his teeth painfully.

Elizabeth was exceedingly pale and felt a sick feeling in her stomach. A liar, a seducer, a man who did not pay his debts and attempted elopements with fifteen-year-old girls! This was the man she had called friend! The man whom she had just that morning been feeling guilty over abandoning. How could she have been so blind? He had flattered her and preferred her, and she had believed and endorsed him. She had slandered the good name of her own betrothed on the basis of that cur's testimony. She was such a simpleton! Stupid girl! She had always prided herself on her character judgments, but clearly she was the one whose character should be examined.

She withdrew from Darcy's arm and walked down to the water, her back to him. They had long passed anyone out enjoying the weather and the only people about were some small children chasing a crab several yards away.

Darcy let her alone for a few minutes before standing behind her and placing a hand on her shoulder. "Are you well, Elizabeth?"

She released a sob and dropped her head to her hands, covering her face. Darcy immediately crossed in front of her and rubbed both her shoulders under his large hands while she shook from the strength of her weeping.

"Dearest, please." He tried to press a handkerchief into her hands but she would not remove them from her face. Finally, feeling desperate and seeing no one about, her pulled her stiffly into his arms and rubbed her back, pressing her head onto his shoulder.

Finally, her sobs relented and she said, "How can you hold me like this? Do you not despise me, and rightly so?"

"Despise you? Why on earth would I despise you?"

"I believed him! I *wanted* to believe him, to satisfy my own wounded pride. I could not have been more blind!" she cried wretchedly.

He continued to console her, not knowing what to say and not fully understanding her. "Mr. Wickham is a practiced liar. Even my own excellent father believed him. You are not to blame, dearest. He has deceived many before and I fear he will continue to do so wherever he goes. It is his way."

She sobbed again, feeling more horrible by his defense of her. "Fitzwilliam, why are you not angry with me?" She looked at him incredulously and began pacing in front of him. "I was so angry with you, with your ridiculous comment! I thought I did not care; I thought the opinion of a strange man should not bother me, but clearly, I have not known myself. Had I been in love I could not have been more blind. But vanity has been my folly! Oh, how vain I have been! How willfully I misunderstood you from the start."

She continued pacing frantically, speaking to him but seemingly speaking to no one and he wondered if she had forgotten his presence.

"The things I said! I supported him! I *agreed* with him! I thought you proud and disagreeable, and he charming and amiable. Foolish girl!"

"Elizabeth." She did not look up. "Elizabeth!" He had her attention. "Am I to understand that you believed Wickham because you disliked me early in our acquaintance, due to a comment I made?"

She stood stock still and pale, looking at his serious countenance and rigid posture. She could not but nod pathetically, her face tear streaked and her eyes wide and sad.

"May I ask what comment it was that set you so against me?" he asked carefully. He was terribly afraid he knew the answer, but he needed to be sure. Little did he know how prideful his features appeared at that moment, how unbending his voice sounded.

"'She is tolerable I suppose, but not handsome enough to tempt me.'"

He closed his eyes as she spoke.

"And, 'I will not waste my time with women who have been slighted by other men.' Or something like that." She looked down at her feet, now half wet from pacing too close to the water, and felt a curious numbness.

He rubbed a hand across his still closed eyes. "Elizabeth, I must beg your forgiveness. I should never have said such a thing and certainly not within your hearing in a ballroom. I am sure you realize by now that you tempt me quite well."

She looked away, surprised by his response. "You are forgiven, sir. Can you find a way to forgive my ignorance and foolishness? My *willful misunderstanding*, as you once called it?"

He walked to her and took both her hands within his own. "Of course, my love. You are not to blame."

"But I am!" she interjected, not willing to let herself off so easily and feeling horribly—not exactly guilty, but something near to that. She could not let him continue to think her an innocent victim. "I am to blame! I did not question him. If his information had come from anyone else I would have thought him too forward, but because I wanted to hear ill of you, because I was discarded by you and charmed by him, I listened to him. I was an all-too-willing participant in his plan to slander you across the country." She dropped her head, beginning to feel exhausted. "Mr. Darcy, I am sorry for what I have said about you in Meryton. It was unfounded and unkind and I apologize. I understand if you do not wish to see me again."

He had been alternately confused and touched at her speech until the last. "No!"

Her head snapped up at his vehement tone.

"Miss Bennet, Elizabeth, do stop trying to cry off! Do you not understand? I want to marry you. You! I did not choose a woman from among a case at the jewelers. There is not a replacement should this one get lost." He took her shoulders in his hands again and held her there firmly, his eyes boring into her. "You are mine, do you understand? I have made my decision and I want you. Do stop trying to change my mind." He spoke fervently, more passionately than she had ever heard him speak.

A smile worked its way across her face, her eyes lightening as she looked upon him, staring at her with such ferocity. Suddenly, she threw her arms around his waist and buried her face in his coat, squeezing him tightly. Stunned, Darcy did not know what to do but return her embrace. He held her to him and dropped his head so it rested on top of hers, his arms pulling her impossibly closer.

They stood like this for some time until Elizabeth pulled back and looked at him shyly. He smiled at her reassuringly and offered his arm, and they made their way back to the cottage.

CHAPTER 16

"Jane, may I come in?" Elizabeth asked as she rapped on her sister's door before bed.

"Of course, dearest. Please, join me." She patted the chair next to hers where she was seated in her dressing gown with a letter open on her lap.

"Who is the letter from?"

"My friend in town, Mrs. Pearson," Jane answered.

"Is she the one with the very eligible elder brother?" Elizabeth asked, wrapping her shawl around her shoulders and settling into the chair by the open window. The only light in the room was the lamp on the table between their chairs and the pale glow of the moon outside.

"Yes, she is. Mr. Walker." Jane looked down self-consciously, then coming to a decision, looked her sister in the eye. "She says her brother has asked after me several times and that she has twice taken the liberty of reading my letters to him."

"Does she?" Elizabeth was slightly surprised with her sister's proclamation, as Jane was usually more circumspect and modest, but she tried not to show it.

"She hints that he is interested in me romantically and wishes to see me when I return to town if it is possible." Jane held the letter out to her sister. "Or do I mistake her?" she added.

Ah, there is the Jane I know. Elizabeth took the letter from her sister and read it through twice before handing it back.

"I do not think you are mistaken, Jane. She sounds very much like she would like to have you in the family and that her brother is eager to perform the job." Jane flushed and looked out the dark window.

"That is what I thought."

"Do you wish to join the Walker family, Jane?"

"I do not know. He is a very kind man, but as yet my feelings are not any stronger than friendship." The name Bingley hung in the air between them, unspoken but not unthought. "His sisters are very kind."

"There is more than one?"

"Yes, he has an older sister living in London. Her husband does business with Uncle. She is very genteel and kind, not unlike Aunt Gardiner, and has the most adorable children." Jane smiled sadly. "There is another brother as well, but I have not met him. He is much younger than the others and is away at school. Martha, Mrs. Pearson, assures me he is a lovely boy."

"Sounds like an ideal family," Elizabeth said softly.

"Yes, they are," Jane said distractedly. After several minutes of silence, she asked her sister, "Do you think it is possible to grow to love someone? I mean someone that you do not love after you know them, but perhaps after knowing them more intimately and for a longer period of time, you may come to love them? Do you think it is possible?"

Elizabeth looked at her sister's worried face, Jane's color high and her blue eyes unusually bright and wide. She answered carefully. "I think it is possible to grow in love, is that not how we all love anyway? But I do not know that it is such an easy recipe to follow. Time and intimacy alone may not accomplish the task."

Jane nodded. "Lizzy, would it be very wrong of me to accept Mr. Walker if I do not love him?"

"I do not think it would be very wrong, no. You like him; you respect and esteem him. Many marriages have been based on far less."

Jane nodded, her eyes meeting her sister's and sharing an unspoken truth. That was not how *they* wished to marry. Or at least it hadn't been before their father interfered.

"So you are thinking of accepting Mr. Walker then?" Elizabeth asked.

"I am giving it careful consideration. I can clearly see how it will be, or as clear as is possible with no formal arrangements. His father and family are all kind and welcoming to me. His mother died several years ago and I imagine I would immediately become mistress of his father's house in London, which will one day be his. It is a large responsibility but one I feel I can take on. He is a good man, of that I am certain, and he knows his own mind, the importance of which has lately been impressed on me."

Elizabeth nodded. "Do you no longer wish for Mr. Bingley, then?"

Jane looked down, then looked at her sister with her eyes full of tears she refused to let fall. "I am trying, Lizzy, trying so hard to forget him! His sisters are not kind like Mr. Walker's, he does not know his own mind, he is blown about by whims and fancies and the wishes of his friends. He is not a man full grown!" she declared vehemently, her eyes clearly showing her distress.

"So you still love him," Elizabeth said quietly, the finality of the words filling the small room.

"I fear it is not something I can control. Would it be wrong of me to accept Mr. Walker, in *every* way," she looked at her sister significantly, "with my heart full of another man? Is it betrayal? Or is it prudence?"

Elizabeth shook her head, unable to answer her sister. Instead she knelt before her, hugging her tightly and stroking her hair as Jane quietly sobbed out her sorrows on her sister's shoulder.

They slept together that night, Jane's head on her sister's soft stomach, as they had done when they were children, and Elizabeth's hand wrapped in Jane's hair, each giving strength and comfort to the other.

In the middle of the night, Jane woke and found her sister by the window, looking out towards the sea.

"Are you well, Lizzy?"

"Yes, Jane, I'll be fine."

Jane watched her sister, then finally curled her legs under her chin and hugged her knees, looking very much like a little girl.

"Do you think you will grow to love Mr. Darcy, Lizzy?"

"I do not know. Sometimes I think I am doomed to a life with a stubborn, intractable, difficult man. Then he is sweet and kind and surprisingly charming and I think everything will be all right in the end." She shrugged her shoulders. "How are you feeling?"

"I feel terrible for bothering you with my troubles. You have your own more difficult situation to deal with and I selfishly burdened you with mine. Can you forgive me?"

"Dearest Jane," Elizabeth said, rising and taking her sister's hands in her own, "there is nothing to forgive. We must go through these things together. Is that not what sisters are for?"

Jane smiled and hugged her, then Elizabeth returned to her own room for the rest of the night where she slept fitfully until late the next morning.

~

The following day was Sunday and instead of attending services, the entire family slept very late and when Mr. Darcy arrived, Mary Bennet was the only family member who received him.

He made stunted small talk with Elizabeth's sister while waiting for his betrothed to come downstairs. Thankfully, she arrived within a quarter hour and whisked him into the garden where she ordered tea. As she poured for him and offered him a small tray of muffins, he couldn't help but think how lucky he was, that he had many more days just like this to look forward to. Even luckier; in less than a fortnight, they would be wed and he would not have to go home alone or even wake up alone. It was not something they had discussed, but he hoped she would consent to share a bed, at least some of the time. He thought he might like to sleep together every night, but he was practical enough to realize such a thing should probably be tried before it was decided upon.

He didn't realize he had been looking in her direction without really seeing her for several minutes until she broke his reverie.

"What has your brow so puzzled, my dear?"

Immediately he brightened. She had never called him that before and seemed quite unaware of having said it herself.

"I was wondering if you snore," he said.

She laughed and quickly set down her teacup. "What?"

He smiled. "It would seem odd for such a delicate person as you, but one never knows about these things."

"I don't know whether to be flattered you think I'm delicate or insulted by your thinking I snore!"

"Why would you be flattered? Are you not often thought of as delicate? I should think it would be quite ordinary by now."

"You might be surprised." She arched a brow and gave him that look he loved. "My mother is not as inclined to think of me as such. She says I am far too wild to be considered delicate."

He scoffed. "As if she—," he stopped, seeing her brow raised and her eyes a mix of censure and amusement. "I, ahem, I'm sure she's mistaken. You are all that is lovely and delicate."

At this, Elizabeth had to laugh. It was a soft, chiming sound, like the wind in the trees in autumn or the church bells at Christmas. Overcome with a sudden rush of affection for her, he blurted, "God, how I love you."

Her retort about him recovering from his faux pas so nicely died on her lips along with her laughter, and she was left looking into his eyes as he regarded her with an intensity she'd seldom seen. She reached across the table and took his hand in both of hers, pressing it firmly and stroking

116

his knuckles with her thumb.

The marmalade cat that made himself at home in their garden took that opportunity to mew loudly at their feet, breaking the moment. She laughed self-consciously and released his hand, busying herself with refilling his cup and then her own.

"When are you returning to London? Shall you accompany us on Wednesday?"

"I'm afraid I must return tomorrow." He was comforted by the slight look of displeasure on her face. "I have much business to tend to before we leave town, and I want to devote the days immediately following the wedding to my new wife." He couldn't help it; he verily beamed with pride at the pronouncement that this exquisite creature sitting opposite him would soon be his wife.

She returned his smile. "What a dutiful and attentive husband I am acquiring."

He smiled at her tease and took her hand again.

"That is something I wished to talk with you about," she said.

"Oh? About me being a dutiful husband?"

She smiled again and tilted her head flirtatiously. "You are getting better at teasing, Mr. Darcy. I approve."

He nodded his thanks and she continued, "I wanted to ask you what sort of marriage you wished to have."

His brows rose quizzically and he sat up a bit straighter. "What do you mean exactly?" he asked, a mad thought running through his mind that perhaps she wished to discuss their sleeping arrangements.

"Well, I mean what sort of relationship will exist between us? Shall we be friends as well as spouses?" She could not bring herself to say lovers. "Meaning, what sort of conversations will we have? What will we confide in each other, if anything? Who will have your first loyalty—your family and friends or me? Do you wish me to come to you with my troubles or to sort them out on my own? What sort of closeness shall exist between us?"

She was in earnest, that was clear to him, and he listened carefully to her words, wondering what had sparked these thoughts and if he should be reading between the lines.

"If I understand you correctly, you are asking if you can confide in me or if I would rather not be bothered?"

"Somewhat, yes."

"Bother me. Every day, every hour, whenever the desire strikes you. I shall always listen attentively and seek to help in any way I can. You know that I love you, dearest, of course we shall be friends, and confidantes, and any other word you can think of. I desire a true partnership with you, not just a decoration on my arm. And it should go without saying that my loyalty is first to you, always."

She sighed in relief, her shoulders slumping down from where they had been raised nearly to her ears.

"Thank you, Fitzwilliam. You've eased my mind."

"Dearest, you seem distressed. Is there something you wished to speak about?" he asked, wishing they were already wed so that he could hold her and comfort her as she so clearly needed.

"It is Jane. I cannot betray her confidence, but I would like to ask you about something."

He nodded.

"It is about Mr. Bingley."

He leaned toward her.

"What sort of man is he? You know him well, do you not?" she asked.

"He is a good sort of man, kind, generous. But that is not what you mean, is it?"

"Not exactly. Last autumn, Mr. Bingley left the neighborhood without saying goodbye to anyone. He said he would be back shortly but never came back. It does not inspire trust. It is not the most… mature… behavior," she said.

Darcy leaned back. "Ah. I think I see what you mean. Miss Bennet met Bingley in town again, did she not?"

Elizabeth nodded.

"And I imagine his attentions were just as pointed to her as they had been in Hertfordshire?"

Elizabeth looked at him but did not respond.

"Without betraying his confidence, I can tell you that Bingley is a young man, and with a sister who excels at management and no estate to be responsible to, he has been allowed to remain a young man. I have no doubt that with time and perhaps a steadying influence, he will grow into a very admirable man, one who would make an excellent husband and father, but if you are wondering if he is there yet, I'm afraid I will have to say no, he is not."

He spoke quietly and Elizabeth understood what he was doing. He was proving his loyalty to her by sharing his private thoughts about his closest friend. He was not breaking a confidence per se, but he was dancing precariously close to the line and she knew he would not have done it for anyone but her.

She squeezed his hand. "Thank you. If I may, one more question about our mutual friend?"

He smiled. "Of course."

"Do you think he is serious about Jane? And if he is, would he then rise to the occasion and be his own man, like you, or would he continue to be bossed about by his sisters?"

"That is more than one question, Elizabeth!"

She shrugged, not sorry in the least. He sighed.

"Miss Bennet has a particularly serene personality and I believe she would be a steadying influence on Bingley. However, I can see how from a woman's perspective that may seem like an enormous risk to take. Allow me to say though, in Bingley's defense, he is not always persuaded by his sisters. The majority of the time their demands fall on deaf ears unless it is something he feels duty-bound to do, and no, not everything falls into that category. And while I think he is not yet ready to be a husband, I do not think it to be too far into the future."

Elizabeth thought on this for a moment and was satisfied at first. After all, in Hertfordshire she had been witness to multiple occasions of Bingley telling his sisters no and doing what he wished to do instead, which, of course, made his desertion all the worse. He could have come back to Hertfordshire. If he was persuaded to stay away, he allowed himself to be.

"Does Miss Bennet doubt his trustworthiness?" he asked, looking curious and slightly uncomfortable.

"Whether she does or not, *I* certainly do."

"And you wield a great deal of influence over your sister."

"Less than you wield over your friend," she said with a knowing look.

His eyes widened slightly. She spoke before he could respond. "I have long suspected you convinced Mr. Bingley not to return to Netherfield and I was angry at first, but my father and I spoke of it and I realized he is his own man. It was his decision to make; he did not have to listen to you. He should have trusted his own judgment, but he didn't. That cannot be laid at your door." She took a deep breath and looked around before resettling her sight on Darcy. "He is not like you."

He looked confused and she continued, "Do stop looking so worried, Fitzwilliam! I am not angry with you."

She smiled and he exhaled gruffly, feeling like he had dodged a particularly nasty bullet. "What do you mean, 'he is not like me'?"

"I mean from the outside, you have similar situations. You are each young men, have already inherited, and are each responsible for a sister, though yours is much younger. But you are a man full grown, while Mr.

Bingley is still in process."

He was looking at her with a peculiar gleam in his eyes and she returned his stare.

"What?" she asked after several moments passed and he said nothing.

"Come."

He stood and took her by the hand, leading her to the path that would take them to the shore. He stopped abruptly in a secluded nook at the end of the garden path before it opened to the stairs leading down. He swiftly pressed her into the niche in the wall and placed his arms on either side of her head, leaning down to kiss her deeply.

It was several minutes before he released her lips, and then he pressed his forehead to hers and caught his breath.

"A man full grown, am I?"

She laughed a bit breathlessly. "As you see."

He smiled and kissed her again, this time more slowly, gently tracing her upper lip with his tongue. She started at the contact and pulled back, then slowly returned her mouth to his. After another minute of exploration, she tentatively traced her tongue along his lips as he had done hers. He moaned and she pulled back again, a question in her eyes, and he pulled her to him, placing one hand behind her neck while the other wrapped around her waist. She placed her hands on his sides and slowly wrapped them around to his back, drawing him closer.

It wasn't long before Darcy withdrew, resting his forehead against hers again, his breathing ragged.

"So that is what a man full grown kisses like. I shall tell Jane to secure one immediately."

He laughed and withdrew, running a hand through his hair and walking a few steps away from her.

"I cannot wait till we are wed, Elizabeth."

This reminder of what was to come silenced her teasing and filled her with a sudden trepidation. She nervously smiled and walked toward the shore trail.

"Come, let us greet the sea today."

CHAPTER 17

Charles Bingley placed the most recent letter from Darcy in the drawer with the others, then leaned back in his chair to think. His old friend wanted to meet him tomorrow at the club. Darcy had sent him a short letter to announce his engagement a few weeks ago and had kindly given him warning when he informed his family, knowing the gossip would circulate town in a matter of hours. Charles had been able to keep it hidden from his sister Caroline for a day or two, then told her after she had a proper meal and the servants were in another part of the house so as not to hear her tantrum.

He'd never seen a person's face become that particular shade of purple before. She trembled with rage and finally threw a small china teacup, watching it shatter on the marble mantelpiece. He stopped her before she threw a figurine in the same direction. After sending her off to be tended by her maid, he had a serious conversation with his brother Hurst. Neither man wanted the responsibility of taking care of Caroline for the long term, and now that her plans to wed Darcy had been thwarted, they agreed it was time to look elsewhere. The season was dwindling to a close and every week there were reports of friends removing to their country estates. There were still some activities and many would not leave town until the middle or end of the month, but they certainly were not spoiled for choice.

Louisa Hurst had an old school friend who had married a distant cousin of her husband's. They were hosting a house party in the summer and the Hursts had been invited. There would be a great variety of guests, including a few single men, and the neighborhood was known to be prosperous. The two men agreed Caroline would make what she could of the remaining weeks in town before accompanying her sister and brother-in-law to the house party in the hopes of finding a man willing to marry her.

Charles Bingley was pleased with his decision and hoped he was one step closer to gaining Jane Bennet's favor.

~

Mr. Darcy left for London early Monday morning and Elizabeth spent the next two days at the shore with her sisters. There was a dinner party to attend but otherwise, the Bennet family was alone. A sense of nostalgia had settled over them as they all recognized that soon, their numbers would be diminished. Elizabeth would marry in a little over a week and Jane was sure not to be too far behind her. The Bennet family as it had always been would end, and the sisters would move away, adding brothers and distance to their family.

Tuesday, the girls took one last picnic down to the shore. The five of them sat scattered across two blankets in a sheltered cove not too far from their cottage. Kitty was sketching Jane and Mary where they sat side by side, the sea at their backs, while Lydia braided long grasses and made crowns for each of her sisters.

"Do you think you will have many children, Lizzy?" asked Lydia suddenly.

"Lydia!" exclaimed Jane. "That is not an appropriate question."

"Why not?" Lydia responded, looking genuinely confused. "We are all sisters here. It is not as if Mr. Darcy were sitting beside us."

Jane acknowledged her point and four sets of eyes turned to Elizabeth.

"I hardly know!" Elizabeth declared, her cheeks slightly red. "One cannot always predict these things."

"Maybe you will have five daughters like Mama!" said Lydia.

"Oh, name one after me!" cried Kitty.

Elizabeth had to laugh at this absurdity, but inside she was worried. How many children did Mr. Darcy desire? How many did he expect? What if she had daughters; would he insist on continuing until there was a son? What if the effort killed her?

Jane placed a warm hand on her arm. "You will have a son, Lizzy, I'm sure of it."

Elizabeth smiled at her sister. "How do you know, Jane?"

"I just know. You will."

"Shall I name him after you?" Elizabeth teased.

"I think a boy called Jane would seem a little odd, but John would not be inappropriate."

"Oh, yes, call him John! Then I shall call him Jack and teach him how to dance!" declared Lydia. She pulled Kitty up and twirled her about, the two of them giggling and laughing. Lydia then picked up the crowns she had made and skipped about her sisters, laughing as she placed the crowns haphazardly on their heads. Mary was still wearing a bonnet and they all laughed at the picture of her braided grass crown atop her straw bonnet.

Elizabeth sighed. She would miss this, miss them, these sisters. Jane's companionship and comfort she would miss the most, but in the six months since her father's change, as she had come to think of it, she had grown closer to them all. She had bonded with Mary over music and singing and had come to appreciate and value her sister in a way she never could have imagined prior to the change. Kitty had become a dear, innocent companion, one that she would miss after she married. Kitty was still a follower at heart and would likely never be an overwhelming presence, or even a strong one, but there was a sweetness, an honesty about her that Elizabeth could appreciate and knew she would miss dearly.

Lydia, quite surprisingly, had become a great source of entertainment and joy, much like she had been as a young child before she had been spoiled so dreadfully. She was still exuberant and likely always would be, but she could curb her tongue in public now, a feat neither of her eldest sisters thought she would ever accomplish, and her need to have her way all the time had greatly diminished. Elizabeth thought it due largely to her no longer being out. As angry as Lydia had been, the change had done her good. She was now in a category of her own, almost, and the lack of competition had calmed her. Kitty was not out either, but only Lydia wore the dresses and hairstyles of a young girl and as much as she had balked against it in the beginning, the change suited her.

That evening, the family prepared for their last dinner together before leaving for London in the morning. The following week would be spent at their Uncle Gardiner's home. Elizabeth would have fittings most days for her trousseau and there would be dinners with Mr. Darcy's family in addition to the usual entertainments.

Dinner was filled with laughter and old family stories. Each sister told a tale of how Lizzy had wronged her as a child by stealing her toy, pushing her into a puddle, or talking her into something they both got into trouble for. Elizabeth blushed and defended herself weakly, all the while laughing until her sides ached.

"You always were an unusual girl," said Mr. Bennet with a wink. He squeezed her hand where it rested next to his on the table.

Elizabeth smiled as she turned to listen to her mother at the other end of the table.

"Well, Lizzy, you have done better than I ever thought you would. Well done, dear. Mr. Darcy is a fine catch."

She smiled proudly at her daughter and sipped another glass of wine, and Elizabeth was not sure if she should feel happy or embarrassed. Her sisters sniggered quietly behind their hands and she decided not to let her mother's words offend her.

"When you were a little girl," Mrs. Bennet continued, "you had the most beautiful hair. It curled all around your face and everyone exclaimed about it. Mrs. Goulding was so jealous! I told her not to worry, her daughter's hair would grow in eventually." Lydia spluttered and nearly choked on her wine. "You were such a pretty child. And now your hair is prettier than ever."

Elizabeth stared at her mother, having never heard her speak in such a way about herself before.

"Of course, you so rarely wear it to your advantage. Why you never listen to me, I don't know," Mrs. Bennet continued.

There is the mother I know, Elizabeth thought.

She laughed quietly to herself and looked across the table to see that Mary and Jane were doing the same, and soon the entire table was laughing.

"What? What is so funny?" asked Mrs. Bennet. This made Lydia laugh louder and soon Mrs. Bennet joined in, not knowing why, but not wishing to be left out of what was clearly a good joke.

CHAPTER 18

The limited number of guest rooms in the Gardiners' London house meant that Jane and Elizabeth shared a room, Mary and Kitty shared, and a very unhappy Lydia slept in the nursery. Her young cousins were much too young to share with. The eldest was only eleven years old. It was almost enough to send her into a tantrum, but just before she lost control of her temper, the nurse offered to allow Lydia the extra bed in her room next to the nursery. It was meant for a wet nurse but there was currently no need for one. Lydia jumped at the chance and happily left her young cousins behind.

They had arrived early and decided to make a quick trip to the shoemaker before dinner. Mrs. Bennet declared they had much shopping to do and no time to waste. Mrs. Gardiner had taken the liberty of choosing a few patterns for Elizabeth that she thought her niece would like, but they still needed to be fitted. Her wedding dress had been made in Margate along with a few other pieces, but her mother insisted that the wife of Mr. Darcy must have an impressive trousseau. Mr. Bennet tried to rein her in, and in the end succeeded a little, but he still cringed at the thought of the bills that would soon be arriving.

Elizabeth made orders for several new pairs of slippers, walking boots, half boots, and a warmer pair for winter. Plans to visit the modiste, the draper, the furrier and glove maker were made for the next few days and Elizabeth already felt exhausted just thinking about it.

Mr. Darcy sent around a card saying he would call Thursday morning if Elizabeth would be available. Mrs. Bennet was torn between telling him there was too much to do to sit around waiting for calls and giving him whatever he asked for to avoid angering him. In the end, it was decided that Elizabeth would stay home with her father and await

Mr. Darcy while her mother, sisters, and aunt went shopping for their own apparel.

When Darcy finally arrived in Gracechurch Street, Elizabeth was seated in the front drawing room where her aunt received visitors. Her father was in her uncle's study; he felt that with both doors open and only a small hall between them, nothing untoward would occur. Elizabeth stood and curtseyed when Darcy entered the room and before she had fully straightened, he was standing before her and taking her hand.

"Dearest," he said softly, "are you well?"

"Yes. And you, sir?"

"Yes, very well now you are come." He pressed her hand to his chest and gazed into her eyes until she flushed from the scrutiny.

"Please, be seated." She sat on the settee and he joined her, sitting close enough to press his leg to hers and rest their still-joined hands on his knee.

"Was your journey pleasant?" he asked.

"As pleasant as a journey with such a large party can be. And yours?"

"As expected."

"Fitzwilliam."

"Yes?"

"You're staring at me again."

"I have missed you."

"It has only been three days."

"Nevertheless."

She smiled and shook her head but squeezed his hand within hers.

"Do you have your week all planned out?" he asked.

"Mostly, yes, but some time can be set aside for you if that is what you are leading up to." She smiled coyly. She quite liked flirting with him. It garnered her the most wonderful results.

He smiled. "That is exactly what I was asking. I'd like for you to meet Georgiana and tour the house, and of course your family should come for dinner."

"I'd love to meet your sister. Perhaps she could come for tea?"

He looked dubious. "We could accomplish two tasks at once if you came to the house for tea. You could meet the staff and interview your new maid if you like."

"Very well. When shall this momentous tea take place?" she asked.

"Whenever you are ready. Mrs. Brown, the London housekeeper, has two different girls she would put forward as your maid. You are to choose between them. Of course, if neither of them is to your liking, we can continue the search."

"Of course, Fitzwilliam, thank you."

"I love that."

"What?"

"The sound of my name on your lips. You make it sound so very appealing."

"Do you not normally find it appealing?" she asked.

"Not particularly. I normally find it cumbersome."

She laughed. "I like it. It is a dignified name, and not one you will find on every other man in the country."

"I suppose that is true. Now," he said, angling his body toward hers, "when shall I get my welcome kiss?"

"Is there such a thing? I have never heard of it. I think you are making occasions up, Mr. Darcy, in order to attain more kisses. Besides, you arrived before I did, so shouldn't you welcome me?"

"Very well, I shall give you a welcome kiss."

She laughed outright. "Fitzwilliam, you are incorrigible! There is no such thing, I am sure of it."

"Of course there is. You simply have not heard of it before; you should spend more time in town."

She watched him with an amused smile as he leaned closer and closer to her.

"Now, I will welcome you to London and you can welcome me to Gracechurch Street. How does that sound?" he suggested playfully.

She could do aught but smile brightly and shake her head, then lean forward to meet him where he was already tilting his head in anticipation of their kiss.

"There is one for your welcome," she said as she pulled away from a quick peck, "and one for mine." The second kiss was gentle and soft and lasted considerably longer than the first.

Darcy sat back with a satisfied smile. "That is much better."

She laughed and rose, tugging him up behind her. "Come, you should greet my father."

~

Friday brought Mr. Bingley to Gracechurch Street. The women of the family were preparing to leave, the hall filled with bustling as five women tied on their bonnets and slipped on their gloves.

Mr. Bingley apologized and asked if it wasn't a good time, and Mrs.

Bennet said it was no trouble at all, Jane would stay behind. Kitty was sent for and told to stay in the corner to give them privacy. Mrs. Bennet whispered the instructions in her ear but she wasn't as good at whispering as she imagined she was and everyone heard. Jane was mortified, but Bingley was glad of the time alone, even if it came at the cost of a little embarrassment. Mrs. Gardiner sent in tea before the two matrons, the bride, and Mary were off to the shops.

Bingley was very pleased to spend time with Jane Bennet. He had enjoyed renewing the acquaintance while in town and after much deliberation, he'd decided that Darcy was wrong about Jane's feelings for him. If she had felt nothing for him, why had she been so nervous when she saw him again? If her heart was untouched, why did she blush so when he touched her in a dance or kissed her hand? No, he was sure Darcy had been mistaken. His friend was just a man, after all.

And if he was right and his friend was wrong about Jane's feelings, it meant he had left her in the lurch, expecting him to come back and likely being grieved when he did not. Was that why she was so skittish now? Why the ease they had enjoyed in Hertfordshire was so difficult to recapture? Could he blame her? Of course not! He would not want an inconstant lover and neither would he wish one for her.

He knew he might make a nuisance of himself, but he couldn't care. Darcy practically oozed satisfaction when Bingley saw him last, and he knew why. Darcy was marrying the woman he loved and perpetually looked like the cat that got the cream. Bingley wished such joy for himself, and he knew he would have it with Jane. He would call again and again until she saw it, too.

~

Saturday arrived bright and clear for Elizabeth's tea with the Darcys. Her mother and Jane were accompanying her. She would take tea with Georgiana and Fitzwilliam, tour the house, and meet with the housekeeper. She would then be introduced to the two women vying for the position of her personal maid.

One worked full time in the London house and the other was a regular seasonal maid who had recently undergone training to be a lady's maid. Elizabeth asked that no further information be given to her about them so that she wouldn't make a biased choice, but she had already gathered that the one from the house in town was a generational employee and had been with the family her entire life.

When the carriage pulled up in front of the large stone house, Elizabeth steeled her nerves and took a deep breath. The house itself did not bother her. However, the idea that she would be in charge of said house and its inhabitants was another story. She squared her shoulders and squeezed Jane's hand, then walked in with her head held high.

"Welcome to Darcy House, Miss Elizabeth," said Mr. Darcy. He was standing by the door and after greeting her sister and mother, quickly took Elizabeth's arm and led her to the drawing room.

He introduced her to his sister, Georgiana, and sat next to Elizabeth on a settee near Georgiana's chair. Jane took the chair next to her and Mrs. Bennet sat across from them.

"This is a lovely room, Mr. Darcy."

"Thank you, Mrs. Bennet."

"The material looks so expensive! Has it recently been redone?" she asked, her hand running over the brocade on the arm of her chair.

"My aunt refurnished it about four years ago, I believe," he answered.

"Your aunt Lady Catherine?"

"No, my Aunt Lady Constance."

"Oh, is she your mother's sister? The daughter of an earl?" she asked eagerly.

Jane's cheeks were red and she stared at the carpet, unable to raise her eyes, while Elizabeth was silently wishing the floor would open up and swallow her whole.

"No, my mother had but one sister, Lady Catherine, whom you met in Kent. Lady Constance is my father's sister. Her husband is Viscount Melburn of Broxley."

Mrs. Bennet's eyes nearly bulged from her head. "Did you hear that, Lizzy?"

Before she could say anything else, Elizabeth clutched Mr. Darcy's arm a little too tightly and spoke. "Forgive me, Mr. Darcy, but might we call for some tea? I'm suddenly very thirsty."

He nodded at her silently and rose to pull the bell and pretended not to hear Mrs. Bennet whispering loudly to her daughters about what a boon it would be to have peers in the family.

Jane tried to shush her to no avail and Mrs. Bennet continued on, ignoring the red face and downcast eyes of Georgiana, until Mr. Darcy finished speaking with a servant and sat back down.

"How often are you in town, Mr. Darcy? Surely you spend the season here," Mrs. Bennet continued in a loud, cloying voice.

"I spend a part of the season each year here, yes, but not all," he replied.

Jane knew the next step in her mother's conversation would be to suggest that he host her sisters or possibly the entire family next season and being the sweet, generous person she was, she threw herself on the pyre to save her sister the same fate.

"Have you seen Mr. Bingley this season?" she asked innocently.

"Yes, I saw him just yesterday, as a matter of fact. He is considering a trip north to visit relations."

Mrs. Bennet was instantly on the scent of a new suitor and Elizabeth mouthed a silent thank you to her sister.

Tea arrived shortly and a very nervous Miss Darcy poured for her guests.

"Two sugars, please," said Mrs. Bennet.

Elizabeth thought the ability to request tea in a shrill voice must be a natural talent.

Miss Darcy was so nervous the cup nearly shook in her hand, prompting Mrs. Bennet to say, "Oh, Miss Darcy! Do not worry, we shall all be family soon."

She gave the girl an exaggerated wink and Elizabeth didn't know whether to be embarrassed that she had pointed out the girl's anxiety or happy that her mother was attempting to show this poor orphaned child kindness in her own mortifying way.

"The first time my Lizzy served tea, she spilled an entire cup on Mrs. Goulding's lap!" Mrs. Bennet tittered and Georgiana looked at her lap, her cheeks ablaze. "These are the most beautiful cakes! Do you have a French chef, Mr. Darcy? Of course you must, you can afford it!"

"Actually, I—" Darcy was interrupted by Mrs. Bennet again.

"Do you have an orangery, Mr. Darcy? If you do not, I must suggest you build one."

"There is an orangery at Pemberley," he said gravely, his expression blank.

"Mr. Darcy, did you not say there was a painting of Pemberley you wanted me to see? Might you show it to me now?" asked Elizabeth, her voice a little higher than usual.

"Of course. Come with me, please," said Darcy.

Georgiana had not spoken more than a dozen words and excused herself to her rooms when the tour began. Mrs. Bennet didn't seem to notice.

Darcy conducted the tour himself. Elizabeth suspected he didn't want the servants to see Mrs. Bennet and spread rumors, or even to know he was willingly marrying into such a family. Or perhaps he wanted to spare Elizabeth additional mortification. Regardless of the reason, he was patience itself and while she did see his upper lip curling in distaste more than once, he was unfailingly polite to her mother. She could not blame him for not being exactly friendly; she was nearly ready to do her mother bodily harm herself and she loved the woman! Mr. Darcy could not be expected to have the same affection for her or to have built up the same level of tolerance for her behavior.

The house was beautiful and Elizabeth had an overall impression of elegance and simplicity, but she was so embarrassed and vexed with her mother that she didn't register half of what she was seeing. By the time the tour was over, she was so tired she just wanted to go home. She pleaded a headache and begged Mr. Darcy to call the carriage and tell the maids she would interview them another time.

He did as she asked and walked the ladies out to the carriage. He handed Elizabeth in last and stopped her briefly before she stepped in.

"Are you well?" he asked quietly.

"I will be," she whispered. "Thank you for your patience today, Fitzwilliam. I will not forget it."

He pressed her hand and with another long look, she was gone.

As soon as they returned to Gracechurch Street, Elizabeth and Jane went upstairs to their room where Elizabeth promptly removed her dress and fell across the bed, hot tears of humiliation running over her cheeks.

"Oh, Jane, please tell me I am imagining things and that she wasn't as dreadful as I thought she was."

"Mr. Darcy was very patient," she answered.

"Oh!" Elizabeth pulled a pillow over her head. "Oh, Jane, if a person could die of mortification, you would be laying me out as we speak."

"Lizzy! Do not joke about such things!" Jane reprimanded.

She sat up on the bed. "I'm sorry, dear. I'm just so embarrassed! I didn't know my cheeks could burn so much." She pressed her hands to her face.

"I know. I'm sure I resembled a ripe apple for much of the afternoon," Jane agreed.

Elizabeth laughed sadly at such a statement coming from her sister. "Jane, I think you must keep mama far away from Mr. Walker and his family. Mr. Bingley has already met her, but surely keeping distance there as well would be advisable."

"As much as I hate to say such a thing about a parent, I think you are correct."

Before they could finish their conversation, a note arrived for Elizabeth.

Dearest,

Would you consider spending Sunday afternoon with Georgiana and me? You didn't have a chance to speak much and she would dearly like to get to know you. Miss Bennet is welcome, of course. Please come, my love.

I eagerly await your reply.

F.D.

Elizabeth quickly dashed off a reply and sent it with the waiting servant.

"Jane, we shall be free tomorrow!"

CHAPTER 19

When they arrived at Darcy House, Jane and Elizabeth were shown into a back parlor they hadn't seen the day before. The windows gave a lovely view of the garden and the room was papered in a warm green pattern. Mr. Darcy and his sister were standing in the middle of the room, a soft smile on his face while hers was turned to the floor.

"Miss Elizabeth, Miss Bennet, welcome."

Elizabeth walked to him and took his outstretched hands, allowing him to kiss her hand before speaking.

"Thank you for the invitation, Mr. Darcy."

He nodded and reintroduced them to Georgiana and promptly called for tea. The four sat and Mr. Darcy engaged Jane in conversation. Elizabeth understood he was giving her an opportunity to converse with his sister and gave the younger woman her attention.

Miss Darcy was tall, taller even than Lydia, and on a larger scale than Elizabeth, again reminding her of her youngest sister who was also on a larger scale than she. Not that Elizabeth was delicate. That word would better describe Mary or Kitty, but she was slender and only an average height, without any of the pleasant plumpness that characterized her friend Charlotte or her youngest sister. Jane was of a similar build, though ever so slightly softer, likely due to the differences in their activity levels. It had always been a point of frustration and hilarity that her mother would go on and on about how graceful Jane's figure was and how beautifully all her clothes fit her when Elizabeth's figure was incredibly similar and she received nothing but criticism from her mother.

Miss Darcy was exceedingly shy and Elizabeth couldn't help but compare the stories Mr. Wickham had told her to the reality before her. *What a fool I was to listen to that man!* They spoke of the activities available in town and Miss Darcy said how she longed to return to Pemberley. Slowly and with great patience, Elizabeth drew the younger woman out by asking her to tell her about Pemberley and her favorite parts of the estate. Unsurprisingly, she loved the music room best and a sitting room that had belonged to her mother and that her brother had recently had redone specifically for her.

Mr. Darcy suggested another tour of the house, this one more intimate than the one the day before. They had remained in the public rooms with Mrs. Bennet. She had asked so many questions about the furnishings and fabrics and whether any of the art was by well-known artists that they hadn't had time to tour the entire house.

Mr. Darcy took Elizabeth's arm and Jane fell back with Georgiana, easily setting Miss Darcy at ease with her gentle nature.

After looking at Miss Darcy's personal sitting room at the back of the house and Mr. Darcy's study near the library, Darcy led them to the master's chambers. He showed them the sitting room at the end of the hallway that connected to his room first. Georgiana became engrossed in telling Jane the family history of a painting on the far wall and Darcy took the opportunity to speak privately with Elizabeth.

"This is part of my private apartment, but I thought we could use it more as our personal sitting room."

"Oh?"

"Yes. I have my study for business and personal use, and of course my chamber if I want to be alone, and there are a number of drawing rooms for entertaining, though if I want to meet with a friend we usually meet at the club."

"So you have rarely used this room at all?" she asked.

"Correct. I had hoped, though, that we might make it our shared retreat. We will often have guests staying with us, Colonel Fitzwilliam and Bingley are both frequent visitors, and of course Georgiana, and I thought it might be nice to have somewhere to relax without intrusion," he said somewhat tentatively.

"It sounds like a charming idea. If the room isn't needed for something else, it seems like a perfectly reasonable extravagance."

He smiled and turned her to the left. "That door leads to my bedchamber. There is also a door in the main corridor that we passed on the way in. Your room is directly across the hall. I took the liberty of having a door to the sitting room installed so that we might both have easy access to it."

He almost hadn't told her that he had installed the door himself and let her think that it had always been there, but something in him needed her to know that *he* had put it there—that he expected to use it, and her to as well, enough to make it worth having done.

She flushed and smiled nervously, then looked around. "And where is the mistress's chamber? Through there?" She pointed to a door.

"Yes. I hope you will like it. The décor is rather outmoded but of course you may change anything you like." He led her into the room. "I had a few things rearranged last month in anticipation of your arrival. I hope it is to your liking."

Elizabeth looked around silently, taking in the grandeur of the furnishings and the room itself. It was easily the size of Longbourn's drawing room and featured ornate furniture and rich draperies. Overall, it was more suited to a woman of fashion than to a country girl, but she found much to be admired in the room. She smiled slightly when she thought how Caroline Bingley would have loved this room and how she would have had the whole thing covered in silk within a week.

"What do you think?" asked Darcy.

"Oh, forgive me, sir, I was daydreaming." She smiled and walked to the window to see what sort of view she would have.

"There is another set of apartments if you do not like this one. They are not as large, but one does have a nice view of the garden."

"Don't be silly, these rooms are lovely." She spun to face him. "I can imagine it in a nice, soft blue paper. It will be very peaceful."

He sighed in relief. Recognizing his nervousness, she walked over to him and reached up to kiss him on the cheek.

"What was that for?" he asked.

"For being such a sweet man."

He raised a brow in question.

"Don't look at me like that," she said teasingly. "It is much better to be a sweet man than a rascal and you know it. I am glad you care for my comfort. It bodes well for the future."

He took her hand and raised it to his lips. "I care about everything to do with you."

Jane and Georgiana joined them and they spoke of wall colors and drapery patterns until Darcy asked if she would like to meet the potential lady's maids. They went downstairs to Georgiana's sitting room and soon the two young women were introduced by the housekeeper.

After greeting them both and asking some preliminary questions, Elizabeth asked if she could speak to each woman alone and Darcy offered his study for the interviews.

Lorraine Smith was a temporary maid who had sought out her own training to be a lady's maid. She was born and raised in London, had a very keen eye for fashion, and was clearly eager to help her mistress make a splash on the social scene. Elizabeth liked her and thought she would likely be very good at her job, and she was well qualified, but she thought Lorraine might be unhappy with the quieter life she envisioned them leading in Derbyshire and the subdued wardrobe and hairstyles she preferred.

Elizabeth asked her about this and was surprised to find that she had actually spent several summers at Pemberley as a child. Her aunt and uncle were tenants there and her parents had sent her to stay with them on more than one occasion. She had fond memories of the estate and enjoyed country pursuits but found that town was where more work was to be found, so town was where she stayed.

Elizabeth thought there might be something of a kindred spirit in Miss Smith, and if they wouldn't clash too much on clothing choices, she would make a good maid.

Molly Sanders was twenty-four and worked in the London house. She had acted as Miss Darcy's maid when the regular maid had a family emergency, and she was intelligent and personable. She had been shadowing the same maid off and on for the last several months and hoped to find a suitable position soon. She had spent her childhood at Pemberley but had moved to London to work in the town house after her father died. She still had family in Derbyshire and looked forward to returning.

Miss Sanders was very sweet and had a motherly quality about her. She reminded Elizabeth strongly of her sister Jane, and that made her wonder if she would be the best fit. Elizabeth was looking for more than just someone to fix her hair and maintain her wardrobe—she was also looking for a friend. She would be all alone in Derbyshire and her maid would be on intimate terms with her; it was imperative they get along and she knew that lifelong friendships of a sort often developed. Or at least they did with those women she knew treated their maids well.

She doubted Lady Catherine's maid felt like a friend.

Elizabeth told both women that she had been very impressed by their knowledge and would take the afternoon to think about it and send them notice tomorrow.

"Did you choose one?" asked Darcy as he walked into the study. Elizabeth sat in a chair near the empty fireplace, staring at a globe on a stand next to her.

"Hmm? Oh, I want to think about it for the day. I'll send them a note tomorrow."

He nodded. "You seem far away. What are you thinking of?"

"It's all very strange, isn't it?" she touched the globe and spun it slightly beneath her fingers.

"What is?"

"This. Us. This house. Me choosing a maid. Just two months ago I had no notion of choosing my own maid, or of even ever seeing the inside of your house. And now we are to be married! It's just a bit strange, that's all," she said quietly.

"Did you truly have no notion of seeing the inside of my house?"

"None whatsoever." She smiled, and then her expression turned a bit sad. "I was woefully blind, I'm afraid. I had no idea you even cared about me. In fact, I thought you disliked me thoroughly!"

"What?" he cried. "How could you think such a thing? After all the attention I paid you." He'd known she was a little surprised, but to be completely unaware? It seemed fantastical to him.

She shrugged. "You were quiet and grave and did not smile or flirt with me. You stared and scowled and generally behaved as if I were in your way." She sighed. "No matter. I did not know you then as I know you now."

He walked toward her slowly and sat in the chair beside hers, reaching out to take her hand and rub his thumb over her knuckles.

"And do you know me now?" he asked quietly.

"As well as can be expected in the circumstances, I think," she said to the floor.

"Elizabeth," he said awkwardly. She raised her eyes to his. "Do you, are you, are you comfortable with the idea of marrying me?" He had wanted to ask the question for some time but had always found a reason not to. It was not like him to avoid introspection, but when it came to his bride's feelings about their marriage and about himself especially, he often found it better to not think on it too much.

"Yes," she said simply.

"Yes?"

"Yes, I'm quite comfortable."

He raised a brow in disbelief and confusion.

She continued, "I will admit that I wasn't in the beginning. You know I was not expecting your addresses. But I am quite comfortable now."

"You are?"

"Yes, I am! Now do stop trying to cry off! I am marrying you!" she cried playfully, repeating his words from their walk on the beach the week before.

He raised her hand to his lips and led her back to their sisters, and not a moment too soon. Elizabeth had meant it when she said she was comfortable, for she was. She'd had time to consider and become accustomed to his presence and she was now comfortable with the idea of their marriage. Beyond that, she couldn't say. And she would really rather he not ask.

~

Comfortable. Elizabeth had said she was comfortable with him. With the idea of their marriage.

Comfortable. Hmpf.

It was a perfectly innocent word, but not the one he would use to describe his feelings about his impending marriage. No, he would use elated, excited, joyful, pleased to an immense degree, eager, happy.

And yet, she did not seem any of those things. He knew her feelings were not equal to his; her father had warned him of it the night he sought her hand. In many ways it was to be expected. They hadn't spent as much time together as he would like and she was very young. He had a moment of regret that he had not properly courted her, in Hertfordshire or in Kent. Of course, at Netherfield he had been fighting his feelings and thought they were conquerable. By the time he realized they weren't, he was under his aunt's watchful eye. He could never court a woman that wasn't his cousin at Rosings.

But still. Had he pushed to marry too soon? Should he have spent more time in Margate? The few days he had spent with her had changed her demeanor around him immensely. Unless he was vastly mistaken, she enjoyed his kisses and his embrace, and both boded well for the future. She teased him and smiled at him and seemed to trust him. What was he so unhappy about? Was a content bride not a good thing?

A good thing, yes, but perhaps not enough. Not for him. He had thought all he needed to do to gain her affection was ask for her hand. No woman would refuse him. Now, oddly, he found himself dissatisfied with what he had always expected. He was immensely happy with Elizabeth herself, but alone in his room, surrounded by darkness, he could admit that he wanted more than Elizabeth in his home and in his bed. He wanted more than to make her a Darcy and make children with her. He wanted more than her at his side and across his table.

He wanted her heart.

He wanted her to love him as he did her. To burn for him, yearn for him, long to be in his presence as he longed to be in hers.

Was such a thing even possible? Did women ever feel that way for men? He had never seen it. Could Elizabeth ever feel that way about him? Could he inspire such a fierce devotion in her?

He was terribly afraid he could not.

CHAPTER 20

The wedding was now less than three days away, a fact Mrs. Bennet reminded everyone of as she bustled about the Gardiners' home in a flurry of activity. Gone was the tranquil woman of the last few weeks and in her place stood the Agnes Bennet her children had long grown accustomed to, though ever so slightly less voluble.

She insisted Mr. Darcy would have plenty of time to see Elizabeth after they were married and dragged her two eldest daughters from shop to warehouse to milliners all day Monday. By evening they were exhausted and collapsed in a heap across their shared bed.

Once everything was complete, Mrs. Bennet relaxed slightly, just in time for Darcy to call Tuesday morning. Elizabeth, Jane, and Mary quickly whisked him away to the park for a walk, barely taking the time to tell their mother where they were going.

Jane and Mary walked ahead toward a small pond while Elizabeth and Darcy lagged behind, strolling leisurely on the shady path.

"How are you, my dear?" he asked her gently. Her hand was on his arm and he placed his free hand over hers and held her as close to him as was possible without impeding their stride.

She sighed. "I am tired," she said softly. She laid her head on his shoulder for a moment, the second time she had ever done so, and he found the action oddly endearing. He squeezed her hand, wishing he could do more, and directed them to a small alcove in the trees where they would be protected from view.

"Will you tell me your troubles, dearest?" he asked once they were secluded.

"I love when you do that," she said.

"Do what?" he asked, trying to control his elation that she had said she loved something about him, even if it was an unnamed action.

"Understand when I am distressed and seek to comfort me."

She smiled so sweetly at him he couldn't help but feel moved by the intimacy of it all and he leaned down and gave her a gentle, lingering kiss.

She anticipated his actions and tilted her chin up to meet him. "I love when you do that, too," she said impishly as he pulled away.

He kissed her once more for good measure before leading her back to the path, too overcome for the moment to speak.

"Fitzwilliam, are you well?" she asked quietly.

He looked at her in surprise. "Yes. Very well." He saw her confusion and continued. "Forgive me if my silence indicated otherwise." He could not tell her how her innocent words and sweet affection had done him in or how he longed to hold her tightly to him and kiss her senseless before continuing on to more agreeable pursuits. Instead he said, "I am very pleased to be walking with you, and even more pleased to be marrying you tomorrow."

"I'm afraid I am not as adept at understanding you as you are me."

"Truly?" He thought she was remarkably good at sensing his feelings and knowing exactly what would restore him to good humor or how to comfort him when he was upset and soothe his anger before it got the better of him. It was one of many reasons they were perfect for each other.

"Truly. I cannot read you as yet. How will I know what you are thinking?" she inquired.

"Easily. If I am smiling, I'm thinking of you," he said charmingly.

She smiled and tilted her head flirtatiously. "And if you are frowning?"

"I am thinking of business. Or my Aunt Catherine."

She burst into peals of laughter. And just like that, she was restored to good humor herself.

~

That evening, the entire Bennet family plus the Gardiners were due to dine at the Darcy townhouse for dinner. Darcy had invited her family, which she had assumed included the Gardiners, and when the thought crossed her mind that perhaps it didn't, she purposely included them to prove a point. Firstly, that her relations were intelligent, kind, genteel people and deserved respect based on their own merits. Secondly, she was soon to be mistress of that house and she wanted to set a precedent. She would not forego her relations for his sake. It was not right of him to ask it of her and she wouldn't agree to it even if he did.

The Bennets and Gardiners alighted from their carriages in front of the tall imposing structure that was the Darcy home. Mrs. Bennet tittered to her daughters until her husband nudged her and they walked up the front steps.

Kitty and Lydia were joining the family. They were given strict instructions not to speak to anyone unless spoken to and to behave with utmost decorum. Lydia rolled her eyes when first being told, but when her father had swiftly said she would not be going at all if that was her attitude, she deftly adjusted her behavior. She was allowed to wear her hair up for this occasion, though her dress was still one suited for a young lady not yet out—not the lower cut gowns of her elder sisters.

In the end, however, it did not really matter what Mr. Bennet had said to his youngest daughter, for she was so awed with the grandeur before her that she was silent and gaping, much like her mother. Kitty fared no better, staring with wide eyes at everything around her. Even the butler was the handsomest such man she had ever seen and she couldn't help feeling that her sister was entering into an enchanted world of some kind, where everything was always polished and sparkling and no one ever spoke above a whisper. She half expected to find royalty in the drawing room when she entered, but there was only Mr. Darcy's family.

Darcy met them in the entryway and led them to the drawing room himself, Elizabeth's arm safely tucked in the crook of his elbow. He entered the room with his head held high, his pride in his bride more than evident. Those that knew him realized what he was doing. He had made his choice and would not be gainsaid. Anyone who stood against her stood against him, and he would not look kindly on her being mistreated.

He introduced the Bennet family, beginning with Elizabeth and her parents and ending with the Gardiners. He had been surprised to see them in the entryway, but now was not the time to discuss who was and wasn't an appropriate dinner party guest. There would be plenty of time to discuss that after the wedding. Elizabeth had likely been confused when he said her entire family was invited. It was nothing but a misunderstanding.

The Bennets bowed and curtseyed and looked very charming, all done up in their finest clothes, the women all in new gloves and slippers. Mrs. Bennet smiled and looked at her daughters proudly. They may not be as wealthy as the painted peacocks before her, but they were the prettiest ladies in the room, she'd bet her dowry on that.

Darcy introduced his family, beginning with his uncle Lord Carlisle, the Earl, and his wife, Lady Carlisle. He was the brother of Darcy's late mother and the father of Colonel Fitzwilliam, who stood in the corner smiling mischievously. Next was Lord Melburn, the viscount, and his wife Lady Constance Melburn, Darcy's paternal aunt.

Elizabeth curtseyed to each and smiled. Lord and Lady Carlisle only nodded, while Lady Melburn graced her with a shallow curtsey. Elizabeth had gathered from Darcy that he was closer to this relation than the others and hoped she would get a chance to speak to the grand lady at some point in the evening.

Lady Catherine was absent, as expected. Lord Carlisle's sons were present, Viscount Linley, the firstborn and heir, then Mr. Michael Fitzwilliam, a rector near his maternal uncle's estate, Colonel Richard Fitzwilliam whom Elizabeth had already met in Kent, and who bowed deeply and kissed her hand with a wink, and Mr. John Fitzwilliam, the youngest brother who was a barrister in town.

Elizabeth smiled and greeted them all, then moved on to Lady Constance's children. The eldest son was not present, but his younger brother, Henry, was, as well as Darcy's cousins Angela and Amelia.

"I hadn't realized your family was quite so large," she whispered to her betrothed as he led her away from his relations.

"Only these two families have four children. As you know, Lady Catherine has only one daughter and my own family is just Georgiana and myself." She nodded and sat on the settee he'd led her to. "My Aunt Gibbons and her husband are not yet here, and they also have only one son and daughter."

"She is your father's younger sister, correct?"

"Yes. Lady Constance is his elder by one year. They were all very close when I was young. Aunt Gibbons, her given name is Amelia—my cousin is christened after her—still lived at Pemberley when my parents were first married. She was very close with my mother."

The pre-dinner hour proceeded without event. The Gibbons family arrived and was treated to the Bennet family lineup while Elizabeth searched Darcy's aunts for traces of similarities. The Fitzwilliam family was obviously where Georgiana got her lighter coloring. As she understood it, the late Mrs. Darcy had been fair-haired like her brother and his children. But Lady Constance and Mrs. Gibbons, the late Mr. Darcy's sisters, were both dark haired and blue-eyed, with defined jaws and perfectly straight noses that came to a soft point at the end, more feminine versions of her Mr. Darcy's.

My Mr. Darcy, when did I start to think of him like that? It is just as well. I am marrying the man tomorrow! I should have begun thinking of him as My Mr. Darcy long ago!

Dinner was smooth and easy, mostly anyway. Lady Constance was acting as hostess for the evening and Elizabeth couldn't help thinking her ease was flawless and utterly superior to anything she could do herself. She hoped she could one day be as effortless in turning the conversation from a difficult topic and seeing that everyone had an enjoyable evening, but at the moment she felt far from that ideal.

When the ladies withdrew to the drawing room, Elizabeth was torn between getting to know Darcy's aunts better and containing her mother. Mrs. Bennet had been, so far, oddly quiet, and like the calm before the storm, Elizabeth was making plans that could be quickly enacted should lightning strike. Her aunt reassured her that she would keep an eye on her mother, and Georgiana had led Kitty and Lydia off to her private sitting room at the back of the house.

Elizabeth sat near Lady Constance and Mrs. Gibbons. The former's daughters, Amelia and Angela, joined them. They asked Elizabeth how she had met Mr. Darcy, whether she played and sang and if she would perform for them this evening, what languages she spoke, who her family were, what her place was among the sisters, and more questions than she could ever remember being asked. They were not as rude or overbearing as Lady Catherine, but the sheer number of questions multiplied by the people asking them was enough to exhaust her for the evening.

After what seemed like forever but had actually been less than an hour, the gentlemen returned. The ladies dispersed and Elizabeth found herself sitting alone. Before she could rise to join her sisters, Colonel Fitzwilliam sat beside her.

"How are you faring?" he asked kindly.

"Honestly, I am a bit tired, but well."

They struck up a conversation easily and before she knew what had happened, Elizabeth was smiling and laughing at the stories he told her, just as she had done in Kent. He was a bit of a kindred spirit and owned a similar personality to herself. She had thought it then and this evening was proving her correct. They lamented on being lost in a sea of siblings, him coming from a family of four brothers while she was one of five sisters.

Darcy watched from near the window where he stood talking to his uncle. The man was going on about some sort of law involving crops or something equally uninteresting to Darcy at the current moment. He was too full of Elizabeth to think of anything else. Her eyes, her hair, her smile—she had been utterly enchanting all evening and he was thoroughly bewitched. Perhaps that could excuse his irrational behavior later, but regardless, it left him significantly less sharp than usual.

Richard was talking to Elizabeth, *his* Elizabeth, and making her laugh. Not polite humoring chuckles, but real, honest laughter. Darcy had never made her laugh like that. They were speaking incessantly, agreeing on nearly everything, and clearly enjoying each other's company. Would it look strange if he were to pull her bodily away from his charming ass of a cousin?

Ah, good, there is Miss Mary, come to take Elizabeth away. I wonder if they shall perform together?

At Lady Constance's request, the Bennet sisters took to the pianoforte. Mary and Elizabeth played the instrument while all three sang together, the performance even better than the one he had heard in Kent. They finished to hearty applause and Elizabeth was swept up by Darcy's cousin Angela before he could get to her. Without realizing how it had happened, he found himself standing next to Mrs. Gardiner.

"Are you looking forward to your visit to The Lakes, Mr. Darcy?" she asked him.

"Yes, quite."

"Elizabeth is so excited. It was very thoughtful of you to remember how she has always wanted to see them."

He nodded, but did not respond.

"I believe you will go on to Pemberley afterward?" she inquired.

"That is the plan."

"Derbyshire is so beautiful that time of year."

He nodded again. *Good God, she's angling for an invitation already! The register hasn't even been signed yet!*

"Excuse me," he said curtly before walking swiftly away.

Mrs. Gardiner looked a little shocked, but quickly pasted on a smile and rejoined her husband.

Elizabeth watched her aunt and betrothed from across the room, wondering what they were talking of. From her viewpoint, it looked like her aunt was doing all the talking and that Darcy was doing everything he could to avoid further conversation. She felt a heat building under her skin but told herself this was not the time nor the place to confront him on his rudeness. *You knew this about him, Elizabeth. Do not be surprised by his pride now.* Still, even though she knew she should have expected it, his behavior toward her nearest relations was upsetting.

Deciding to think no more about it at present, she returned her attention to the other guests.

After escaping the scheming of Elizabeth's aunt, Darcy joined his uncle Mr. Gibbons in his conversation with Mr. Bennet. After a few minutes spent debating wine vintages and where to buy them, they were joined by the earl and Mr. Gardiner. Darcy was offended by Mr. Gardiner's effrontery in approaching his uncle, likely for his own gain. *Does this tradesman have no shame?*

"Here now, Gibbons, Mr. Gardiner says he has a man who can get that port we were talking about at the club," said Lord Carlisle eagerly.

"Really? Do tell, man!" Gibbons replied.

Darcy couldn't believe the gall of the man! He was talking and laughing with his relatives as if he was one of them. How dare he abuse Darcy's hospitality so? He had to admit the Gardiners weren't too awful and they were certainly dressed fashionably, which is likely why his family spoke to Mr. Gardiner as they did. They didn't know he wasn't of the gentry.

But Darcy knew. And he was disgusted by this upstart behavior. He excused himself from the conversation before he said something intemperate. He was getting married tomorrow; he wouldn't allow anything to mar the occasion.

Elizabeth watched Darcy out of the corner of her eye. She could tell by the set of his shoulders and the way his mouth flattened into a thin line that he was angry. What he was angry about she could not say. Then he looked at her uncle, his nostrils flared and his eyes narrowed ever so slightly, and she knew.

The source of his disquiet was her very own family, her most treasured uncle, her godfather and blood who had been nothing but kind to her the whole of her life. The man who gave her sanctuary when her mother became too much, who always remembered her favorite fruits and got them special for her when she visited, who had told her stories of castles and knights and dragons when she was but a small girl and enamored of her daring uncle. He had fed her thirst for adventure and always treated her with respect and kindness, as if she were a person that mattered and asked intelligent questions and not as an annoying child. Besides her dearest Jane and her father, he was the person she loved most in the world. She could not imagine getting married without him there, and she certainly could not imagine living the rest of her life without his presence.

Suddenly she felt as if ice had dropped down her back. Would Darcy forbid her from seeing them? Surely he wouldn't! But she saw the look on his face. He was paler than usual and his jaw was clenched, a sure sign he was angry. She saw him excuse himself from the gentlemen and a fear she had never felt before engulfed her. He had been so kind to her parents and sisters that she had come to think better of him. It had never occurred to her he might cut her off from her family. But it was suddenly all so clear. He could not divorce the Bennets, they were entirely too closely related for that to work, but he could cut off an uncle and aunt. He could forbid her from calling on them and bar them from his house, her future home.

At the thought of being kept from her most treasured family, her fear turned to rage the likes of which she had never experienced before. She was giving up everything—Everything!—to marry him. She was subjecting herself to scrutiny and criticism from his family and she expected it would come from many of his friends as well. She was giving up on love—Love!—to be his wife. Because her father asked it of her and because Darcy loved her so dearly—she had thought enough for both of them. But now she questioned even that.

How could he love her, *truly* love her, if he disdained her very roots? How could they spend a lifetime together peaceably with such different ideas of what made a person worthy?

She could not look at him. She wanted to say things, so many things, but she could not say them in a crowded drawing room. She could not tell him how conceited she thought him, how selfish she found his disdain for the feelings of others. She quickly excused herself and made her way into the hall, relief flooding her as soon as she escaped the stifling room overfilled with his presence.

As suddenly as it came, her rage left her and she was filled with a deep sadness as she moved into a dark corner to have a moment of privacy.

She had been right all along about him. Of course her mistaken assumptions about his past with Mr. Wickham had been proven false, but her impression that he was rude and unpleasant and thought himself above his company was depressingly accurate. He could be kind when he chose to, she herself had been the recipient of his kindness, but that made it all the more deplorable when he was so rude to her relations. He knew better and she knew he could do better, but he simply wasn't willing to take the trouble to be kind to people he thought beneath him, no matter their relation to her. Not even for her sake.

She spared a moment for the irony of it all. She was considered beneath him by many, yet he had offered for her! Why would he do such a thing if he were so concerned about his precious connections? Had he not thought this would happen? That he would be thrown into the company of lowly tradesmen? She feared she had been right when she sent him that first letter. They would not suit. It was too late now; they would be married in the morning. She would be bound forever to a man who hated the very people she loved most and who disdained perfectly worthy people not because of their actions or behavior, but because of a silly sense of rank and entitlement.

She felt sick and warm all over and had the disturbing feeling that she was about to cry.

She forced herself to calm and took deep breaths, feelings of vindication in being right warring with a desperate desire to be wrong. She didn't want to be right about this; after all, she was bound to him now, there was no escaping it.

She recited a silly poem to herself to lighten her mood. When that didn't work, she recalled moments of her childhood that she found particularly funny or lighthearted: Mary falling in the mud and being so angry about it she pulled Elizabeth in with her and they both dissolved into girlish giggles; Lydia as a baby laughing hysterically while Elizabeth made funny faces for her just to hear the delightful sound; Jane trading her sampler for Elizabeth's when their mother was inspecting their work, knowing hers was better and not wanting her mother to be disappointed in Elizabeth.

Finally, Elizabeth felt composed enough to re-enter the party, but her reprieve was short lived. Darcy entered the hall a minute later and she rolled her eyes at his attempt at chivalry. Would that he understood a true gentleman would not chase his betrothed into the hall because he would not have caused her to escape there in the first place.

He took her arm and led her back to the corner. "Will you not tell me what is wrong?"

"I do not understand, Mr. Darcy, how you can proclaim to love a woman so passionately while at the same time detesting her relations wholeheartedly. How does one accomplish such a feat?"

She was satisfied with the shocked look on his face and quickly gathered her skirts and pushed past him, leaving him wide-eyed in the corner.

He quickly turned and grabbed her arm. She spun around to face him in a swirl of skirts and righteous indignation. Her eyes were ablaze and Darcy felt a moment of fear when he looked at the rigid set of her face.

"What do you mean, madam?" he asked.

"What do I mean? Surely you know you have been less than civil with my aunt and uncle. You have nearly been hostile! What can you mean by it? How can you behave so poorly to my dearest relations?"

Darcy took a deep breath and released it through flared nostrils.

"Your aunt was hinting at an invitation to Pemberley. It was unseemly. Did you ever think that perhaps I was not the one being uncivil?"

"She what? I find that very difficult to believe."

He huffed. "She commented on the season and how beautiful Derbyshire was likely to be. She clearly wished to see it for herself!"

"Oh? Are you sure she didn't say Derbyshire *is* beautiful this time of year, not likely to be?" He looked thoughtful for a moment. "She hails from Derbyshire, Fitzwilliam! It is her home! Which you would likely know if you had deigned to speak with her more than two sentences before today. She was likely trying to converse with you, but you had to be taciturn with her and assume the worst. Why would she need an invitation to a county filled with her family and friends? And even if she had been hoping for an invitation, which I sincerely doubt, would that be so wrong? I am her niece! She has known me since I was a babe! Is it so unusual for her to want to see where I will live out my days and ensure I am well settled? Is care and genuine interest in another's life so foreign to you that you see nothing but artifice and manipulation?"

"Manipulation? I am not the one pretending to be something I am not, a lesson your uncle clearly needs to learn."

She gritted her teeth. "When did dressing fashionably and behaving politely become so offensive?"

He drew himself up tall and a deeper shade of hauteur overtook his features. "You should not have invited them without speaking to me," he declared.

"I told you how much my uncle means to me. You *knew* he was important. And yet, you still treated him like dirt on your boot." *Not unlike how your aunt is treating me,* she thought.

"You told me no such thing!"

"Yes, I did! In our letters, I told you about the necklace he gave me and that we shared a special bond. He is my godfather. He is my *family,* Fitzwilliam."

Darcy was red with anger and didn't know what to say. He stood staring at her, breathing and trying to calm himself, his feelings utterly at war. He had been so happy just a few moments ago; his future seemed so bright. Now, he could not believe she dared to speak to him in such a way; he was terribly offended. And he thought her incredibly beautiful in her righteous anger and felt outrageously attracted to her, all at the same time. But how dare she speak to him thus in his own home!

It will be her home tomorrow. And did you not say you wanted a wife with spirit, not one who would cower every time you frowned? he thought traitorously. He glanced at her in time to see a single tear track down one red cheek as she took a shuddering breath.

Feeling cut to the quick by the sight of her, he wondered if she was correct, and if she was, what did that say about him?

"I, I," he breathed, unable to settle on any one emotion from the several roiling within him. "My God, Elizabeth!" He pulled her to him and crushed his lips against hers, holding her so tightly his arms ached from the effort.

At first she was stiff against him, her small fists at his chest, but when he didn't let her go after a minute, she pounded her hands against his shoulders. Finally, he released her mouth and looked at her with wild eyes. Her angry retort stopped on her lips as she saw the fire in his gaze. He was breathing hard, as was she, and his desperation was palpable. Had he always loved her so fiercely?

After a few moments she relented and wrapped her arms about his waist, holding him just as tightly as he held her. She laid her head on his chest, and he kissed the top of her head and rubbed her back slowly.

"I cannot give up my family, Fitzwilliam. I cannot," she whispered. "I love them too much."

In the end, it was the soft sound of her voice gently entreating him that pierced his heart. "Of course not, my love. I will never ask it of you. You have my word."

She nodded silently, trying to keep the tears at bay. Tentatively, she put her hands on his shoulders and stood on her toes, pressing a gentle kiss on his lips.

"We should return and say goodnight. We've likely already been missed," she said.

"You go ahead. I will call for your carriage."

"Thank you."

Before she knew it, Elizabeth was being handed into the carriage by Darcy who gave her hand a quick squeeze before waving them off.

~

Though she was no longer seething with anger, Elizabeth was far from calm as she prepared for bed that night. She paced back and forth, her nightgown twisting around her ankles, muttering to herself and gesticulating wildly.

"What has you so distraught, Lizzy?" asked Jane from her seat at the dressing table.

"My betrothed and his ridiculous pride, that's what!" she exclaimed.

"But you've been getting along so well!" cried Jane.

"Yes, until I saw his true feelings. I cannot believe his opinion of my family! I'm surprised he lowered himself to offer for me, with my degrading connections! Is he not afraid the smell of Cheapside will rub off when we kiss, or is the Darcy name enough to cleanse me for his exalted society?" She took a shuddering breath, surprised at her own vehemence.

"Elizabeth," said Jane gravely, "surely he did not call your family a degradation."

"He didn't have to say it, Jane. It was written all over his face."

"Are you sure that's what he meant? You couldn't have misunderstood him?"

"Jane! You weren't there. You didn't see the look in his eyes or how he spoke so dismissively of the Gardiners."

"I'm sorry, Lizzy. This must be difficult for you."

Elizabeth sighed. "It is. But it is done."

"I'm sure it isn't all bad. Mr. Darcy is desperately in love with you. If you ask it of him, I'm sure he will take the time to get to know our relations and see their merit. He cannot fail to see their worth if he knows them, surely. His pride cannot be so important to him."

"You don't know him, Jane. His pride makes most of his decisions, I fear."

Jane shook her head. "But he chose you, Elizabeth. His heart *must* be stronger than his pride."

Elizabeth looked at her in surprise, and her heart lightened ever so slightly.

CHAPTER 21

Elizabeth stood outside the church on her father's arm, her pale blue dress fluttering in the light morning breeze. She took a deep breath and let her father lead her into the unfamiliar building. She would be Mrs. Darcy in less than half an hour. She had a slight urge to take off running down the street, but knew deep down it would do no good. This was her destiny. She could do aught but face it head on.

Darcy stood at the front of the church next to Charles Bingley. His family sat in the pews behind him, whispering quietly as they awaited the bride. The other side of the church was less populated than his. Her mother and sisters were there, as were her aunt and uncle and a handful of people he assumed were acquaintances of her family in town. Comparing it to his own side of the chapel, hers looked rather sparse. His entire family from the evening before had come as well as the cousins that had not been present. In addition, several of his friends from school and the club were there. *Her friends are probably all in Meryton and couldn't make the journey*, he thought.

Suddenly, he wondered if she would have liked to marry from her home. He was slightly abashed that he had not thought of it before. But had not her own father suggested London as the location? Or had it been Darcy, himself? He couldn't remember. He felt like he'd lived a lifetime since that fateful day in Kent. No matter, it was done now and there was nothing he could do about it. He would ask Elizabeth later if she would have preferred marrying in Hertfordshire and if she said yes, he would apologize. Problem solved.

The doors to the church opened and there she was. She was resplendent with the sun shining at her back. Her satin gown glowed in the soft morning light and her hair seemed auburn one moment and brown the next as the light from the stained glass windows danced across her visage. Her face was tilted down and shaded by a bonnet, so it was difficult for him to see her clearly, but he knew she would be lovelier than he had imagined.

The ceremony proceeded in the usual way with Darcy scant noticing anything about the goings on. He only noticed how her hand trembled when he took it in his, and how her voice sounded when she agreed to love him forever, and the light blush that tinged her cheek when he slid the ring on her finger. When all was done, they exited the church to congratulations from the assembled guests and climbed into the carriage that would take them to his aunt's house for the wedding breakfast. She had insisted on hosting it, saying Gracechurch Street was too far from the church and that she would stand in place of his parents who surely would have wanted some part in the festivities had they been alive.

Darcy was touched by the gesture and had no difficulty convincing Mr. Bennet to allow his family to host the event. Now, he sat across from Elizabeth in a carriage on their wedding day, headed to Lady Constance's home for the wedding breakfast, from whence they would leave for their wedding night. He could hardly wait. He knew the breakfast must be endured, but he did not want to linger overlong and hoped Elizabeth would be in agreement.

She twisted the ring on her finger, watching the light catch on the gold, mulling over the changes in her life. *It is happening.* She had thought about it and knew it would come, and she had grown closer to her betrothed and thought more highly of him, but now that the day was upon her, she found herself overwhelmed and wondering if she'd known what she was about when she'd accepted him.

It is just nerves, Elizabeth. All will be well, she admonished herself. She had to admit to a great amount of trepidation for the days to come. Mr. Darcy passionately loved her, of that she was certain. And while she had no direct experience, it wasn't difficult to imagine that a man with such feelings would often want to be in her company, throughout the day and night. She was nervous about what was to come and nervous about the life she would now lead, and nervous about leaving her family and the only home she had ever known to live somewhere she had never seen.

At this thought, she felt her courage rising. She would not be intimidated! She would not! He was just a man, Pemberley was just a house, and the new would only be strange for a little while.

"Here we are," said Darcy. Elizabeth looked up in surprise. They had gone the entire way, though it was short, without saying a word. He had silently observed her while she mulled over her thoughts, thinking she was still upset about the evening prior. "I know we did not speak much last night and there is more to say. We will have plenty of time after the breakfast to say whatever needs saying."

She nodded and he helped her down.

~

The breakfast was a great success, or so Darcy's aunt would call it. The same people from the church were there in addition to a few others. A group of musicians played constantly and the food was elegant and abundant. Lydia, Catherine, and Georgiana all escaped to a sitting room on the next level while Jane spent a great deal of time speaking to Mr. Bingley.

He wore a blue coat, a few shades lighter than Darcy's, and Jane thought his hair was unusually attractive that day. One curl in particular kept falling across his forehead and she hated that she found such a simple thing so endearing.

"It is good to see them so happy, is it not?" Mr. Bingley said to Jane as they stood to the side of the crowd.

Jane raised an eyebrow and glanced at her sister. Elizabeth looked as if she would bolt to the nearest exit any moment and Mr. Darcy looked like he also wanted to leave, but for entirely different reasons. How did Mr. Bingley not notice it? Perhaps he was just making polite chatter.

"Yes, it is a lovely breakfast," she replied.

"Miss Bennet, do you plan to be in town long?"

"We return to the seaside the day after tomorrow. Why?"

He shifted from one foot to the other. "I had hoped to see you again, perhaps plan an excursion. May I call on you tomorrow? Or would you like to go to the menagerie? I've heard the most wonderful things about it and would love to see it with you."

She couldn't help but smile at his enthusiasm. "I would love to see the menagerie with you if my mother has no need of me."

His smile took up half his face and she laughed lightly, feeling her traitorous heart give a little tug in his direction.

~

They stayed at the wedding breakfast longer than Darcy wanted. It was clear to Elizabeth that he wanted to leave, but she could not bear to say goodbye to her family just yet and she lingered long.

She spent considerable time with Colonel Fitzwilliam, who gladly took her around making sure she knew everyone and kept her mightily entertained throughout. At one point she laughed so hard she had to stop to catch her breath. Two of his brothers proved almost as jovial and she was incredibly relieved to be gaining such cousins.

She talked for three quarters of an hour with her mother, suddenly missing the dear, maddening woman who had raised her. Mrs. Bennet looked on her daughter with such a softness in her eye and expression that Elizabeth was nearly moved to tears. Her mother had finally shooed her off to spend time with her new family, and Elizabeth didn't miss that Mrs. Bennet dabbed a handkerchief at her eyes when she turned away from the room.

Once Elizabeth found Jane, she could hardly let her go. She was suddenly wishing Jane was to accompany them on the wedding trip, but she could not do that to her sister. She should stay close to the men who were trying to win her. But oh! How she would miss her dearest sister! When the two finally parted, both needed handkerchiefs and Mr. Bingley was quick to offer his to Jane, looking unusually understanding and compassionate. *Perhaps there is more to him than I suspected*, thought Elizabeth.

She went upstairs and spent nearly half an hour saying farewell to Lydia and Kitty, giving them all sorts of advice. Kitty cried when Elizabeth hugged her goodbye while Lydia reminded her to send them souvenirs from The Lakes and to write down everything she saw so they would feel like they were there. Elizabeth promised she would and left tearfully, after Georgiana quietly gave her a peck on the cheek and wished her well.

The celebration was still going when she came downstairs. Colonel Fitzwilliam and his brother Michael were singing rather boisterously at the instrument with two female cousins Elizabeth couldn't remember the names of, but that she vaguely remembered being told were on Darcy's mother's side of the family. She smiled at their antics and seeing her sister Mary nearby, took her by the arm and pulled her into a dark corner of the hall.

"Lizzy, what is it?" asked Mary in a hushed voice.

"Mary, I want you to do something for me," whispered Elizabeth.

"Of course."

"Keep an eye on father."

"What?"

"I suspect something may be wrong, with his health. I don't know what, but I have long noticed some changes and I can't help but suspect that he turned his household on its head for a reason." Her sister's eyes were wide. "Just promise me you'll watch out for him. Write to me if he looks pale or sleeps more than usual, or if anything else out of the ordinary occurs. Will you do that for me?" asked Elizabeth.

"Yes, of course," replied Mary.

"Promise!"

"I promise!"

Elizabeth pulled her sister into a crushing hug. When they pulled apart, they shared a resolute look and linked arms before walking back into the party.

Elizabeth joined her father where he stood next to several of the other men discussing some sort of hunting. She linked her arm with his and leaned her head on his shoulder, a gesture that made two of the older men smile fondly. He excused himself and sat with her near a window where they stayed close and conversed about all manner of things silly and important for a quarter hour until Mr. Bennet said, "Shall you be well, my dear?"

She smiled wanly. "Yes, Father, I shall." She sighed and returned her head to his shoulder. "I am very tired today, that is all. Do not worry for me."

"It is a father's prerogative to worry for his daughters," he replied. "Now tell me the truth. How are you faring?"

Quietly, she said, "Some days it is very hard. I confess today has been trying. But I believe that some good rest and time to become adjusted to each other is all that is needed."

"Truly?" he asked.

"Yes, truly. He is a good man, I think. He will be kind to me."

"Of that I have no doubt. I could not have let you marry him if he was anything less," said Mr. Bennet in his soft, deep voice. "But that does not mean it will not be a difficult transition for you. I have looked at the calendar, and if all goes well with the harvest, we will come visit you in late October or early November if it suits."

"Oh, Father! Of course it suits. It will be perfect! How long will you stay?"

He smiled at her enthusiasm. "I cannot say. It will depend on the weather and how long it will be wise to stay from home."

"I wish you could stay for Christmas, but I know it will be difficult to travel in the colder weather."

"We shall see. Now I believe there is a man over there desperate to steal you away but hesitant to interrupt us. Why don't you put him out of his misery?"

He smiled and kissed her cheek and she did the same, trying not to cry when he escorted her to Mr. Darcy's side and they said what felt like their final goodbye.

As they were leaving the party, she pulled her father tight for one last embrace and whispered in his ear, "Write to me, Father. You must promise."

"I promise, dear girl."

His eyes were suspiciously shiny as he stepped back and let her husband hand her into the carriage, giving up his rightful place to another. His heart was full of prayers that he had not sent off his favorite daughter to a life of misery just to save the others. *God forgive me.*

The party continued after the couple had departed but Mr. Bennet had no stomach for it. He went to the library and sat near the window with a book he had read to Elizabeth as a child. He got no further than the first few pages when he let his grief take him and shuddered as a sob tore through his body. He let his sorrow have its head for several minutes before pulling himself together and wiping his eyes. He stayed near the window, looking outside but seeing nothing, his mind filled with a bright-eyed little girl, her chestnut ringlets tied in a shiny blue bow, proudly showing him the flowers she had picked or the letters she had managed to write or the wobbly curtsy she was learning to master.

"My darling girl, be well. Be happy. Find your courage and learn to love him. You'll be better for it."

~

Elizabeth was tired. In fact, she was exhausted. The last week had been nothing but travel and shopping and dinner parties and anxiety. Now, it was all over and the truly exhausting part was to come. She now had to live with Mr. Darcy. *All the time.* In the same house with adjoining bedchambers. She felt like she was having an attack of her mother's nerves and had the strangest desire for smelling salts.

Why was she so upset now? Had she not made peace time and again with the idea of marrying Mr. Darcy? *The idea of doing something and actually doing it are not the same thing*, she thought.

Now here she was, sitting in her new room in her new house, brushing out her hair. She was worried about so many things. Would she be a good mistress to the Darcy properties? Would she like his family and friends and would they like her? Would she like Pemberley? Must she be presented and if so, when? What was wrong with her father and if she wasn't there to watch him, who would? Was it possible for him to sink further into whatever was plaguing him and be seriously ill before anyone noticed? Would she ever see him again? She swallowed down a lump at the thought and tried to remind herself that nothing was certain. He may be perfectly well and live many years more.

Her maid left at her request and she wondered if she had made the right decision there. The most immediate concern was for her wedding night. They arrived early in the evening and neither had wanted food. Darcy requested a tray in their sitting room some time later, but she knew not when that would be. When would he come? How would he behave when he did?

Stop thinking about this, Lizzy! She chided herself. *You'll know soon enough.*

~

Darcy was a nervous wreck. He and Elizabeth had had hardly any time to talk. First they'd been at the church, then the carriage was quick and silent, then the breakfast was bustling with family and friends, all who wanted to congratulate him and meet his new wife. They had barely spoken two words to each other! He'd hoped there would be time to speak about their quarrel the night before, but there wasn't. She had seemed reluctant to leave her family and he couldn't blame her. The family would be returning to the seaside soon and a few days later they would be off to The Lakes. It would be months before she saw them again and she was facing a great many changes in the interim.

He thought she had seemed happier lately, well, except for last night, but otherwise, she had seemed quite happy to be in his company and enjoyed his kisses. He could hardly wait to make her his. His hands kept clenching and unclenching at his sides and he ran his fingers through his hair as he paced his room.

He'd never been with a maiden before. He didn't want to frighten her and he knew he must be gentle, but he was so overwhelmed with every conceivable feeling that he was afraid he would lose control of himself and hurt her. What if it was so bad she didn't want to do it again? What if she cried?

"Pull yourself together, man! Just be calm, be patient, be kind and gentle with her. The rest will come," he recited the advice his uncle had given him a few days prior in what had to have been the most awkward conversation they'd ever had. But despite its having been incredibly uncomfortable to speak of such things, he was glad for it. His uncle had given him good advice and he meant to heed it. "I will not rush. I will not demand. I will entice. I will lead her, surely and steadfastly, and all will be well."

He quit talking to himself and walked through the door to the sitting room and onward to the door to her chamber. Taking a fortifying breath, he reached up and knocked.

"Come in," he heard her say quietly.

CHAPTER 22

Elizabeth stood between the vanity and the bed, as if she had been walking between the two and somehow froze on the way. She wore a silky robe that came to her ankles under which he was sure was an enticing nightgown. Her hair was loose around her shoulders and the lack of petticoats was obvious in the way the gown clung to her figure. Her eyes were wide and watched him warily, and her hair hung in long curls down her back.

She looks skittish, like a colt that might bolt any minute. He took a step toward her and she leaned away a tiny bit, but didn't move her feet.

"Are you hungry?" he asked.

They had eaten at the wedding breakfast and he had instructed his housekeeper to have a late supper ready for them to eat in their rooms later, but he wanted to say something.

"No, I am well, thank you," she replied.

What was wrong with her? She seemed suddenly so scared and quiet. This was not the Elizabeth he knew. Perhaps she was still upset about the night before? Should they discuss it? *Now?*

"Elizabeth, I have wanted to tell you all day, but there never seemed a moment, or any real privacy, but I have wanted to tell you that I am sorry for upsetting you last night. Especially as it was the night before our wedding."

She looked up at him warily, unsure of his motives.

"Are you sorry we quarreled, or sorry about your behavior?"

"My behavior?"

She crossed her arms over her chest. "Yes! You know what I mean, Fitzwilliam, please don't make us go through it again. You were rude to my relations. I want to know if you are sorry about that or if you still think they are beneath your notice and only said I may continue to see them because men agree to things that they later regret while they are kissing women!"

How does she know such a thing?

His confusion must have shown on his face for she said, "Remember? You said that you would give me anything I asked for if I kissed you."

She smirked and he flushed red.

"Are you saying you were not sincere in your affection last night, but were only acting a part to manipulate me into doing something you wanted?" he cried.

She flushed. "No. I am merely reminding you of something you said to me. I was sincere in my affection, as I always am. You were very… compelling." She finished quietly and looked down before raising her head again to glare at him. "That does not mean I am not also upset with you."

He pinched the bridge of his nose. This was not at all how he had envisioned his wedding night proceeding.

"What do you want from me, Elizabeth? Please, just tell me." He sighed in exasperation.

She clenched her teeth and finally bit out, "I want you to be kind to my family. I want you to get to know them and learn to respect them on their own merits, of which there are many. I want them to be welcome in our homes and for you not to restrict me from going to theirs. That is what I want."

"Done. Now may we put this behind us?" he said quickly in clipped tones. He'd almost said, "Now may we get on with it?" but he stopped himself before making such a foolish blunder.

She sighed and shook her head. This wasn't going well at all. This day had been wearing, as had the week leading up to it, and the night was to be filled with new and possibly painful and definitely strange experiences. She truly did not wish to begin in such an inauspicious manner.

"Fitzwilliam, might I beg a reprieve?" she asked tiredly.

"A what?" he cried, shock evident in his tone.

"I am exhausted, it has been a very long day, and I would very much like to not begin our married life in a quarrel or with harsh feelings between us. It does not engender warmth."

He huffed and looked to the side, knowing she had a point. He also knew that he agreed with her; he did not wish to begin tempestuously either. But how had they gotten here? Things had gone terribly wrong.

He heard his uncle's voice in his head. *"How you handle this night will long define your relationship with your wife. A man who is warm and loving will be welcomed by his wife with open arms. A man who is quick and cold will be met by dread. Which do you want to be?"*

Was she already dreading this part of their relationship before it even began? He purposely gentled his tone and forced his rigid posture to relax somewhat. *Entice, do not demand.*

"Elizabeth, I know it has been a trying time lately, for you especially. I propose we start over. How does that sound to you?"

"Start over?" she questioned.

"Yes. Why don't you lie down and rest for a bit, and I will return in an hour or so. Will that suit you?"

She looked toward the window where the sun was nearly hidden and then looked back at him skeptically. "You will return in an hour?"

"Yes, if you wish it."

"Very well. I will see you in one hour." She stood waiting for him to leave so she could climb into the very comfortable-looking bed, but he just looked at her expectantly.

Finally, he took her hand and guided her to the edge of the bed. She climbed up onto it and he tucked the covers around her before placing a gentle kiss on her forehead.

"Sleep well, my love," he whispered.

She snuggled into the blanket and within a few minutes was fast asleep.

~

A short time later, Elizabeth woke just as her dressing room door closed. She noticed a tray with a fresh pot of tea near the empty fireplace and rose to refresh herself and make a cup. She was just taking her first sip when the door to their shared sitting room opened and Fitzwilliam stepped in quietly.

"It's all right, I am awake," she said from the settee. She smiled at him shyly and he returned it.

She was grateful, really. She knew he did not need to give her time to adjust, he did not need to be patient with her or have tea sent up. But he did these things because he was a good and kind man and while she was wounded from the events of the previous day, she decided not to let it overcloud her good judgment.

So he was proud. What of it? Now he was also her husband and she should focus on his good qualities and hopefully, with time and a little effort, his pride would wane.

"Did you sleep well?" he asked her softly, afraid to startle her.

She felt her heart soften a little more.

"Yes, quite well. Thank you for the time. It was very restorative," she said the last quietly, hoping he understood her meaning.

He looked at her softly but kept his position near the fireplace. "You are welcome."

"Would you like a cup of tea?" she asked.

"No, thank you. I am well."

She replaced her cup and stood, looking around before settling her eyes on him. She supposed this was the part where she was supposed to welcome him to her bed, but she had no idea how to go about such a thing. Should she turn down the coverlet for him? Plump his pillow? Climb in first and hold out her arms? It all seemed utterly ridiculous!

"What—what should I—what do you wish —" she was flustered and incoherent and making no sense at all. "You must think you've married a dunce, Mr. Darcy."

He smiled and took her hand, coming a little closer. "I think no such thing."

She had so many questions: What he expected of her, what she should expect of him, what the protocol was for this entire affair. Would he sleep with her after? Should she invite him to stay? Or ask him to leave? Which did he expect? Which did he *prefer*? Should they speak? Remain silent? Wouldn't that be terribly awkward? To be silent for half an hour altogether? Suddenly she was filled with apprehension. Did it take half an hour? Less time? More time?

"Dearest, what troubles you?" He rubbed his thumb along the back of her hand, inadvertently making her more nervous.

"I, oh, I have so many questions!" she blurted. Her eyes widened in shock at her admission and he laughed lightly. "Forgive me."

"There is nothing to forgive."

She fidgeted nervously, glancing between him and the floor repeatedly, her face getting pinker by the moment.

"Really, Fitzwilliam, it isn't necessary for you to laugh at me so! You have me in a very delicate position! You could be gentlemanly about it," she said with a pout.

He stopped himself from making a joke about the *delicate position* he'd rather have her in and sat on the settee, pulling her down beside him.

"Now, tell me about these questions you have," he said.

"I couldn't possibly! It's unseemly!" she cried.

He raised a brow. "More unseemly than me being in your private chambers in our nightclothes?" The line between her eyes appeared as she frowned. "Elizabeth, our roles have changed now. I would like us to be free with each other—especially here. To speak, to act, to share whatever we like. These are our private rooms. You have my word that nothing you say to me here will go beyond these walls."

"And you will not mock me?" she asked suspiciously.

"I will not mock you. I promise." He suppressed his grin at the adorable look of resolve on her face. "Now, what is your first question?"

Taking a deep breath, she decided to forge ahead. "How long does it take?"

Darcy flushed and spluttered before saying, "It depends. Sometimes it may be rather quick. No more than a few minutes. Other times, the act could stretch into hours."

"Hours!"

"Well, including all the activities, not just the portion where—it can be different each time."

She nodded. "Will it always be here? Do you expect me to come to your room sometimes?"

His eyes took on an interested glow. "Whatever you like, my dear. I am perfectly amenable to you coming to my rooms whenever you like."

"And do you want to… sleep with me… after?" she asked quietly.

He pulled her closer to his side and she snuggled into him, seeking solace in a form of affection she was familiar with. And from this angle, he couldn't see her face or how often she blushed during this very awkward conversation. She hated how he made her anxious and yet she wanted to be close to him at the same time. Were all men so maddening?

"I believe in the beginning, it would be nice to sleep together. I cannot bear the idea of ever leaving this room, now that I have seen you in such a state." He touched her hair and ran a hand down the length of her arm while she blushed. "In the future, we may want to sleep separately. I think we can decide as we go. I will certainly not impose my company on you if you'd rather be alone. I hope you know that."

"Of course. I would never think it of you," she said quietly.

"Good."

"I heard," she hesitated and fiddled with the lapel on his dressing gown, "I was told that perhaps it happens more than once in a night, especially in the beginning, and that might be why you would wish to sleep with me. Is that true? Can it occur more than once in a night?"

He shifted. "Yes, it can, and yes, it likely will be like that, especially in the beginning, but I would not want to sleep with you merely to have you near for convenience's sake." He shifted so she could see his face. "Elizabeth, I love you. With all my heart. With everything I am. I want to be near you, for no other reason than to bask in your presence. Don't you see that by now?"

"Fitzwilliam," she whispered. She felt overwhelmed by his words and reached out a hand to touch his face softly. She ran her fingers over his nose, along his jaw, and traced his lips lightly, all the while keeping her eyes trained on his as they grew blacker by the second.

Slowly, he bent his head to hers. His lips were surprisingly soft and tender. He had kissed her before, but this kiss was different somehow. She felt it in her toes, if such a thing were possible, and quickly realized the difference between this and every other kiss he'd given her.

This time, he had no intention of stopping.

CHAPTER 23

When Elizabeth woke a little after dawn, she felt terribly awkward. Fitzwilliam was in her bed, sleeping with one arm outstretched and taking up an inordinate amount of space. She saw her robe lying on the floor and quickly put it on, wincing a little as she walked. He had been gentle and kind and patient, just as everyone thought he would, but she had been right about it being a little painful, though thankfully not too bad. It was, nonetheless, so very strange.

She tiptoed to her dressing room and saw the tub being filled and sat gingerly at the dressing table to brush her hair while she waited for the remainder of the water to be brought up. The two maids carrying the buckets were quick and efficient, nodding in her direction but not looking at her. She must remember to learn their names.

Her maid, Molly Sanders—chosen because of her motherly, Jane-like qualities, bustled in and poured a few drops from a small bottle into the steaming water.

"Are you ready, Mrs. Darcy?"

"Yes, thank you, Sanders. What was that you added to the water?" She was helped out of her robe and into the steaming water.

"Lavender, madam, to ease the muscles."

Elizabeth sank into the water slowly. "Very thoughtful, Sanders. Please come back in a quarter hour to help me wash my hair."

"Yes, madam."

Elizabeth sank down and leaned her head back on the towel that rested on the tub's edge. The copper bath was one of the refurbishments Darcy had seen to before her arrival. She must remember to thank him.

What an odd night it had been! Her skin flushed just thinking about it, but she told herself the hot water had something to do with it. They had kissed for an incredibly long time, longer than she thought was even possible, and he had touched her in places she had never thought anyone would touch. Her feelings about this new activity were rather mixed. Many of the things her new husband had done with her—and to her—body had been pleasurable, but it had all been so new, and so very surprising, that she spent half the time overcoming her shock. Just as she got over the newness of a sensation enough to enjoy it, he was shocking her with something even more intimate.

The feel of him on top of her had been indescribable and she felt both profoundly close to him and a little bit scandalized. She told herself this was nothing to be concerned with. After all, a lifetime of modesty was not done away with in a moment.

She wondered if she would have felt differently about it all if she loved him as she had always hoped to love her husband and, as she was realizing, he deserved to be loved. Would she have leapt into his arms as soon as he entered her chambers? Would her shock have been replaced with excitement? Would she have relished every moment in his arms, without worry or confusion? She could not know, of course, but for the first time since her engagement began six weeks ago, she wished she did love him.

Not in the general "I want to marry a man I love" way, but in an "I wish I loved *this* man" way. *Perhaps I will grow to love him*, she thought. *It is possible, surely. I already like him significantly more than I used to.*

Afterward, they had eaten some fruit and cold meat laid out in the sitting room. He had then accompanied her to her bed. She was unsure if he was going to sleep with her or if he wished to lie together again. In the end, he had climbed into the bed, cuddled her close and stroked her hair, and fallen asleep rather quickly. Elizabeth had lain awake, wondering if she would even be able to sleep with this man in her bed, clinging to her so. She eventually fell asleep with her head on his chest and his arm wrapped tightly around her.

She hadn't heard any sounds from the bedchamber and thought Darcy was likely still asleep. She scrubbed her skin, frowning at the small swirl of red drifting off her intimate places. She was also surprised to see small red marks on her décolletage and looking in the mirror, she saw two on her neck as well. She could not fathom what these marks were until a memory niggled its way to the front of her mind. She was fourteen and sneaking a biscuit from the kitchen. One scullery maid was assisting the other with tying a scarf around her neck so Cook wouldn't see her "love bites." She hadn't known what they were talking about and dismissed it, but now she wondered. *Love bites...*

"Are you ready for me to wash your hair, Mrs. Darcy?" asked Sanders.

Elizabeth opened her eyes and leaned forward. "Yes, let's."

Sanders removed the braid and before she could say anything, Elizabeth sunk down into the water to soak her hair, blowing bubbles out of her nose.

Sanders had been bending to retrieve a bucket of water to tip over her head and the look of surprise on her face made Elizabeth burst into laughter.

"It's quite all right, Sanders. I shan't drown! Save the fresh water for the rinsing. It would take buckets of it to wet it to the scalp. This way is much more efficient."

Her maid quickly removed the shocked expression from her face and began washing Elizabeth's hair, scrubbing her head in the most delicious way. After she was rinsed, Elizabeth leaned forward to allow Sanders to scrub her back and Elizabeth rubbed her fingers along her neck and rotated her sore shoulders. She thought they were likely in such poor condition from the odd angle she slept at last night.

"Would you like me to rub your shoulders, madam?"

"Are you good at it?" Elizabeth asked. Mary had tried to rub her shoulders once and she winced through several minutes of torture before telling her sister she was better now and to please stop.

"My sister says no one's better," said Sanders proudly.

"Very well then."

Elizabeth leaned forward and pulled her hair over one shoulder and Sanders proceeded to work out the knots and soreness from her neck and shoulders. Elizabeth nearly sank into the water from the sheer pleasure of it and sighed contentedly more than once. A maid of her own was a glorious thing indeed.

After she was dried and her hair combed out, Elizabeth wondered what she should do. Normally, she would sit by the fire to dry her hair, or in summer, as it was now, she would sit by an open window and read for a bit. Once or twice she'd even snuck outside to let it dry in the sun, a wonderful but improper way to dry thick hair such as hers.

She looked toward the window and saw that it had started to rain, making sitting in front of an open window impractical. The fire hadn't been lit when she'd left her room, but if the rain brought colder temperatures, it might be lit now. She didn't want to wake Fitzwilliam by ordering one done, however. Who would have thought such a simple thing as drying one's hair could be so complicated? Marriage was already requiring adjustments and suddenly she wished he had slept in his own room to spare her this ridiculous decision making.

"Shall you sit in front of the fire to dry your hair, madam?" asked Sanders.

"Is there one lit?"

"The one is your chamber is bright as can be," said the maid cheerfully.

"Then yes, I will. Do you know if my husband is awake yet?" It sounded strange to say the words. *My husband.*

"Yes, madam. The master is in his dressing room."

"Thank you, Sanders. It usually takes about half an hour to dry, and then I shall need your help dressing. I believe I'll wear the new pink gown today."

"Yes, madam. I'll have it pressed and ready."

Sanders opened the wardrobe and removed the dress while Elizabeth tightened the belt on her soft blue dressing gown and went into the bedroom to dry her hair. She sat by the fire, absently running a comb through her hair, turning her head from side to side while her thoughts wandered.

~

Darcy awoke slowly and wondered where he was. The crown above this bed did not match the one in his chamber and then he remembered yesterday had been his wedding and he was in his wife's chamber. *My wife.* Just thinking it gave him a deep feeling of satisfaction. He reached out to his side, searching for her, but met only a cold sheet. There was a brief moment of panic when he wondered if it had all been a dream. He sat up and looked around the room, then heard Elizabeth's laughter coming from behind the dressing room door.

A smile he wasn't aware of slowly worked its way across his face. He was married. To Elizabeth. To a woman he loved in a marriage of genuine affection, not a calculated union of convenience. His relief was immeasurable, his joy boundless. He rose and went to the dressing room door, his intention to see his wife, but he heard her maid's voice and what sounded like water being poured into a tub and decided to follow his wife's example and bathe. He would give her privacy for now; he could suggest bathing together at a later time when she was more accustomed to his presence in her intimate life.

He was incredibly cheerful and his valet stifled more than one smile as he watched the master of the house grin like a fool while bathing, combing his hair, and getting dressed. He'd barely been able to stop long enough to be shaved.

Darcy reentered his wife's room with a spring in his step. She was sitting before the fire with her hair around her like a curtain, much of it still damp, and a comb in her hand. Her expression was blank as she stared into the flames.

"Good morning, dear." He placed a swift kiss on her cheek. "Are you hungry?" he asked.

"Hmm?" she asked, suddenly surprised at his presence.

"I asked if you were hungry. There is breakfast in the sitting room."

Just then her stomach released a loud growl and they both laughed.

"I suppose that answers the question. Come." He held out a hand and she followed him into the room between their private chambers. A selection of breakfast items was laid out on a side table and she quickly filled a plate and sat across from Fitzwilliam.

"Did you sleep well?" he asked.

She flushed. "Yes, I did, thank you. And you?"

"Better than ever." He grinned, of course.

She nodded and looked down as he winked at her, her face impossibly red now.

"What shall we do today?" she asked a few bites later.

"Whatever we like. There is no set schedule. I thought in the days to come it would be nice to give you an in-depth tour of the house, and of course you'll want to meet with the housekeeper and cook, but otherwise, we are at our leisure."

She nodded. She felt as if she was doing a lot of nodding lately. He looked entirely too satisfied with himself. She would have been irritated by it if he weren't being so charming. She shook her head, another thing she was doing a lot of these days. Would she ever fully understand her husband?

"I would like to meet with the housekeeper and cook tomorrow, if I may," she said.

"Of course you may. You are the mistress of the house; you may do whatever you wish."

She smiled and he returned it. He seemed utterly at ease and almost annoyingly happy. She never thought she would say it: Fitzwilliam Darcy—Man of Merriment. She almost made herself laugh with the thought. Why was he so much more comfortable than she was? Did he often have breakfast with women in his private sitting room? Had he been married before?

"Am I your first wife?" She was sure she was, but she wanted to double check.

He choked slightly on his tea. "Pardon me?"

"I'm sure I would have heard if I wasn't, but it suddenly occurred to me that I never asked you before and I wanted to know."

"Yes, you are, of course. What on earth would make you think otherwise?"

"Well, you seem so comfortable. As if you've done this a hundred times before. I just wondered if perhaps you had." She shrugged and took a sip of her tea.

"If you'd like to know why I seem so at ease, it's because I have done this a hundred times before."

Her head shot up and she looked at him with worried eyes.

He really should not enjoy this so much. His features softened into an odd mixture of tenderness and mischief. "I have been imagining this morning, and last night, and yesterday, for months. Your place has always been here, across the table from me, in bed next to me, living with me. You belong here, Elizabeth. How can I be anything but pleased that you have finally come home?"

She stared at him, unable to speak, feeling unexpectedly touched. He found her hand on the table and kissed it tenderly. She squeezed his hand in return.

"I have been meaning to ask you," he asked softly, "are you well this morning?"

It was impossible to mistake his meaning. "I am a trifle sore, but nothing overwhelming." He looked relieved. The desire to tease could not be resisted. "And you, sir? Are you well?" He looked at her in surprise. She pressed on, "You were very… active last night. You did not sustain an injury?" She looked at him sincerely, her mouth slightly twitching in the corner the only hint that she was teasing him.

Immensely pleased to see her playful after such a serious day and night, and on such a subject, he smiled and joined her game. "I assure you, Mrs. Darcy, your husband is not in such poor condition that one night of activity will render him lame. I am fit for activity again as soon as my lady may accommodate."

"Are you now?" she asked in a playful tone. "What a lucky lady I am, to marry a man of such strength and stamina."

"You have no idea, Mrs. Darcy."

At this he rose and pulled her from her chair, her surprise mounting as he bent down and picked her up, her feet flying from the ground as she shrieked.

"Fitzwilliam! Put me down this instant! What are you doing? Are you trying to hurt yourself?"

She kicked and even hit his shoulder more than once, but he did not release her until they were in her chamber and he dropped her into the center of the freshly made bed. She yelped as she landed and he quickly plopped down next to her.

"See? I am perfectly fit." He smiled boyishly and she couldn't help but laugh at the picture he presented.

~

Finally, when the sun was high in the sky, Elizabeth was dressed in her new pale pink gown and awaiting her husband who had promised her a detailed tour of the house.

"Sanders, do I look different to you?" she asked her maid after she latched a delicate bracelet on her wrist.

"Different, Mrs. Darcy?"

"Yes. I fear I am walking strangely. What do you think?" She walked a few steps away and turned back. "Do you notice anything amiss?"

"No, madam, other than looking a bit careful, you seem the same as yesterday."

"Careful. Hmm. Thank you, that will be all. I'll ring when I need you."

The maid curtsied and disappeared, leaving Elizabeth wondering what exactly a person looked like when walking carefully. Like the way Jane walked when she sprained her ankle three years ago? Surely she wasn't limping! Or perhaps it was similar to how she walked when she fell out of a tree in Sir William's orchard when she was fifteen and landed on her backside. But of course she hadn't really seen herself walk then, either. She would describe the way she moved then as careful, though.

She tried to see herself in the large mirror in her dressing room, but the room was of such a size and the mirror in such a location that she couldn't make out anything useful. She decided to move it into the bedchamber where there would be more space and wider angles. She grabbed the mirror on either side and lifted, but it would not budge. She considered calling a footman, but how would she explain what she was doing? In the end, she tilted the mirror and braced it against her hip while leaning back and pulling with all her might. She had to stop once, but she did eventually get it into the bedchamber and placed in the corner.

So settled, she walked away from the mirror, looking over her shoulder at herself the whole way. She adjusted the mirror and her direction and tried again. She didn't look *very* different, just strange with her head turned round.

"What are you doing, Elizabeth?"

She jumped and her hand flew to her chest. "Fitzwilliam! Do you not make noise when you walk?"

He raised a brow and gestured toward the mirror. "Did you move that yourself?" he asked.

"I didn't want to call a footman and it wasn't too heavy."

"Hmm." He walked toward the mirror and lifted it, making another face at her when he realized its weight. She shrugged sheepishly and he shook his head at her.

"Are you finished? Shall I return it for you?" he asked.

"Yes, please," she replied, grateful to get him away from the topic of what she was doing.

He lifted the mirror easily and walked into the dressing room with it, reappearing a moment later. "Now, what exactly were you doing? Watching yourself walk? You're not trying out some ridiculous new sashay, are you?" he asked worriedly.

She laughed. "No, of course not! I was merely observing something."

"What were you observing?" he inquired.

"Nothing of consequence. Now, where shall we begin the tour? The guest wing?"

"Why won't you tell me?" He continued to question her.

"Tell you what?"

"What you were doing," he replied, slightly annoyed at her avoidance.

"Must you know everything that I do in the privacy of my own rooms?" she asked, now irritated herself.

A hurt look ran across his features before he straightened his shoulders and said stoically, "Of course, madam. Forgive me for intruding on your privacy. Shall we?"

He opened the door to the hall and she stepped through, noticing that he looked steadfastly over her head and refused to look at her face.

"Fitzwilliam," she said softly. He finally looked down when she put her hand on his arm and met her worried expression. "Have I hurt you?"

He released a breath and had a moment of struggle with his pride, but then decided he would risk speaking to his wife. "Forgive me, Elizabeth. You have every right to privacy. It is only my overzealousness to be close to you that wants to know everything, and I admit it stung when you did not want to tell me." He shook his head. "It is a very strange thing—being in love with a woman."

He looked at her and she felt something inside her soften a bit further.

"I want to give you everything, share everything with you. I have never been in such a situation before. I'm afraid I do not always handle it properly.," he said.

"I think you handle it beautifully most of the time," she said, and reached up on her toes to kiss his cheek. "I apologize for being thoughtless. I did not realize your intent."

"You have nothing to apologize for. I invaded your rooms, not the other way round."

"Nevertheless," she said. She placed her hands on his chest and played with the lapels of his jacket. Did she feel his heart speed up beneath her hand? "Dearest, can you keep a secret?" There was definitely a quickening beneath her palm now.

"Of course."

She looked around the deserted hallway to ensure they were alone before speaking quietly. "I was trying to look at my walk."

"Your walk?" He looked utterly confused.

"Yes. I felt like I was walking differently and I wanted to see if it was noticeable to others. That is all."

"Why would you be walking diff —" He stopped and looked at her flushed face and downcast eyes. "I see. It seems I have more to apologize for today. My intrusion now seems doubly rude. You were only trying to examine the damage I caused and then I had the nerve to question you." He shook his head in disgust and looked away. "Forgive me, my love. I will not intrude again."

"You are forgiven," she said, smiling sweetly at the look of relief on his face.

"I did not mean to injure you. Are you very sore? Would you rather we rest instead of touring the house?" he asked contritely.

"No, I've had enough of my room for the day. I'd like to stretch my legs. Shall we tour the guest rooms? We didn't see them when I visited before."

And so they were off. He told her stories about the rooms and who usually stayed in each and when they were last changed. She made mental notes of the furniture and which coverlets looked like they should be replaced soon. She was pleasantly surprised to find that the rooms were beautifully done but were not garish. *This is true elegance*, she thought. *Where beauty and comfort are the goals, not the display of wealth.*

When the tour was complete she said, "There is one room I have not seen yet."

"Which is that?"

"Yours."

He hesitated but a moment. "This way."

He took her arm and led her rather swiftly through the halls so she was practically skipping to keep up with his long strides.

He opened a door and led her in, saying, "My lady's wish is my command."

She stepped into his bedchamber and looked around, curiosity getting the better of her. There was a leather chair by the fireplace and a soft fur rug in front of it. She noted the door she presumed led to his dressing room and another that led to a balcony outside. She opened it and looked out, the rain preventing her from exploring further.

"It extends to the sitting room that direction." He pointed to his right and she looked obligingly, her eyes catching sight of the bed.

It was covered in a deep green counterpane with curtains of a similar shade pulled tight to the posts. There was a small table on either side with a lamp. She quickly looked away and noted the round table in the center, presumably for dining in his chambers and another chair in the corner. Altogether, it was rather sparsely furnished and she wondered if it was by design or if he hadn't really noticed it.

"You do not have much furniture," she observed.

"No. I do not like clutter."

She nodded and walked to the other side of the room, feeling the plush rug beneath her slippers and sliding her hand along the smooth wood of the table.

"May I?" she asked, reaching for his dressing room door.

"Of course."

She stepped inside the small room. It was similar to hers in that it was surrounded by wardrobe doors that she was sure were filled with elegant clothes, but the style was rather different. Hers was done in pale, light colors while Darcy's was a rich blue.

"I'm surprised it isn't green to match your chamber," she said as she looked at the oddly-shaped chair in the corner she assumed was for being shaved in. She had seen an advertisement for one once.

"I do not like too much of the same color. It becomes monotonous," he said.

"You do not like clutter and neither do you like single color schemes. What else shall I learn about you today?" she asked playfully.

"Do you have a bathing tub?"

"Yes, it is through there," he replied, gesturing to a door in the corner. "You may look if you wish."

She opened the door and stepped onto the cool marble. The copper tub gleamed against the pale floors and a small window let in a thin ray of light.

"Mr. Darcy!" she exclaimed. "That tub is enormous!"

He smiled. "Yes, I ordered it when we became betrothed. It only arrived a few days ago. Do you like it?"

"I think I might drown in it! Thankfully mine is smaller. Is your old one in my chamber now?"

"No, I wanted you to have a new one as well. The tubs that were in our bathing chambers have been moved to guest chambers."

"Ah. I'm sure the guests will appreciate it! Most only offer a hip bath. This is quite luxurious." She ran her hand over the lip of the smooth copper appreciatively. "Tell me, why is this one shaped differently?"

Her tub was higher on one end than the other, allowing the user to lie back. This one was high on both ends with a dip in the center, presumably for entering the tub.

"This one is designed for two people. That is why it is so large," he said simply.

Her eyes widened. "Two people! But why would two people want to bathe together? It hardly seems efficient."

He chuckled at her innocence. "When one is bathing with another, efficiency is generally not on one's mind."

"Oh," she said, suddenly comprehending and blushing a light pink. "And have you had many inefficient baths, Mr. Darcy?"

He was taken aback by her question, but answered. "No, actually I have never tried it. But I am convinced it shall be enjoyable."

She blushed brighter. "Thank you for showing me your rooms, Mr. Darcy. I believe I would like to see the gallery again. We went through it so quickly last I was here." She bustled out of the room quickly and he ambled behind her, a small smile on his face.

Dinner was a subdued affair. It was their first meal downstairs. They ate in the small dining parlor next to the music room rather than the large dining hall which would have felt cavernous with just the two of them. This table comfortably seated six and could be expanded to hold twelve if necessary.

"Do you like the room?" he asked her after catching her looking around for the third time.

"Yes, very much. The paper is particularly pretty."

"My mother chose it shortly before she died. The paper came in after the funeral but my father did not hang it. I found it a few years ago and had it put up. It suits the room admirably, don't you think?"

"Yes, it does. And how perfect that you can have such a pleasant reminder of your mother on a regular basis," she said.

"Yes," he said plainly, looking at his plate.

"What shall we do the remainder of our time in London? We leave in five days, correct?"

"Yes. Did you want to do any shopping? It might be a good idea to order a new coat and fur lined boots. We have no plans to return to town before winter."

"I suppose I could. I imagine I have enough new gowns for some time, but of course I will need more now that I have married such an important man."

"You certainly shall. Important men never like to see their wives in the same dress twice."

She laughed. "You are getting very good at teasing, Fitzwilliam."

"I have an excellent teacher," he replied and took her hand on the table. She blushed unexpectedly and looked down.

"Are you ready to retire, Elizabeth?"

She looked up and recognized the look in his eyes. "Yes, Fitzwilliam. I'm ready."

CHAPTER 24

Bingley collected Jane at the Gardiners early the day after the wedding. Mary and her Aunt Gardiner accompanied them as chaperones. Jane was grateful her mother was too tired from the wedding to want to do the job herself.

It was fairly early in the day and the menagerie wasn't too crowded. She held Bingley's arm as they walked around and looked at the animals, commenting on their size or coloring and whatever else came to mind.

"I've always thought it interesting that the male animals are more colorful and showy than females. So different from the way people behave," Jane mused.

"It truly separates us from the animals," said Bingley. Jane gave him a quizzical look. "Our women are so beautiful," he said softly, looking directly at Jane.

She blushed and moved on to the next exhibit. "How are your sisters?"

"Louisa is well. She just informed me last week that she is expecting a child this Christmas."

Jane smiled brightly. "That's wonderful! Please give her my congratulations."

"I shall. She and Hurst plan to leave for his estate shortly before attending a house party in July. They will remain in the country for the rest of the summer. She hasn't yet decided if she will return to town for her lying in."

"Will Miss Bingley accompany them to the country?" she asked. She leaned over to look at a small monkey of sorts sitting in the bottom of a cage.

Bingley moved closer. "That is undecided. It depends largely on what I do this summer."

"Oh?" she asked distractedly as she moved around the cage to get a closer look.

"Yes. I usually spend a large portion of the summer at Pemberley with Darcy, but obviously, this summer is not usual."

Jane sent him a small smile of understanding before returning her attention to the primate.

"I was thinking of visiting the seaside," he said uncertainly.

Jane straightened and looked at him seriously. "Whereabouts?"

"I had considered Margate. Your sisters said how beautiful it was and I would like to go where I have acquaintance in the area." Jane nodded with what he thought was a disappointed expression and he stepped toward her. "Miss Bennet, I'm saying this all wrong. I would like to see you this summer, and since you are in Margate, thither I will go. Would you allow me to call on you there?"

She studied him for a moment before speaking. His jaw was slightly tense and his nostrils were flaring a bit with the strength of his breath. His shoulders were straight but rigid and the tips of his ears had gone red.

"Will your sister accompany you?" she asked, and moved to look at a lizard-like creature in another cage.

"I am undecided. I would be able to entertain if I had a hostess, but I do not know that the town would suit her."

"Have you asked her opinion on the subject?" Jane asked.

"Not as yet. I had thought I would wait for my plans to be fixed before asking her what she wished to do," replied Bingley.

"What if she wished for you to accompany the family to the house party?" she asked as she moved to yet another cage holding a red exotic bird. Her voice was light, but her shoulders were tense and her eyes strained.

"I have no desire to go to the house party. Caroline will go there, looking for a husband, but what I am looking for is soon to be in Margate," he said warmly.

"Oh," she said softly, her cheeks flushed and her eyes wide.

"Miss Bennet, I want to call on you. My intentions are entirely honorable. If you do not wish for my attentions, I beg you tell me now and save us both the mortification of me following you about unwanted," Bingley said fervently.

Jane looked at him in shock, stuttering over her response. "I, I, Mr. Bingley, I do not, that is, I rather like, I mean," she stopped and took a deep breath. "I would be pleased to receive your call in Margate, Mr. Bingley." He beamed at her and she added, "*Without* your sister."

~

Dearest Jane,

I know you are wild with curiosity so I will put your mind at ease. I am well. My husband is very well, too, and very kind to me. Do not worry for me, dearest. Mr. Darcy is very gentle and attentive and I have great hopes for my felicity in this marriage. It is still all very new and strange, and I suspect it will take me some months to become accustomed to living with a man such as he, but it is not overtaxing and I find myself enjoying his quiet company and wry humor. We are proving good companions and I can't help but think that bodes well for the future.

I wish I could have met your friend Mrs. Pearson before we leave for The Lakes, and especially her brother Mr. Walker. I could not visit anyone the day after my wedding, but believe me I very much wished I could—if it had been another day, of course.

I was glad to hear you enjoyed visiting them before you returned to the seaside. She sounds a very kind friend and Mr. Walker an amiable man. Are you still confused there, dearest? Do you know what you will say should he offer his proposals? Know that I am with you in spirit if not in body and that you are welcome to join us wherever we are if you find yourself in need of respite.

Where is Mr. Pearson's estate? If it is not too far from Derbyshire perhaps you could see your friend when you visit me—but of course I am getting ahead of myself. We have not even settled the dates for your visit and I am already planning your life! Forgive me, dear sister.

I am wild to know what Mr. Bingley means by saying he will go to Margate. Shall you choose him, then? Oh, dear sister, what a choice you have before you! Only you would have two amiable, handsome, wealthy men chasing after you. Perhaps it is as Mama has always said. You could not be so beautiful for nothing!

I can hear your voice in my mind telling me to stop teasing you, so I will desist now. Take care of your heart, Jane. I will support you no matter your choice.

We leave for The Lakes tomorrow and I am all excitement to see them, though I confess to some nervousness over the journey itself. I will be in a confined carriage with Mr. Darcy for days. Do join me in praying my tongue does not run away with me. It would be awful indeed to be trapped with an angry Mr. Darcy for so many days at once.

Give my love to my sisters and parents and scratch the ears of the marmalade cat in the garden for me. I must close and check my trunks for the journey. Here is the direction of where we shall be. I will write you when we have arrived safely.

Your sister,
Elizabeth Darcy

P.S. If you want Mr. Darcy to speak with Mr. Bingley, all you need do is ask. I'm sure he would be happy to oblige.

Elizabeth pressed her seal into the wax and was just placing it on the salver when she felt strong arms encircle her waist. She smiled and leaned into him.

"To whom are you writing, my love?" Darcy asked.

"My sister Jane. May I ask why you are sneaking up on me in such a way?" she responded, closing her hands over his arms.

"I wanted to see if you'd like to take one last walk in the park before our journey. I imagine you will not like the confinement."

"You are beginning to understand me, Mr. Darcy."

"As I should, Mrs. Darcy. What kind of husband does not endeavor to please his wife? And is not understanding her needs the first step in meeting them?"

"While that may be very sound indeed, I do not think it the usual way, though I am happy to be the recipient of your efforts." She smiled happily and he kissed her neck, reveling in the freedom to do so.

"You make me very happy, Elizabeth," he said.

"How long do you suppose it will last?"

"What? My happiness? Decades, I should hope," he said, somewhat surprised at the question.

"No, I didn't mean that. Of course I want you to be happy always. I meant this joy you feel in kissing me, especially in public rooms of the house."

He shrugged. "I cannot explain it, but kissing you like this pleases me tremendously."

"Perhaps it is the novelty of being able to do what was forbidden only a week ago?" she asked.

"Perhaps," he answered as he continued to kiss her neck, seemingly unperturbed by her words.

"It is all so very new and exciting. Surely I will become commonplace soon enough."

"Never!" he said vehemently. "There is nothing common about you, my sweet."

"You say that today. Mayhap after nearly a week in a carriage, you will feel very differently."

~

The first day in the carriage was easy enough. They played a simple word game Elizabeth had learned with her sisters, slept a bit, and read from their individual books. Darcy told her that they would travel the longest distance in the first days while they still had the stamina for travel. Once they had been on the road three days, they would slow their pace and see a few sights before arriving at The Lakes in a week's time.

Elizabeth found this plan agreeable and spent the first day pleasantly engaged with her husband. She could not say she loved him yet. Circumstances had been too strange, emotions too raw, and her own nature too distrusting to love him so quickly, but she did feel a soft sort of tenderness toward him. It was a warm feeling that filled her with a gentle sensation when he was near and made her fondness for him grow rapidly. He was a good man, she had realized that long ago, but the longer she was near him, the nearer she was to him, the more obvious it became. And the more ridiculous she felt for her previous bad opinion.

Never one to focus on mistakes of the past, she brushed it aside and focused on today, on her growing respect for the forthright man who would be her companion throughout her life.

The morning of the third day, Elizabeth awoke to find she had begun her courses, a very inconvenient thing to have happen while traveling such a long distance. She grumbled at her ill luck and lamented the absence of her maid, who had gone on ahead of her to prepare the cottage where they would be staying. Grateful it had at least begun while she was at an inn and not on the road where she would have had to ask her husband to stop and the whole thing could have been mortifying, she gathered what she needed and prepared to leave. She asked the maid at the inn for some sleeping powders, knowing it would all be so much simpler if she could rest through it, then stepped outside to await her husband.

Darcy collected his wife and led her to the carriage, happy to be on the way and that much closer to their destination. Today would be their last day of hard travel. He was enjoying being in Elizabeth's constant company, but he missed spending nights with her. They could not share a bed in an inn; it was unseemly. It would be especially awkward for Elizabeth who was so new to such activities and still very shy with him. The last week had taught them much about each other and acclimated them somewhat to the marriage bed, but it was all still quite novel.

After the first day, he no longer came to her during the day. He limited such things to the evenings after his complete mortification at witnessing her examining herself for injuries at his hand—well, at his *something*. He had barely been able to restrain himself, but the anticipation made the nights that much sweeter.

Now, he was denied even that. She had sat next to him the day before and laid her head on his shoulder while she slept, which had been sweet torture to him. He had stroked her hair and stolen a few kisses, but nothing more. This was to be their last day in such close confines where he was able only to look and barely touch. The distractions of the next few days seeing the sights should help occupy his mind, and he imagined there would be plenty of places to steal a kiss or two and hopefully more. The first night of the journey, they had both been exhausted and knew they had an early morning, so he had kissed her goodnight and left it at that. The second night, he had hoped for a little affection before retiring, but she had practically fallen asleep at the table and he could not bring himself to demand anything of her when she clearly needed to rest.

Now, he was beginning to think his notions about showing affection in a carriage were a bit silly. So what if it wasn't entirely proper? He was quite sure people did all sorts of improper things all the time. He'd been very improper prior to their wedding. But since they had wed and he had full access to her person each night, it seemed greedy somehow, selfish, to demand affection from her every hour of the day, and there was something in Elizabeth's demeanor, some intuition that made him stop, but he tried not to think about that. Perhaps he was overly concerned and she wouldn't be as scandalized as he had feared. This was Elizabeth after all.

The ride started easily enough. They discussed the books they had been reading and whether the night had been comfortable at the last inn. At the first stop to change horses, Elizabeth refreshed herself—not an easy thing to do in a busy inn—and stretched her legs, walking slowly around a small herb garden behind the main building. She mindlessly watched a maid gathering vegetables into a basket while she rubbed her lower back slowly, trying to ease the tension. Traveling was rigorous enough on the body without the added trouble of courses.

Darcy asked if she wanted tea and she said no; the sooner they reached their destination the sooner she could get a hot brick and lie down. She had hoped they would be at the cottage before this started, but clearly it was not to be.

"Are you ready to depart? The carriage is awaiting us," came Darcy's voice from behind her.

She sighed and removed her hands from her back, lifting her face to catch a few rays of the sun before returning to the covered carriage.

"Yes, I am ready."

Darcy followed her into the carriage, sitting beside her instead of across. She didn't worry about the change. She had just taken a sleeping powder at the inn and thought she would drift off soon. Her husband would make an admirable pillow.

"May I rest my head on your shoulder? I should like to sleep," she said.

Surprised, he said yes and she curled up next to him and he wrapped an arm around her, his hand resting on her lower back. Suddenly having an idea, she asked him, "Fitzwilliam, would you mind placing your hand just here?" She moved his hand to cover the sore spot on her back. "The heat of your hand eases my soreness."

"Of course. I didn't realize you were in pain. We could have stopped longer at the inn," he said kindly.

"No, it isn't necessary. A little rest will help immensely. I will feel much better when we reach the inn tonight and I can have a hot brick."

He nodded, wondering what the problem was. She had been fine the day before. She was tired, certainly, but traveling had that effect on everyone and she had not gotten as much sleep as usual the last week. *Another thing I am responsible for*, he chastised himself. *I must take better care of her.* But this was not merely fatigue; she had said she was sore. Was it the carriage? He thought it was very well-sprung, though not as well as the larger one. Had he made a mistake in choosing this conveyance?

Just as he was working himself up into a fit of worry over his wife, she made a slight noise and burrowed her head into his chest. She was asleep already. He leaned himself back into the corner and pulled her so that her head was on his chest and her body between his and the backrest of the carriage. He kept his hand pressed into her back as she'd asked and placed a kiss on her head before closing his eyes and joining her in slumber. *Sleep is a much better idea than fretting like an old biddy.*

Several hours later, Elizabeth was still asleep but Darcy was awake. He'd opened a book and held it in one hand while the other gently stroked his wife's back. He was surprised she was sleeping so long, but if it brought her relief, he supposed he should be glad. The sun was dipping toward the horizon and it would be full dark in less than two hours. They wouldn't be driving much farther. Would she be able to sleep this night?

Suddenly a smile broke across his face before he even realized what he was smiling about. Elizabeth would be very well rested when they reached the inn this evening. Surely after sleeping half the day in the carriage, she would be able to stay awake later into the evening. Why hadn't he thought of it before? It was the perfect solution! Sleep in the *carriage*, remain awake at the *inn*. What a stupid man he was! But in his defense, he had never taken a long carriage ride, or any carriage ride for that matter, with a woman he was in love with or even mildly interested in. With this new solution in mind, and happy thoughts of being alone with his wife occupying his attention, he continued reading contentedly, not understanding more than one word in five.

Elizabeth was groggy. Her mouth felt a bit sticky and there was motion around her. She was pressed against something warm but slightly scratchy and it was…. Moving? Where was she? *Ah, I am in the carriage with Fitzwilliam on the way to The Lakes.* She stiffly tried to sit up and touched one hand to her head.

"Are you well?" Darcy asked.

"Yes, I just felt dizzy for a moment. Probably from all the motion," she said.

"And you haven't eaten much all day. There are some biscuits here. Would you like some?"

"Yes, please."

She nibbled on the biscuit she'd chosen from the tin and looked out the window.

"It's nearly dark. Will we be stopping soon?" she asked.

"Less than a mile now," he replied.

They pulled into the drive of a rustic looking inn. There were roses to the left of the entry and she breathed in the fragrant scent gratefully. It was comforting after so many hours in the carriage. They had been driving with the windows closed to keep out the dust. Once they slowed their pace, they would be able to open them, but for now, she was happy for a bit of fresh air.

They were shown to a suite of rooms including a sitting room where Darcy ordered their supper be served as soon as it was available. Elizabeth walked to the large window overlooking the back garden and threw open the sash.

"A servant can do that. You needn't bother yourself," said Darcy.

"It's no bother. I need the air."

She leaned slightly out the window and took several deep breaths, willing her headache to recede and her aches to subside. She excused herself to freshen up and went into her room, once more lamenting the absence of a maid. Luckily the owner had sent someone up to help her change out of her traveling clothes. Wearing a light day dress and having the chance to bathe quickly from a basin did much to liven her spirits and she rejoined her husband with more energy than he had seen from her all day.

The meal was quite good for an inn and she ate the roast beef and vegetables with relish. The bread was particularly welcome as it had just come out of the oven. Darcy watched it all with a small grin, thinking her renewed spirits and returned appetite suited his after dinner plans.

When they were through, she asked if he would accompany her on a short walk to stretch her legs and he readily consented. When they returned, the fires were lit in the individual bedchambers and Elizabeth walked toward hers, saying she would ring for the maid to help her prepare for bed.

"That isn't necessary, Elizabeth. I can help you," said Darcy.

Stopping in her path with her back still to her husband, she said, "I already told her I would ring for her later. It will only take a moment."

"Surely I can manage a few buttons!" he exclaimed, thinking she was trying to spare him an unnecessary duty.

"You really needn't bother, Fitzwilliam. I shall join you here when I am ready," she said quickly as she made for the door. She was through it and had closed it soundly behind her before he could think of a response.

Has she just run from me? What on earth is going on? Annoyed but trying not to let it overtake him—he had learned something from their first awkward day together—he went into his room and changed into his nightshirt, loosely tying his dressing gown over it. He had a sip of brandy and returned to the sitting room, staring out the window at the darkness while he awaited his surprisingly changeable wife.

Had he offended her in some way? He went over their conversation in the carriage, over dinner, on their walk. There was nothing out of the ordinary. She had asked him about the book he was reading; he had told her. She had asked him about something being discussed in parliament that she had seen him and her uncle and father reading about in the broadsheet; he had told her what he knew of it. She had asked him about the plans for the morrow, and again, he had told her. What had he possibly done to offend her? Was she even offended? Was she nervous that he would try to lie with her at an inn? *Ah, that must be it*, he thought. She had been raised a modest lady and they were very newly married. The thought of such intimate activities in what was so public a place must be unnerving to her.

Well, he should set her mind at ease. He had not planned as far as that. Yes, he had wanted to kiss her and hold her a bit, and perhaps feel certain assets under his palms that he had recently become acquainted with, and he wasn't *completely* sure he would be able to stop himself from going any further, but he wasn't *planning* it. He could restrain himself. He would restrain himself.

The door to his right opened and Elizabeth stepped out, a dark grey dressing gown covering what looked to be a very serviceable plain white nightgown beneath. He frowned. She had been wearing silky, soft, enticing gowns each night of their marriage. They hadn't stayed on her long, but he had certainly appreciated the picture they created. Were these her travel things? The last two nights he hadn't seen her as they had not talked after dinner but gone straight to bed.

"Do you think they have chocolate here?" she asked. She was settled into the chair by the fire, looking at him expectantly.

"I'm sure they do. Shall I ring for it?"

"Please."

The maid arrived shortly and he requested chocolate for his wife and port for himself.

"Are you looking forward to seeing the ruins tomorrow?" she asked.

"Yes. I haven't seen them since I was a child."

"It will be nice to be out of the carriage for a little while," she commented absently.

"Yes, it will."

"It's too bad you didn't bring your horse. You could have ridden part of the journey at least," she offered.

"Then you would be alone in the carriage," he responded.

Was it his imagination or did she look like that idea wasn't particularly bothersome? He walked toward the fireplace and sat in the chair in front of her, leaning forward with his elbows on his knees. She looked at him in surprise.

"Elizabeth, are you well?"

"Why do you ask?" she said. She scooted back in her chair and looked aside nervously.

"You seem distracted. You slept half the day in the carriage. You —" he gestured aimlessly with his hands. "Forgive me, you just don't seem yourself."

She sat up a little straighter. "Traveling is tiresome. I thought a sleeping powder would help me rest so I took one at the first stop. There is nothing wrong with me." *Nothing that won't be over in a few days.*

"Sleeping powder!" he cried. "Why would you—if you were tired wouldn't you sleep on your own?"

She shrugged and looked away uncomfortably.

"Ah, I see," he said grimly.

She startled and looked up. "You do?"

"Yes. Forgive me for intruding on your rest, madam."

He withdrew and stood looking out the window, his back to her. She was utterly confused about what had just happened. She stared after him for a moment, then decided to ignore the problem. Her sisters often behaved similarly. They would get in a snit about something, not tell anyone what it was, then huff off to pout until someone came to find them and cajole it out of them. Well, she wanted no part in such games. If he wanted to act like a child, she would not participate.

After several minutes of her sitting in silence and him staring out the window—what was he looking at, anyway?—her curiosity got the better of her. Fitzwilliam did not usually pout and he was normally nothing like her sisters, so she thought it right to ask him of his troubles.

"Fitzwilliam, is something troubling you?" she asked carefully.

Only the realization that my wife of nine days is already tired of me. "No, I am perfectly well," he said flatly, still facing the window.

"Truly?"

He turned to face her. "I am as well as you, Mrs. Darcy," he said with a slight nod in her direction and what she could swear was a mocking look in his eyes.

Elizabeth sat motionless at his words, stunned that he would speak to her in such a way. "What are you implying?" she asked.

"Nothing, my dear. Absolutely nothing," he replied. She was sure his tone was mocking her now.

"Please don't call me dear when you are angry with me. It ruins it," she said somewhat sharply.

"As you wish, madam," he said as he turned back to the window.

A few minutes passed in silence—neither spoke nor moved. Finally, Elizabeth could take it no more.

"Is this how it is to be then? You will take offense at some imaginary insult and will not tell me why you are angry, but will stand at the window and sulk? How long is it to last? How frequently does this happen? Should I take to carrying a book with me at all times in case you decide to shut me out at an inopportune time?"

He whirled around, his face pinched with the anger that had finally come to the surface. Though it was the slightest bit frightening, she felt triumphant at forcing a reaction from him. She had never been able to abide stoicism.

"Me? I am the one being silent? *I* am withdrawing? That is a rich tale you weave, Elizabeth."

"What are you talking of?" she asked, confused and irritated. Her head was starting to pound again and the cramps in her lower back were getting stronger. She squinted her eyes to relieve the pressure in her forehead, unknowingly making herself look incredibly angry.

Frustrated, tired, and disappointed, Darcy decided to end her games here. "Is my company so tiresome you had to send yourself to sleep to avoid it?"

"What?"

"I see clearly now why you have been avoiding me, why you won't come near me. Why you are wearing that!" He pointed to her nightgown and she clutched it to her chest.

"What are you talking about? I'm not avoiding you!" she exclaimed. Her hand rubbed her temple and her eyes closed against the pain in her head.

"Are you not? Then why have you become a different person on this journey? The first day you were my Elizabeth. Then yesterday you were tired and silent. I thought it was just fatigue, but today you hardly spoke three words. You were happy to let me do all the talking while I prattled on, ignorant of your growing disdain." His voice grew with each accusation and before he knew what he was about, he had worked himself up into a frenzy.

She gasped at his outburst and stood to face him. "If I was avoiding you, would I have asked to cuddle with you in the carriage? If I was avoiding you, would I have eaten with you and specifically asked for your company on a walk? If I was avoiding you, sir, would I have come out this evening to sit with you despite the pain in my head and the ache in my back? You spoiled, hateful man!"

Elizabeth clamped a hand over her mouth, shocked by her own words, and ran from the room, shutting her door with a thud, the lock making a clear snick as it latched into place. He could hear her sobbing from the sitting room and wondered what he had done. He stood there, wondering when he had become intemperate and volatile. Just a few hours ago he had held her while she slept in the carriage. He had led her peacefully through the garden. They had eaten a pleasant meal together and he had so looked forward to spending the evening with her in his arms. Is that what this was about? Had he become a spoiled child who threw a tantrum when denied a treat? Was he hateful as she had said?

He paced and ran his hands through his hair, all the while hearing Elizabeth's muffled sobs through the door. It sounded like she had buried her head in a pillow but he had always had keen hearing. After several minutes the sobs subsided and there was a knock at the door. He answered to find a maid there with hot chocolate for his wife and port for himself.

The young woman bobbed and said, "The missus says to tell the lady that she'll have what she requested shortly and one of the maids will bring it up. Sir." She bobbed again and was away before he could question her further.

Taking a sip of the port to fortify his nerves, he took up the chocolate and rapped on the door.

"Elizabeth, your chocolate is here." There was no reply. "Dearest, please open the door. I'm sorry, my love. I didn't mean to upset you. Please open the door and let me talk to you."

Elizabeth debated whether or not she should let him in. She was very angry with him, and he was being very difficult. But they were also very newly married and she did not want to set a dangerous precedent. Her parents often argued and then would be silent, her father locked in his bookroom and her mother ignoring him whenever they were in a room together. She did not wish such a marriage for herself. She would hear her husband. Even if it took more patience and humility than she currently possessed.

He stood there for what felt like ages before he heard soft footsteps and the click of the lock. She pulled the door back and stood behind it, using it as a barrier between them. He stepped in slowly and placed the chocolate on the table by the bed.

"Elizabeth, I —" he looked at her, her eyes red and her cheeks wet, and felt himself the worst sort of brute. "God, Elizabeth, I am so sorry! I

don't know what came over me! I didn't mean it, truly. I was just—
please, my love, forgive me?"

She looked at him warily, not sure what to believe or that she even
understood what was happening. She'd never seen a lovers' quarrel
before and this was more than they'd experienced in their courtship,
which had been far from smooth. He'd actually raised his voice to her!

"I hate to see your tears. Please, let me make it better," he pled.

"How do you plan to manage that?" she asked skeptically.

He looked dumbfounded for a moment and she found it irritatingly
endearing. "I will start by apologizing profusely."

"I believe you're well on your way there."

He took a small step toward her, a contrite look on his face. She
responded with a step closer to him.

He made up the remaining distance and tentatively took her in his
arms. Her arms hung limply by her side, not returning his embrace.

"Will you forgive me for being a brute?"

"Of course." She brought her hands up to rest lightly on his elbows,
not prepared to go further just yet.

"I am so sorry, my love. You are right. I was being spoiled. I didn't
get what I wanted and acted like a child. Forgive me."

"You are forgiven, Mr. Darcy. I apologize for calling you hateful. It
was unkind. Forgive me?" She looked up at him, completely drained and
wanting nothing more than for them to make peace and go to bed with
her chocolate.

"Of course. This whole thing was my fault."

He held her a little distance away from him and observed her while
she played with the lapels of his dressing gown. Finally, she spoke.

"Can you tell me why you thought I was avoiding you? And what
offense you have taken at my dressing gown?" she asked, confused.

He flushed. "You have been quiet. It is unlike you and you have also
usually worn... different types of gowns to bed and coupled together I
thought you were trying to put me off."

He flushed a bit and looked around self-consciously and she
understood it cost something of his pride to make the confession.

"Oh. I see. Well, since we are being honest, I *was* trying to put you
off," she said to the floor.

He stiffened beneath her palms and his hands clenched where they
held her elbows.

"You see, I have not been feeling well because, because my time is
here," she said quietly.

"Your time?"

"Yes. My courses. Are you familiar with such things?"

"Oh, I hadn't realized. Naturally you would, I don't know why I didn't think," he trailed off, embarrassed.

"Yes, well, I shall feel better in a few days, but for now, I ache in my middle and have a headache and not much patience I'm afraid." At his dismayed expression, she added, "It is not always so painful. Most are not so bad, but I think this one is exacerbated by the travel and perhaps all the excitement of late."

He nodded. "I feel dreadful, Elizabeth. What a terrible husband I've been, and we've only just begun!"

"Do not say such things," she said firmly but kindly. Her hand stroked his cheek as she continued. "I could have told you earlier and avoided this misunderstanding. I was embarrassed and didn't know how to have such a conversation with a man, let alone one with such intimate access to my person." She blushed at her speech but held his gaze.

He placed his hand over hers on his cheek and smiled at her lovingly. "Is there anything I can do for your comfort? Anything you require?"

"I have asked for everything I need and hopefully the servant will bring it soon," she replied.

"Oh, that reminds me, the maid said they have what you requested and will bring it later this evening."

"Very good. It is a most inconvenient time to be without my maid!"

"That was also my idea because I wanted you all to myself. Is there no end to my selfishness?"

"Stop it, Fitzwilliam! I didn't know this would happen. If I had, I would have asked to keep the servants with us. You must understand that I am no child who needs everything done for her. If I need something, I can and will say something. You mustn't take care of me like an infant. All right?" she said firmly.

He smiled. "All right." He kissed her hands one at a time and asked, "Does that often happen? It arrive unexpectedly?" Darcy liked to be prepared and if they would need to always travel with his wife's maid in future, he wanted to know.

"It is not completely unexpected. It is once a month. The exact day varies, but not by more than a few days. I thought it might begin at the end of our journey and I was hoping it wouldn't happen until we arrived, but it was not to be."

"Forgive my impertinence, but how long does it usually last?" He flushed as he asked and she would have laughed at his discomfort if she hadn't been so uncomfortable herself.

"Usually four or five days."

"At least you will be able to enjoy The Lakes right away then."

"Yes, that is one happy turn."

There was a rap on the door and Darcy left her to the maid's attention. He paced back and forth in the sitting room, disgusted with his own spoilt behavior, relieved they had reconciled, disappointed that his lovely wife was unavailable for the immediate future, and feeling a tendril of hope that it would all be well once they got to The Lakes.

CHAPTER 25

The Bennets arrived at Margate without much trouble. The house was just as they left it and even the marmalade cat was awaiting them in the garden. All but Mrs. Bennet were subdued, thinking how they were one person less on this journey. Mrs. Bennet could speak of nothing but her daughter, Mrs. Darcy, and how well that sounded and how much pin money she would have and how many grand parties she would now attend. Her other daughters nodded and smiled and agreed where necessary, but even Lydia was quiet. Who would sneak her biscuits now that Lizzy was gone?

Mary entered the room she had shared with Elizabeth, now her room alone. She sat on Elizabeth's bed forlornly and looked around, wondering what she would do now without her sister's lively conversation or her assistance in practicing music or the faces she made at the table when no one was looking.

Mary was joined shortly by Jane, who sat beside her and placed her arm around her younger sister.

"I feel quite lost without Lizzy," said Jane. "What are we to do now?"

"I haven't the slightest idea," Mary replied.

Kitty poked her head around the corner and knocked lightly on the frame. "May I join you?"

"Of course," said Jane.

Mary scooted over and the three sat on Elizabeth's bed, their absent sister's scent and sense all around them.

"I feel like she will come in at any moment and tell us to get off her bed," said Kitty.

"She would likely drag us outside to walk on the shore," said Mary.

"Do you suppose she will drag Mr. Darcy about like she was always doing to us?" asked Kitty.

"I doubt it. Mr. Darcy doesn't strike me as the type to be dragged anywhere," said Jane.

"Can you imagine her trying, though?" said Mary with a smile.

Kitty laughed and stood, doing an impression of Elizabeth when she wanted to go for a walk and everyone refused to go out.

"What are you doing in here?" said Lydia as she walked into the room.

"Talking about Elizabeth," said Jane.

"Kitty thinks she may try to drag Mr. Darcy on walks like she does all of us," added Mary.

Kitty again made her annoyed-Elizabeth face and Lydia immediately put on a stoic expression, drawing herself up as high as she could go and pushing out her chest, her back tight and her gait stiff. "Now, Elizabeth, you know proper young ladies do not run about the countryside," she said in a deep voice, impersonating Darcy.

"Oh, but Mr. Darcy! The sun is calling me! I must greet it!" Kitty said in an exaggerated characterization of Elizabeth.

Jane and Mary laughed.

"Nonsense!" cried Lydia in her deep voice. "The sun shall await a time convenient to me. Do you not know that I own half of Derbyshire and all must obey my command?" Though exaggerated, her impersonation was alarmingly accurate.

Jane was laughing silently now, holding her stomach and turning pink.

"Oh, might I walk all of it?" Kitty said with batting eyes and a flirtatious smile. "I am a very great walker, you know."

Lydia patted Kitty's head and smiled condescendingly. "Of course, my darling, anything for you. Just give me a kiss first." She puckered her lips out and leaned forward, making Mary laugh so hard she fell back on the bed howling.

Kitty was still playing her part and blushing and looking down coyly. Jane joined Mary in her uncontrollable humor until finally Lydia and Kitty broke down into fits of giggles and the four of them ended up in a heap, shaking and crying, they laughed so hard.

~

Mr. Bennet took a quiet walk on the shore by himself, his mind full of reflections of the days past. Elizabeth had sent him a short note that arrived just before the carriage pulled out of Gracechurch Street.

Dear Papa,

I know you are worried, but do not be. All is well. Fitzwilliam is very kind to me and I will be fine. Take good care of my sisters and watch out for Jane. She is conflicted about the men in her life and needs patience and understanding.

I will write more soon. Don't forget you said you would write to me in return. I have not forgotten your promise!

All my love,
Lizzy

P.S. I think Mr. Bingley may be more than first appears—don't discount him just yet.

He fingered the note in his pocket and stared out at the horizon. He prayed his daughter would not have a marriage like his had been. He wanted her to always be able to respect her partner in life. Mrs. Bennet had never asked, not once, how her daughter was faring, how she felt about Mr. Darcy, whether or not they got along or had similar dispositions or hopes for life. No, all she could think about was pin money and carriages and houses in town and country.

A moment later he chastised himself. Mrs. Bennet was a silly creature, yes; she always had been. She was not blessed with intelligence, but she had no malice in her. She meant no harm to anyone and loved her daughters in her way. Unexpectedly, his plan to fashion his daughters into marriageable women had had a similar effect on his wife. She had always been trivial, but she had not always been shrill nor had she complained so much.

No, if he was honest, he had to admit that his sarcasm and disdain for her lack of abilities had created a chasm between them. As it grew, so did her grievances. Before long she was complaining loudly and calling for her salts. Could it have been him all along? Did his withdrawal of affection and respect lead her to become what she had—shrill and ridiculous?

He had to admit the evidence pointed to that being true. Since he had given her a modicum of guidance, shared the burden of raising five daughters with her, and showed her sincere and gentle affection, she had complained less, been less grumpy and irritable, and embarrassed the family significantly fewer times than she had before. She had, in fact, become pleasant company again. She wasn't the smartest woman and never would be, but she sometimes made amusing observations and she had a good sense of humor if the topics weren't too complex.

She did take good care of him. He felt a wash of shame come over him as he realized that she always had, even after he had begun ridiculing her in front of her own children and mocking her to her face and others. She made sure his favorite dinners were served on Sundays, and when there was a dish he didn't like, there was always a small serving of something he preferred brought just to him. She gave him gifts that he liked and used; fine handkerchiefs with his monogram, a new tooled leather saddle for his birthday three years ago, and his favorite, the painting of his mother and sister, painted a year before the latter's death, restored and framed after it had been damaged by a leaky roof.

When had he become such an ass? When did the honest affection of a beautiful woman cease being enough for him? He shook his head and gazed out at the sea. He was doing better now, and he would continue to do so.

Hopefully, his Lizzy would escape the trap he had fallen into, one largely of his own making. Firstly in choosing an ill-matched partner, then in behaving badly towards the one he had chosen. He was certain she could love Mr. Darcy if she only let herself. Failing that, they could at least have a solid friendship. That would be a lot better than many had in marriage.

~

When the Darcys arrived at the cottage, it was late in the day and they had been traveling since eleven after touring a castle early that same morning. Elizabeth was dirty, tired, sore, and desperate for a bath. Before she even toured the house she escaped to her room to wash her hair, which hadn't been scrubbed since they left London six days ago. She was so relieved to see her maid she nearly hugged the woman.

Once her trunk was delivered, she locked the doors to her chamber—she did not want to risk her husband coming in at an inopportune moment—then she slid into the tub. She immediately dunked her head and blew bubbles in the water, inordinately happy to be getting clean. As Sanders washed her hair, she closed her eyes and truly relaxed for the first time in several days. Her courses had finally ceased a few hours ago and she knew she would be spending the evening with her husband, ready or not.

Spending time in a close carriage with him had been an interesting experience. As she feared, they had clashed and suffered awkward moments, but as her father had said, being alone together had forced them to converse on topics they otherwise wouldn't. She felt they had learned each other a bit better, but she was also slightly weary of his company. Not horribly, as she was admittedly exhausted and cross from her physical state, but she did not know him very well yet and she still felt a little strange being alone with him. They would be married a fortnight tomorrow and that simply wasn't long enough for her to feel completely at ease, especially since half that time had been spent traveling.

Perhaps it is not Fitzwilliam at all, she thought. *Maybe I just need to be alone altogether.*

She had not enjoyed a solitary walk since several days before the wedding, and she had arguably gone through the most tumultuous time of her life in the last month. Surely she was entitled to a little air and privacy? Deciding it would be better to have some time to herself to regain her equilibrium before snapping at her husband, she dismissed her maid and told her to tell Mr. Darcy that she would meet him in the dining room for supper after her hair had dried.

She stepped out onto the balcony off her bedchamber and looked at the sun glowing orange as it set and breathed in the clean air gratefully. She made herself comfortable in a lounge chair and leaned back with her eyes closed.

She fell asleep quickly and finally awoke when she heard muffled voices in a nearby room. She sat up and looked around, suddenly wishing Fitzwilliam was with her. *What a changeable creature I am!*

"Good, you are awake," said Fitzwilliam as he stepped onto the dark balcony.

She looked around groggily. He was arranging dishes of food on a table to her right. A few candles were lit, but most of the light was provided by the moon.

"What's this?" she asked.

"Supper. I took the liberty of having it sent to my room." He nodded in the direction of a door on the other side of the balcony. "After I saw you were asleep, I thought this would be better."

She looked down and saw a small, soft blanket was draped around her. "Thank you," she said, pointing to the cover.

"You're welcome."

He continued to fill the plates in silence before eventually handing her one and sitting down across from her with the other plate. She nibbled slowly, still waking up.

"It's very peaceful here, isn't it?" she said after some time.

"Yes, very. That is one of the reasons I thought it would be a perfect location for a wedding trip, besides you having wished it, of course."

"Have you been here many times before?"

"Only twice. Once while at Cambridge and then with my father six years ago. He was a close friend of Mr. Lansdowne, Sr."

"It was very kind of him to share it with you."

"He is a kind man. I hope to introduce you before we return to town. The family has an estate in Staffordshire, not fifty miles from Pemberley."

"And what is fifty miles of good road?" she asked with a smile.

"When there is money enough to make traveling easy, it is as nothing," he rejoined.

They both chuckled lightly and continued with their meal. Elizabeth stole glances at Darcy between bites. She was having the oddest sensation. She felt the most peculiar desire for her husband's presence. She wouldn't call it missing him, exactly. Indeed, that would be absurd. But she did feel it had been a horribly long time since he had held her. They hadn't even kissed properly since beginning the journey. Once she told him she was on her courses, he had touched nothing but her hand and that only slightly. She didn't know what to make of it. Did he think she was somehow more fragile at this time? Or perhaps he found it all revolting. She certainly didn't enjoy it. But surely he knew she wasn't going to slap him if he kissed her, didn't he?

She studied him, and while she was staring at his freshly washed hair and the way it fell over his forehead just so, he looked up at her. His face was friendly, but his eyes were filled with such trepidation, such longing, that she felt her heart reach out for his.

Wordlessly, she set her plate and glass of wine aside and scooted in next to him on the chaise lounge. He was surprised, but made room for her by opening his arms. She placed her head on his chest and snuggled close to him, one hand over his heart.

"Can we see any more stars here than we can in Hertfordshire?" she asked.

"A few, but not many," he said in a soft voice.

"Show me?"

"Of course."

They lay back and looked at the stars, Darcy pointing out the constellations he knew and the dimmer stars that could not be seen further south. They spent an hour lying together and talking, watching the night sky.

"What would it be like to go there?" she said suddenly.

"Where? To the stars?"

"Yes. I should like to see a star up close, I think. Or perhaps the moon. Do you think we shall ever go there?"

"No, of course not!"

"Not 'we' you and I, 'we' mankind. Do you think we will ever make the journey?"

"It must be quite far. I should think it would take a very long time. And of course there is the small problem of not being able to fly."

"Don't be impertinent, Mr. Darcy. That's my job," she said as she jabbed him in the ribs.

He laughed and hugged her closer.

"Maybe someone will find a way to fly one day," she wondered aloud.

"Like a bird? Perhaps someone could design wings, I suppose. Though I imagine our arms would get very tired," he said.

"Maybe the wings wouldn't have to move, but only glide. Like a kite."

"I have seen a hot air balloon that can take a man into the sky, but it is hard to direct and quite dangerous."

"Really? I should like to see that," she said, her voice filled with interest.

"If I hear of one nearby, we shall go see it," he said with a kiss to the top of her head.

"Thank you, Fitzwilliam," she said feelingly.

"You're welcome." He suspected she meant more than just the balloon, but he didn't want to fish for information.

"What is your favorite constellation?" she asked.

"My favorite? I don't know that I have one."

"How can you not have one? That is like not having a favorite color."

"I do not have a favorite color."

"What?" she exclaimed. "How is that possible?"

"It's quite easy, really. I simply do not have one," he replied.

"You are a queer creature, Mr. Darcy," she said fondly.

"What is your favorite constellation?"

"I think Cassiopeia."

"Why?"

"The story is so tragic. And who would like to sit upside down half the year? Plus it is easy to find in the sky."

He chuckled and pulled her closer, kissing her hair again. She rubbed her hand along his chest, snuggling closer.

"Would you like to know something strange?" she asked.

"Yes."

"I feel like I miss you. Is that not absurd?"

"Not so absurd," he said quietly.

"But we have been together nearly every moment for a fortnight!"

"Not *every* moment."

"Most moments."

"Well, it is possible to miss certain aspects of someone or something. Like I have missed holding you this week," he said softly. His voice was gentle and a touch unsure.

"Then we are in accord because I have missed being held by you."

"Truly?"

"Yes. It is a very enjoyable sensation," she said with a teasing smile. She leaned up and placed a quick kiss on his cheek. "You are very warm and there is something about your arms that I quite like."

"Is there now?" he asked with a raised brow.

"Mhhm," she nodded. "Something about them makes me feel safe and loved."

"You are safe and loved," he replied, pulling her closer. She sighed contentedly and returned his squeeze, so close she was half on top of him now. "Elizabeth?"

"Yes?"

"Are you still in your time?"

"No. I have just finished," she replied softly, her voice full of promise.

"Will you come to bed with me?" he asked.

"Of course."

"No," he said forcefully. She looked at him in surprise. He sighed and closed his eyes, trying to find the right words to say. "Elizabeth, I know you believe certain things to be your duty and that lying with me is one of them. But *I* do not want to be a duty to you. I would like our coupling to be joyful and desired by both of us. If you do not want to be with me in this way, please do not pretend for my sake. I would ask you to promise me, for the rest of our lives, that you will never allow me to take you when you do not truly wish it. I could not bear to be resented for such a thing. Please, promise me."

"Very well. I promise," she said gently.

He sighed and closed his eyes, resting his forehead on hers.

"Fitzwilliam?"

"Yes?"

"Will you come to bed with me?"

He looked up and saw her eyes sparkling at him and her teasing smile about to break through. "Gladly."

~

Elizabeth noted something different about their lovemaking that night. He was as tender and gentle as he had been every other time, but there was something else there. A closeness, a sense of togetherness that had not been there before.

It would be some time before she realized that the change was not with them, but within herself. Did Fitzwilliam even recognize it?

~

Darcy felt that he was going slightly mad. He had run the gamut of every possible emotion in the last week and he was looking forward to a month of relaxation now that they had finally arrived. His marriage was in many ways more than he had ever hoped for. Elizabeth was delightful. Her arch manner, the way her eyes twinkled just before she teased him, the way her lips parted just so when she was surprised. He could not get enough of looking at her, touching her, having her. He almost felt intoxicated, so enamored of her was he.

But there was something in the way of his complete happiness. He did not like to dwell on it, and he wasn't completely sure, but he felt that Elizabeth herself was not as enamored as he. He especially noticed it in their most intimate moments. At first, this did not bother him. Indeed, he was so overwhelmed by his own feelings he barely registered hers. Everything was so new—especially to her—he knew there would be a period of adjustment, that she would take time to become accustomed to his physical presence. When he thought about her position, how she was the physically weaker of the two, younger than he, and completely inexperienced, he could understand how a woman might feel vulnerable in such an intimate situation—that she would need to trust her partner deeply.

To that end, he had been kind and loving with her. He had been affectionate for the fortnight they had been married, at least to the extent he could be once her wretched courses had come, and when he lay with her he had been tender and gentle, assuring her of his devotion in every touch to her soft skin and every kiss to her sweet lips.

But despite his trustworthiness and utter devotion, she had not responded as he thought she would. He was mature enough to realize people did not always behave the way he wished them to, but he had such hopes with Elizabeth that he thought, just this once, his faith might not be mislaid.

She wasn't cold to him, quite the contrary. She often touched him throughout the day, leaving a tingling sensation on his arm or shoulder or wherever she had placed her hand. She laughed and teased and sparkled for him without reservation. She never turned him away and accepted each of his kisses if not always enthusiastically, at least happily. He truly had nothing to complain of. He had heard stories from other men of wives who locked their doors at night and turned their faces when their husbands leaned in for a kiss. His Elizabeth would never do such a thing, he was nearly sure of it.

What was truly bothering Darcy, as much as he hated to admit it, was that her personality was not coming through in their lovemaking. If he was honest with himself, and Darcy always was, he had dreamt of her teasing him and raising that impertinent brow as she slowly slid her nightgown off her shoulders. Or sitting in the center of the bed, surrounded by white downy blankets and pillows, wearing nothing but a smile as she waited for him to come to her. Or playfully tormenting him with innuendo and suggestions throughout the day, culminating in fervent coupling that night.

But none of that had happened. She had consented to him coming to her every night she was not indisposed, even Sundays. She had consented to him sleeping in her bed afterward. She had consented to being completely bare with him, something she had been embarrassed to do but had agreed to after gentle encouragement and assurance of his affection and the dimness of the light.

As he sat being shaved the morning of the second day at The Lakes, Darcy berated himself. She simply needed time to become accustomed to the marriage bed. As her confidence grew, so would her comfort. Or perhaps it would be the other way round. Anyway, he was sure he was worrying over nothing. So Elizabeth had not met his mind's imaginings within a fortnight of being married. Was that really something to complain about? They had plenty of time—they had a lifetime together.

He smiled at the thought.

Perhaps he could lead. If he was more playful with her, then mayhap she would reciprocate. Only, the problem was Darcy had never excelled in being playful. *Fortune favors the brave, old man.*

He would try. If it meant making Elizabeth more comfortable and making their marriage more enjoyable, he would do anything—even if he was likely to make a fool of himself in the process.

CHAPTER 26

The cottage at The Lakes was everything Elizabeth had hoped it would be and then some, though as cottages go, it was rather large. It was comfortably furnished and thoughtfully laid out. There was a lovely view from every window. Everywhere she looked, she was greeted with beauty.

The morning of their second day, she toured the house on her own, quietly leaving the room while Fitzwilliam was in his dressing room. Her mind couldn't help but wander to her new husband and how he had arranged this lovely trip. It really was very thoughtful of him to remember that she had always wanted to see The Lakes and to secure such a nice place to stay. Away from nearly all of society, they would become accustomed to each other in private, without family or society pressures and obligations. She was very grateful for his foresight and his kindness and generosity towards her.

And he truly was very patient with her. She could tell he was befuddled by her sometimes, but she didn't always know how to make sense of her own thoughts and feelings, let alone explain them to him. She felt badly about it and tried to be as receptive as she could to his affection. She was affectionate herself in turn, not holding herself back when she wanted to touch him. She had always been a very tactile person, always wanting to touch things and regularly laying a hand on the arm of the person she was speaking with. Her mother had chastised her for this habit and told her not to flirt with everything that stood on two legs. At the age of twelve, she had not understood what her mother meant, but by sixteen she comprehended fully and learned to keep her hands to herself.

With Mr. Darcy, she did not hold back. If she was excited and happy about something, she smiled at him brilliantly and squeezed his hand or touched his arm or gave him a swift kiss on his cheek. The last always made him smile and sometimes blush, and she thought she was on the right track there. This thought made her pause as she wandered onto a terrace at the back of the house. Did he need more encouragement from her? Was that partly to blame for the quizzical look she sometimes saw?

She could do that. She was a very warm person, after all. Being affectionate with her husband would not be difficult. She would start today.

~

At breakfast, Darcy asked her what she would like to do that day.

"If you are tired, we could simply relax here, perhaps take a stroll. Or if you are feeling energetic, we could take the small boat out onto the lake."

"If you're feeling up to rowing me about, I would like to take the boat out," she replied.

He smiled and assured her he was up to the task and they were soon off.

The lake had few occupants as they were already in a rather quiet location and the hour was still early. Elizabeth put on her straw bonnet and lace gloves and took a parasol to protect her from the sun. Darcy smiled when he saw her in her simple white dress with small yellow flowers on it.

"You look like sunshine, my love," he said.

She smiled softly in response and blushed a lovely pink color.

"Come, the boat is ready," he said as he led her to the dock and onto a small rowboat with three benches. Oars stretched across the narrow center bench and a hamper filled with food rested in the bottom. A blanket lay rolled up and stuffed under the wider front bench.

She stepped into the boat gingerly and a footman pushed them off, wishing them a good day on the high seas, to which Elizabeth laughed gaily. Darcy rowed them leisurely for some time, and finally headed toward a small island not too far away.

"Do you want to go ashore?" he asked.

"Yes, let's. I've never been on an island," she said.

He smiled at her anticipation and pulled as close as he could to the shore.

"I'll have to pull it in the rest of the way," he said once the boat had dragged the bottom.

She nodded and watched in fascination as he steadied the boat and stepped out, careful not to rock her. She held onto the sides and he gave her a grin and a wink before heaving the boat toward the shore, leaving Elizabeth duly impressed. He stopped a dozen feet from the bank. He could have pulled it farther, but he didn't want to push it back out through the muck.

"Will we picnic here?" she asked.

He agreed and she passed him the blanket and hamper. He came back for her and she wrapped her arms round his neck while he held her to take her across the shallow water and onto the shingle.

"How strong you are, Mr. Darcy," she teased as he stepped carefully across the rocky lake bottom.

"Nonsense. My lady is as light as a feather," he said playfully. Her laughter was his reward and he smiled brightly at her.

She reached one hand down to touch the water and neatly flicked a bit of it onto her husband.

"What are you doing, wife?"

"Nothing, husband," she said mischievously.

He took two more steps and she flicked him with water again, this time onto his face.

"Elizabeth," he said warningly.

"What?" she said innocently.

He loosened his grip and pretended to drop her, catching her just before she hit the water.

"Fitzwilliam Darcy! Don't you dare drop me into this water!" she called laughingly.

"Oh? You don't want to refresh yourself in the cool lake?" he teased.

She laughed again. "No! I would like to remain dry. Do not —" he pretended to drop her again and she screeched and kicked her shoe into the water, sending a spray of water into his face.

He spluttered and closed his eyes at the assault while Elizabeth tried to hold in her laughter, which was impossible to conceal when he was holding her and feeling every repressed shake of her body reverberate across his chest.

"Forgive me, Fitzwilliam. I did not mean to get you *so* very wet," she apologized brightly, her eyes twinkling.

He gave her a rueful look. "I will repay you for that, madam," he replied, but before he could finish the final words, he stepped onto a slippery rock and lost his footing.

For a wild moment, they flailed in the air, her clinging to him tightly, him waving one arm frantically for balance while the other clutched his wife. They both fell in with a spectacular splash.

Elizabeth's cry quickly turned into laughter as she put herself to rights. They were both soaked through from the waist down and half-covered in muck. Darcy had the disadvantage of being on bottom and the entire back of his shirt was wet and dirty as well as some of his hair. His hat floated a few feet away. Darcy scowled as he stood and placed a hand on her elbow to steady her. She scooped up his hat as they walked the remaining few feet to dry land and handed it to him with a sheepish expression. She could not contain her laughter when he looked at the poor muddied hat with an expression of disgust and dismay.

He eventually laughed with her and they pulled the bits of leaves and other debris from each other as they stood on the grassy shore, dripping and cold.

"We'll have to sit in the sun to dry out," she said.

"We'll never dry in all these layers."

He removed his jacket and waistcoat and hung them on the low branches of a nearby tree. Thankfully, the day was sunny and warm, so they would dry quickly. Elizabeth removed her shoes and stockings, placing the former in the sun and the latter over a branch. She then shimmied her petticoat out from beneath her skirts and hung it up as well, followed by her damp bonnet. It had thankfully kept her head dry, and much of her torso was dry but for a few splashes, luckily, but she still did not enjoy the feeling of her wet skirts across her legs. She quickly laid out the blanket and lay back on it, turning her face to the sun and closing her eyes.

"Are you going to join me?" she asked.

He swiftly lay down beside her in a similar position.

"You may as well take off your shirt. It's wet and can't be comfortable." She looked over at his wet linen and grimaced. He looked doubtful. "No one will see you. This island looks deserted."

He looked around and pulled his shirt over his head, leaning back on the blanket next to his wife in nothing but his breeches. Elizabeth smiled at him and closed her eyes, reveling in the warmth of the sun. They eventually flipped over to dry their backs and turned their heads to face each other, smiling and talking about silly nothings.

Elizabeth opened the hamper and began doling out food while Darcy poured them each a cup of wine from the cask. They ate the cheese and bread in relative silence until Elizabeth leaned over and popped a grape into Darcy's mouth. He smiled and returned the favor and soon he had his head in her lap while she fed him small bites of strawberries and more grapes. When they'd had their fill of fruit, he closed his eyes as she ran her fingers through his hair, humming softly.

Eventually she stopped humming and began exploring her husband's shoulders and neck. She ran her fingers over his skin lightly, noticing how it felt warm from the sun and was slightly lighter than the skin on his face. Her hands drew circles over the tops of his shoulders and dipped down to his arms, feeling the gentle firmness of his muscles and tracing the outline of a triangle on the outer edges of his arms. She idly wondered if such muscles were from riding or if her husband was an avid swordsman. Somehow, the latter seemed to fit him and the thought was not displeasing.

She continued her explorations down his chest and across his ribs. He was very broad, her husband. His waist was narrower than his chest, but only barely. His ribs stood high off the ground and rose and fell steadily with his breaths. His chest was covered with soft, dark hair, not so much that he felt furry but not so little as to call it a smattering. She ran her fingers through it and felt his heartbeat beneath her palm.

She had never touched him so blatantly. When they were together intimately, he was always touching her, moving over her still body. Afterwards, she would often rest her head against his chest until they fell asleep. But it was always dark and she never felt as free or able to touch him as she did now, nor had she felt such a desire to do so.

His hair stopped just below his breast except for a dark line that traveled down his center. She traced it for a moment until it disappeared into his breeches and continued on with her discoveries. His shoulders were hot to the touch and solid beneath her hands. His ears were surprisingly soft and his hair seemed in need of a cut. She had touched it many times before, but always in the heat of passion. She was enjoying this slow assessment of her husband's form.

Darcy was also enjoying it—immensely. He had begun to drift off to the soothing feeling of his wife's nimble fingers in his hair and her sweet voice humming a tune. Then those same fingers began a new circuit around his shoulders, arms, and chest, once even drifting dangerously close to his hips. She could not know what she was doing to him. He had chanced a peek at her, finding she was all curiosity and studiousness. It was clear it was not an erotic game she was playing but rather a curious woman's investigation into the male form. Of course, he was happy to broaden his wife's mind in any we he could, but if she didn't stop soon, he'd hardly be able to hold himself back from doing some investigating of his own.

Taking a deep breath, he slowly opened his eyes as if waking from sleep. He didn't want to discourage her explorations or push for more than she was ready for, but he would not be able to remain still much longer.

"Do you think our clothes are dry now?" he asked.

"Most likely," she said. He sat up and she rose to grab her stockings and petticoat off the branch she'd hung them on. "These are dry. Shall we head back?"

He looked at the sky and the grey clouds in the distance that were moving their direction.

"That's probably best."

Within an hour, they were returned to the cottage and requesting baths. Elizabeth stood in the sitting room while she waited for the water to heat, remembering something her husband had said about baths when he'd given her a tour of the London house. She thought of joining him in his bath, but did not feel bold enough today. But soon, she would. It would be a perfect goal. She would aim to surprise him in his bath within the week. If that was not encouragement, she didn't know what was.

CHAPTER 27

Dinner that evening was a lively affair. They teased each other about their escapade on the lake's small island and laughed until their sides ached.

Elizabeth shocked Darcy quite happily when she said, "And of course I alone received the pleasure of seeing you lying in the sun without the encumbrance of your shirt." Her eyes gleamed wickedly and for a moment, he couldn't breathe as his heart took off at a gallop.

"I daresay it wasn't as enjoyable as seeing your bare legs through your wet dress," he said calmly before taking a sip of his wine.

Her mouth dropped open and she flushed before grinning and laughing softly. When the footman came in with dessert, she gestured him to her side and whispered something in his ear. The young man nodded and left the room, dessert still in his hand.

Darcy looked at her quizzically and she stood, her chin out but her cheeks slightly flushed, giving away her nervousness.

"I've asked for dessert to be served on the terrace outside our chambers. I thought we could eat it after changing into more comfortable attire, if that suits you?" she asked, her voice steady but for the tiniest shake.

There is my bold Elizabeth. "Yes, it suits me very well." He rose and offered his hand, pulling her close and kissing her knuckles before leading her down the corridor.

As he prepared for bed, though the sun was only just setting, he smiled to himself. His plan had worked. He had been playful and carefree with Elizabeth today and look what had happened! She had all but requested his presence in her private chambers. He had hoped for positive results from his campaign, but never that they would happen so soon. He would not question his good fortune. He was already wearing comfortable breeches, not the incredibly fitted ones that were so in style in town, and he changed his shirt for a loose linen one and dismissed his valet for the night, telling him he would ring for him in the morning.

Darcy padded out to the terrace in bare feet and settled into a chair by the table where dessert had just been laid. He poured two glasses of wine and looked at the sunset while he waited for his wife.

Elizabeth had her maid take off her light summer dress and let down her hair. Sanders pulled a tiny section from either side of her face and braided it, then wrapped it around her head to hold the rest of her hair out of her face but still maintain the look of tumbling, riotous curls.

"Which nightgown, madam?" asked Sanders.

Elizabeth looked back and forth between the gowns, trying to decide between a soft rose and a deep blue.

"Which do you think will look better at sunset?" Elizabeth asked with a glance at the window.

"I think the rose, madam, but the blue would be best in moonlight." Sanders had a light flush to her cheeks but was otherwise the picture of professionalism. Elizabeth couldn't help the laugh that bubbled forth.

"I shall wear the rose, then."

Dressed and brushed and recently bathed, Elizabeth stepped out onto the terrace and saw her husband sitting in the light, watching the sunset intently. She approached him quietly, sliding her hands around his shoulders and hugging his back as she leaned over and gave him a kiss on the cheek.

"Hello, darling," he said lowly. Then he reached around and pulled her in front of him and into his lap before she could do more than gasp in surprise.

She instinctively hung onto his neck and cried out, "Fitzwilliam!"

Before she could say more he had covered her mouth with his and she responded as he wished her to, with fervor and hunger. He leaned over her, kissing her with relish before pulling back and settling himself into the chair so she was above him, all the while never releasing her lips.

She pressed her breasts into his chest and got as close as she could, her arms wrapping more tightly around his neck, one hand playing in his dark curls. Her legs had been over the side of his chair and as he moved, she was at an awkward angle. To steady herself, she went up on her knees, his head tipping back as she leaned over him, her hands coming to grip his jaw and wrap around to the back of his head. He ran his hands up the back of her leg, skating beneath the silk of her gown and ghosting over her thighs. He tried to nudge her legs apart and the movement made Elizabeth reach one knee to the other side of the chair so she was effectively straddling him, his form sinking lower as she towered over him.

He was so thrilled by this development he could hardly breathe, but he was thankful he had worn the looser breeches.

Elizabeth was enthralled by the feeling of power she had as she knelt over her husband. She could feel how much he enjoyed what she was doing. His heart was pounding against her chest and his hands trembled when they touched her. The evidence of his arousal was obvious beneath her and his breath was ragged in her ear as she kissed his jaw and then further down his neck. She felt something overtaking her, she knew not what, but just as she was about to question her actions, Fitzwilliam called her name and captured her lips in another kiss and all rational thought fled as she felt and followed and in turn led her husband.

~

The sun finally down, they sat side by side on the lounge chair, Elizabeth half on his lap so they would both fit. Darcy was nibbling on a biscuit filled with strawberry jam as she sipped a glass of water, half-wondering what had come over her not an hour before.

"Are you well, wife?" he asked gently.

"Quite well, husband. You?" she returned with a smile.

"*I* am ecstatic," he said with a seductive smile that had her blushing to the roots of her hair.

Before she could respond, her stomach rumbled and Darcy laughed, suggesting she eat her dessert. The staff had brought a trifle as well as a tray of fruit, cheese, and biscuits. They were very well prepared, these servants.

She smiled and popped a small chunk of cheese in her mouth and washed it down with a sip of wine.

Darcy had a brief image of drinking wine from her mouth and eating off her delectable body—he thought her back might make an especially fine plate—but he shook his mind free and focused on the present.

Elizabeth had requested his presence, then had returned all his passion as she rode him to glory. He had never felt better.

"Dearest?" she asked some time later after they were both full and the tray held nothing but crumbs.

"Yes, love?" he asked, smiling at the endearment.

"Would it be utterly ridiculous to go to bed? It has been a long day and I think I am still tired from the journey." To illustrate the truth of the matter, she released an enormous yawn and stretched her arms above her head, her robe slithering delicately over her skin.

"Of course not. I'm rather tired myself. Would you like to sleep in your chambers or mine?" he asked, not even considering they might sleep apart.

"I have never slept in a man's chamber!" she said brightening.

"I should hope not!" he cried in mock indignation.

She smacked his arm and all but dragged him into his room. They curled up in the center of the bed, the open terrace door letting the sounds of the night and a light breeze blow gently into the room. She rested her head on his chest and he held her close, sighing in contentment before drifting off, only to waken and repeat the events from the terrace twice more before morning.

CHAPTER 28

Bingley took care of what business needed doing in town, and eight days after Darcy's wedding, was on his way to Margate. He had arranged a room at the same hotel Darcy had stayed at when he visited. He wasn't sure how long he would stay, but he vowed he wouldn't leave without Jane's agreement to marry him. Nothing but her absolute refusal could cause him to depart sooner. Maybe they could even marry at the seaside. They could go on to honeymoon nearby, perhaps in Ramsgate or Brighton, and avoid excess travel. But Jane would probably not wish to marry without Elizabeth there, and he knew the Darcys would be visiting The Lakelands through the end of July.

He shook his head of his fanciful ideas and told himself to focus on getting Jane's agreement first. Everything else could be sorted out later. After checking his appearance for the fifth time, he made his way to the Bennets' little blue cottage.

"Mr. Bingley! How nice to see you!" called Mrs. Bennet from the front garden where she was snipping flowers with a small pair of shears. She held a basket over one arm and waved to Bingley with the other. "I shall be in momentarily. Jane is around the back with her father."

He thanked her and made his way around the side of the house, thinking that Mrs. Bennet really was an uncommonly pretty woman, especially for her age. It could only bode well for his future with Jane.

"Mr. Bingley! You are welcome to Margate," cried Mr. Bennet as he came around the corner.

Jane turned to face him and blushed, greeting him softly. She thought he looked happy and nervous, or maybe it was just her imagination.

Bingley joined them for tea. Mr. Bennet invited him into the discussion they were having on a book Bingley had luckily read while at Cambridge.

"Do you think Reginald should have yielded to his friend?" asked Mr. Bennet, referring to the protagonist in the story.

"His friend's judgment was sound, and he was certainly in possession of more information, which Reginald should have taken into account. But I cannot think it good to so wholly surrender your own judgment, regardless of the closeness of the relationship." He looked at Jane as he said the last, his eyes serious and steady.

"I must agree, Mr. Bingley," said Jane. "While it is good to acquiesce to a friend, especially when they are in need, acting against our own judgment for someone else's sake, I think, would rarely lead to a good end."

The couple smiled at each other and Mr. Bennet leaned back with a grin. His little Jane was going to be quite all right.

Mrs. Bennet joined them then and invited Mr. Bingley to stay for dinner, to which he gladly agreed, as he would each night for the next several days.

~

Mr. and Mrs. Bennet were happier than they had ever been. Well, perhaps they had been happier in the first blush of love, when she was seventeen and he seven and twenty, but this was different. That had been heady and passionate, full of big dreams and starry eyes. But now, both quite settled in middle age, they knew one another better. And while Mr. Bennet still did not think he had chosen *wisely*, he was beginning to think he had not chosen *badly*, either. If he took the trouble to look, he was able to find attributes worthy of affection in his wife. The two were often found taking walks along the shore at sunset, or she would read to him as he rested his eyes in the shade of the back garden. She put flowers in his room and he complimented her regularly, telling her how the sea air was making her complexion positively glow and what a good job she had done in dressing their girls and (almost) maintaining the new budget.

She basked in his praise and thrived on his attention, not wondering about the cause of his change in behavior but only grateful for the result. Such was her nature.

Jane watched her parents with a wary eye. She couldn't help but feel all of their camaraderie would end soon, and she waited, sadly prepared to comfort her mother when it did. She didn't mind attending her mother, and she was moderately pleased that others found her presence comforting, but she did have her own pursuits and her mother did have three other daughters at home. Jane simply didn't understand why *she* should always be the one to give consolation. Surely it was a skill that would benefit her sisters? Was it not something everyone would have call to do at some point or other? For the first time in her twenty-two years, Jane felt resentment at always being the responsible, comforting one. Sometimes, she thought it might be nice to just be Jane, without having to tend to those around her. The thought was so foreign it left her very unsettled.

She told herself she was worrying for nothing. Her mother had been remarkably calm this entire journey. It was only her own innate sense of responsibility, and perhaps an inability to trust all the new ideas and feelings she was experiencing, that made her anxious for the future. Sometimes, though she would never tell him this, she wished her father had never begun his mission to educate and civilize his daughters. She saw the benefits, and was beyond glad not to be mortified by Kitty and Lydia in public any longer, but she could not be happy that her own ideals and beliefs had undergone such a radical change, and were undergoing it still. Her rational mind told her it had been likely to happen at some point regardless, but she could not be comforted. Just for a little while, she would be unhappy about it. Then she would smile and go about her day, thinking of it no more.

After all, she could not change the world.

~

Mr. Bingley proved to be a constant suitor. He came to the cottage most mornings shortly after breakfast. For a fortnight, he accompanied Jane on slow walks by the shore and organized outings for the entire family to visit nearby gardens and ruins. He even hired a boat for the afternoon for all four Bennet sisters, which could have only ended in disaster and, in fact, did. After four dripping, disgruntled girls made their way back to the cottage, Bingley returned to his hotel with a silly smile on his face he could not remove, no matter how hard he tried.

Somewhat to his own surprise, he dearly wanted to join the Bennet family. Yes, Mrs. Bennet was louder than she ought to be and was entirely too in awe of status and wealth, but the latter described more than half the women he knew. Her other embarrassing behaviors had been tempered of late and she was not cruel, something he couldn't say for many other women of his acquaintance or even in his family.

The Gardiners were amiable and intelligent people and he could picture many nights spent in entertaining dinners full of lively conversation. Mr. Bennet was a congenial fellow, though a bit dry for Bingley's tastes; he was a more straightforward man. He didn't manipulate those around him or pretend to feelings he did not have. Despite their differences, Bingley found the older man's company stimulating and enlightening, and he enjoyed playing chess with such a skilled opponent.

The Bennet girls would make excellent sisters, Bingley decided. They had been great fun on the water. Even after the boat tipped and they were all sprayed with sea water, they had laughed and maintained their spirits. It was only as the wind picked up and they were cold and shivering that they had become grumpy. Even then, they weren't half as bad as Caroline on an ordinary day, without the inducement of a near-dunking.

He knew they had small dowries, but he intended to copy his friend Darcy and suggest Jane's portion go to her sisters. With both he and Darcy as connections, surely the other three would find decent husbands. Even if only one of them married, supporting two women would not be terribly difficult.

He shook his head to clear his imaginings. He had not proposed yet and Jane had not accepted. He could kick himself for not proposing at the Netherfield ball last November as he had thought about. Just as he was about to whisper the sweet words into Miss Bennet's ear, his sister had approached demanding his assistance with some problem or other. The moment passed, and now here he was, having chased his love to Margate, desperately waiting for a sign that she would be amenable to a proposal.

~

"Good morning, Mr. Bingley," said Jane sweetly as Bingley joined her on the terrace after breakfast.

He smiled at her widely. "I have news," he said with restrained enthusiasm, tapping a letter against his palm.

"Oh? From your sisters?" Jane asked.

"From Louisa. She tells me Caroline has met a gentleman at the house party. He has shown an uncommon amount of interest in her and asked Hurst about her situation. My brother says he believes a proposal is imminent."

"After so short a time? Is that wise?" Jane asked, concerned.

"Normally, I would say no. But Caroline seeks an advantageous match, not a romantic attachment. I believe she would be comfortable with being nothing but friendly with her husband."

Jane shook her head. "I know it is the way it is often done, but I cannot imagine doing so. It must be very strange to live in such close quarters with someone you know so little of."

He shrugged. "Probably, but everyone has different expectations and they will come to know one another better soon enough. And he is not a total stranger. They have met at dinners and balls in the past, but nothing ever came of it. He is a friend of Hurst's, which relieves my mind in terms of his suitability. I would not agree to marry my sister to a stranger, but a respected friend is another matter."

Jane nodded. "Your care does you credit, sir."

He looked away. "I wish I could agree, Miss Bennet. I feel I should have done much more long ago." He looked down, a chagrined expression on his face. "I am not naturally forceful. I can manage my servants and take care of my business, but I do not like to force issues with those who should know better, and I do not like to practice strategy on people."

"I believe you're saying you are honest, Mr. Bingley," said Jane with a soft smile.

"Perhaps. Caroline would call it otherwise," he said quietly.

"I think it is refreshing," said Jane. "Who wants to constantly worry whether others are trying to manipulate us or force those who would rather not into good behavior?"

"You are wise, Miss Bennet. Strategy is best left to the chess-board. I prefer my interactions to be simpler."

She smiled and he took her hand in his.

"For example, when I admire a woman, she will know it by the way I hold her hand, and have eyes only for her." He looked at her meaningfully and she blushed scarlet. "I will be straightforward in my addresses, but patient and in tune with her desires. She will know how cherished she is by how I give her all of my time, all my attention," he kissed the back of her hand slowly, "all my heart."

Jane gasped, her breath coming rapidly.

"Miss Bennet, say the word and I will cease speaking this minute," he whispered urgently.

She swallowed loudly, but said nothing, her eyes wide and her lips parted.

"Miss Bennet, Jane, I must tell you how much I love and adore you. I loved you in Hertfordshire, but that was as nothing compared to what I feel for you now. I promise to treasure you above all else. Will you do me the very great honor of being my wife?"

Jane's heart practically leapt out of her chest, and she wanted to fall into his arms, but she forced herself to stop and think rationally for a moment. She closed her eyes, feeling his hands tighten around hers. Could she rely on him always? Would he be able to stand his ground against his sisters and officious friends? Would he be a true head of the family, or would she be constantly prompting him to lead and exhausting herself in the process?

An image of Mr. Walker came to mind. He was more like Mr. Darcy: dependable, predictable, reliable, and very in control. And yet, she felt nothing when she thought of him. No butterflies in her stomach, no hitch in her breath, no gooseflesh on her arms. He was pleasant and good company and nothing more.

Finally, after Bingley was sure he had aged five years, she slowly opened her eyes and smiled angelically at him.

"Yes!" she cried.

The word was barely out of her mouth before he stood and pulled her up with him, embracing her and spinning around. They laughed together and Jane felt tears of joy on her cheeks. He tenderly wiped them away with a handkerchief and she laughed nervously.

"I must go to my mother," she said.

"I'll go to your father," he replied.

Smiling at each other again, they went into the house.

CHAPTER 29

Mid-July, Mrs. Bennet sat down to write a letter to Elizabeth. She had put a note on her husband's previous letters, but this was the first she had written on her own. Her daughter had been married a month and she thought it would be a good idea to inform her of what to look for if she became with child. If she was anything like the Gardiner women, she would be in the family way before the end of the year.

Mrs. Bennet told Elizabeth that her courses would first seem late before she would realize they were not coming at all. She may feel overly tired and want to sleep more than usual. Certain smells and foods could turn her stomach, and she may even be sick. Mornings could be particularly bad for some women, but her experience had always been sporadic throughout the day. Her breasts would likely grow fuller and heavier and would be more tender, possibly painful.

Eventually, her appetite would increase and she would notice she was becoming fuller all over, not just in her middle. Mrs. Bennet told her that with three of her five pregnancies, she had enlarged primarily over her legs and bottom before her belly grew at all. Her skin would likely change, too, taking on a more milky appearance and her cheeks would eventually fill out, though likely not for some time.

She also told her the signs of a miscarriage, which she had thankfully only experienced once, and informed her that a drop or two of blood was nothing to be concerned about, but perhaps it was a signal to relax a bit more and run about a bit less. If there were painful cramps, call the midwife.

Mrs. Bennet paused in her writing as she remembered the painful miscarriage she had suffered between Kitty and Lydia. She had been sure it was a boy. Everything in her told her it was so. Her sister told her she had thought so before, but Mrs. Bennet knew this time was different. Alas, it was not to be. In her fourth month, she had been gripped with terrible pains, the like of which she had only experienced when delivering her girls. The midwife was called, and within a few hours, Agnes Bennet was no longer with child.

The tiny babe had been buried in the family graveyard at her insistence. She had not looked at the half-formed child, but the midwife confirmed what she had known all along. The child had been a boy. She called him John, after her grandfather, and wept bitterly for weeks.

Her next pregnancy was very careful and though she knew in her heart the babe was another girl, she did not want to take any risks. Lydia became a much-prized infant after a deeply-felt loss.

Mrs. Bennet sighed and pulled herself together to finish her letter. Elizabeth would be more successful than she had been, she knew it. She was fortune's child, that girl. To be so wild and still catch such a man as Mr. Darcy, she had to be very lucky. There was no point at all in giving her tips—she did not need them.

Agnes Bennet looked down at her own traitorous body. The sunlight from the window above the desk where she sat illuminated her clearly and she sighed. Her bosom was lower than it had been, and her midriff was almost painfully flat. She would not flush with new life or swell with a child ever again. Lydia's difficult birth had made sure of that.

She sighed once more. Her daughters would do better than she had. She knew it.

~

After a fortnight of glorious weather and excellent company, Elizabeth sat in their private sitting room, finishing her breakfast and looking over her letters. Darcy had gone for a morning ride and she was enjoying a few moments to herself. She had learned her new patterns well enough now to know that while she needed this time to remain equable, she would begin to miss him after an hour or two spent in solitary pursuits.

She opened the letter from Jane, nearly shrieking when she read of the engagement. She was thrilled for her sister. She experienced many thoughts and feelings but was surprised by the lack of one she had been expecting. Loss.

Elizabeth had been sure Jane's marriage would remind her of the sacrifice she herself had made and that she would be both happy for her sister and a little sad for herself. But she did not feel so. Yes, she was happy for Jane, but to her very great surprise, she was glad her sister would *also* have a good marriage with a man she esteemed.

Choosing not to dwell overlong on that thought, she opened the letter from her mother. Slightly shocked by the content and its delivery, she was surprised at how helpful and informative it was. There was no talk of lace or advice on how to keep her husband happy—just womanly advice from mother to daughter, and good advice at that.

She knew not what to make of it, but sat down immediately to respond.

As she was writing, she thought about having a baby. Specifically, having a baby with Mr. Darcy. Of course, she had known for some time that if she had children, he would be their father and the likelihood of having them was extremely high. But still, it was a very different thing to think about after the wedding than it had been before.

She found herself wondering what their children would look like and presumed they would surely all have curly hair, since both she and her husband did. His was less so than hers, but she would be very surprised at a straight-haired child. Just as Jane and Bingley would likely have angelic blond children with sweet dispositions, the Darcy children would likely all be dark and either very mischievous or very serious. She found herself laughing at the picture.

She placed her hand over her abdomen and felt its flatness, wondering what she would look like swollen with child. What would it feel like to have a babe growing inside her?

"What are you doing, love?" Darcy asked as he wrapped his arms around her and placed his hands over hers.

"I was thinking about having a baby," she said absently.

He stiffened and turned her to face him. "Are you?" he glanced down to her belly. "Are we going to…?"

"Oh, darling, I'm sorry! No, I'm not with child. I didn't mean to mislead you. I was just thinking about the possibility."

He nodded, his expression slightly dazed. "What do you think of the possibility?" he asked quietly, holding her close enough that she couldn't see his face.

"I think it would be lovely. And a little frightening. And exciting."

He pulled back and looked at her.

"But I think I would also miss this time when it is just the two of us," she added.

He smiled. "Truly? I will miss it, too," he said, pulling her close again and resting his head on her hair. It was some time before he realized she had called him darling for the first time.

Elizabeth caught their image in the mirror hanging across from the table. They looked so very *right* together, so content in each other's presence, and suddenly she was struck with a startling realization. He was the man, in disposition and talents, who suited her best. Her liveliness was already making him easier and more pleasant in company and his greater information benefitted her immensely and engendered a respect she doubted she could ever feel for another man to the same degree.

We're perfect for each other.

Stunned by her realization, she failed to respond to something her husband said. Were there bees in the room? Is that why she heard buzzing?

"Elizabeth! Are you well?" He was placing a hand to her forehead and looking at her worriedly.

She only stared back at him blankly.

"You suddenly went pale. Come, lie down." He turned to lead her toward the settee but she didn't move.

He looked at her worriedly, and suddenly she blurted, "I think I love you." His eyes widened and she closed hers in mortification. "I'm sorry, that was badly done."

"You—you think… what?" he asked.

"Fitzwilliam," she said, eyes shining and color restored, "I've fallen in love with you."

"You've," he swallowed. "You've fallen in love with me? When?"

The urge to tease was nearly overpowering but she knew now was not the time. "I do not know exactly when, just that I know now. I believe it has been coming on so gradually I barely noticed."

He crushed her to him and pressed a steady kiss to her hair.

"Dearest, loveliest Elizabeth. You are my very heart."

She squeezed him back as hard as she could. "My Fitzwilliam."

He sighed. "You do realize what today is?" he asked after a long silence.

"What is it?"

"Your birthday."

She gasped. "How could I have forgotten?"

"We have had no sense of time here. Anyhow, it seems I am the one who got the gift." He tucked a tendril of hair behind her ear.

She leaned into his hand with a soft sigh and he couldn't stop himself from sweeping her into his arms and taking her straight to his bedchamber.

~

Two hours later, they were sprawled in Darcy's bed, speaking of inconsequential nothings.

"When would you like your birthday present?" he asked.

"I thought the concert and the fireworks tomorrow were my gift," she replied.

Darcy was taking her to an event a few miles away and there were to be fireworks over the lake afterward. Elizabeth had never seen them before and he couldn't wait to see her experience them for the first time.

"That is part of the celebration, but not the gift."

She sat up, suddenly curious. "So what is the gift?"

"Wait here."

He left the bed and went into his dressing room, returning a minute later. He handed her a folded piece of paper. She took it and looked at him quizzically.

"Go ahead, open it," he encouraged.

She opened the paper and began to read the short letter, reading it twice through to make sure she understood.

"Fitzwilliam," she said shakily, "is this real?" She held up the paper. He nodded. "You would go to so much trouble for me?"

Her eyes filled with tears and he pulled her into his arms. "Oh, darling, I didn't mean to make you cry. Of course I would go to the trouble for you. I would do anything for you, surely you know that."

"Fitzwilliam! This is the best gift anyone has ever given me. I cannot wait to see them completed." She read the letter again in excitement, marveling over the idea that her husband would commission a Bennet family portrait and accompanying miniatures of the individual members. "Has he really already begun the sketches?"

"He has. He sent me a few suggestions for poses. I thought you might want to see them before he begins the final product."

He showed her a few sketches of her father outside the cottage. In one he was in profile, looking at the sea; in another, he was reading in his favorite chair on the terrace; in the final sketch he was next to her mother and the two of them were laughing, her mother's hand on her father's arm. She reached out and touched the picture, suddenly missing her family and unbelievably touched by her husband's gesture.

"He will come to Pemberley and sketch you once the rest of your family is completed," he said quietly.

"Will he sketch you, too?"

"I am not a Bennet," he said.

"But you are my family. If it is to be my family portrait, I would wish you to be in it. And Mr. Bingley, too, if he would like."

"If you wish it, my love, consider it done," he said thickly.

She fell into his arms and held him tight. "Thank you, Fitzwilliam. It is absolutely perfect."

CHAPTER 30

In what was a surprising turn, though perhaps it should not have been, Bingley and Jane announced they would like to wed as soon as possible, right there in Margate. He said he did not care if his family or friends were there, as long as he was married at the end of it. He could invite a friend in London to stand up with him and preferred his sisters not attend.

Jane agreed. They had spent enough time waiting and thinking about each other; she was ready to begin their life together. She would have liked Lizzy to be there with her, but she knew her sister was in the middle of her wedding tour and very far away. It would take her a week to get to Margate, only to return north after a few days. Not wanting to subject her sister to such rigors, she sent a letter asking if Elizabeth would mind terribly if she married without her, and she and Bingley would visit Pemberley after their tour.

Mr. and Mrs. Bennet had no choice but to agree with the young couple. Mrs. Bennet bemoaned ever being able to decorate the chapel at Longbourn and have all her Meryton friends see one of her daughters wed. She was resigned to it soon enough, though, when Lydia blithely suggested it was much less likely Mr. Bingley would disappear again if they married quickly. After that, Mrs. Bennet threw herself into planning a simple but beautiful wedding, and Mr. Bennet was pleased to save the cost of a lavish affair. He only wanted to see his very worthy daughter well settled.

The same dressmaker that made Elizabeth's wedding gown was commissioned to make Jane's, and Mary was to stand up with her. The friends they made in Margate were all invited and the Gardiners would come for the week of the wedding. The new couple would leave immediately after for Brighton. Bingley had let a house there for the remainder of the summer. All was put together rather quickly and before anyone really knew what had happened, Jane Bennet was Jane Bingley, waving to her family from the coach as they pulled away from their small but elegant breakfast.

~

"Fitzwilliam!" Elizabeth called as she rushed into his dressing room.

"Yes?" he replied, amused at her entrance and at his valet's quick exit.

"You will never believe what Jane is doing!"

"I thought she was marrying my friend Bingley. Is that not the case?" he asked sardonically.

"Ha ha. You may think you are funny now, Mr. Darcy, but I know something you don't know," she said in a sing-song voice.

"How do you know I don't know it? It's likely I have a letter from Bingley waiting for me as we speak."

"Fine. If you're so sure you have no need of my information, I shall leave so you may finish preparing."

He smiled at her as she flounced out of the room. Once he was finished dressing, he looked in his room for a letter but saw nothing on the table where a letter would usually be found. He then checked the salver near the door and nothing was there but a packet on its way to Georgiana. He asked a footman if there had been a letter for him that day and the man said there had not been, but that Mrs. Darcy had received three.

Gritting his teeth, Darcy turned and found his wife in the sitting room, seated by the window and reading a letter with a look of pure happiness on her face. He sat down and watched her, saying nothing for several minutes. She bit her lip and laughed out loud and gasped more than once at what she was reading. Finally, he could take it no longer.

"Any news?"

"Hmm? Oh! Just something with my family. I'm sure it wouldn't interest you," she said simply.

He caught her lip twitching but was impressed by her ability to keep up her little game this long. Usually she could hold nothing in when she was excited.

"That's all right. I should come to know your family better. What says your father?"

"They are planning to return to Longbourn in early September. Mother wants him to stop in London for a week and he is trying to find a way to avoid it."

Darcy smiled. "Has he been successful?"

"Not yet." She gave him a look he'd seen often before. Half sympathy, half mischief. *Lord, she is delightful!*

"Tell your father they may stay at Darcy House if they wish. It would be tight at the Gardiners," he said.

Her head snapped up. "That is very generous of you. Are you sure you wish to do that?"

"Of course. I shall write to your father if you prefer."

"No, that won't be necessary. I can take care of it. Thank you," she said sincerely.

He nodded in response. He had won; his wife was no longer teasing him. He waited, wondering how long it would take for her to tell him the news.

"Jane and Bingley have decided to marry in Margate, in three weeks," she said. "Two weeks now. Can you believe it?" Her eyes went back to her letter.

"Are you sad to be missing the wedding?" he asked.

"A little. I had always thought I would stand up with Jane. But she stood up with me, something I never thought would happen, so I suppose it is all right in the end." She shrugged her shoulders. "They wish to visit Pemberley in the autumn and then go on to Scarborough for Jane to meet his family. They will return when my family arrives for Christmas."

"That sounds wonderful. We will see more of them on a visit than if we were to go to the wedding."

Elizabeth nodded. "Are you sorry to miss it? He is your closest friend."

"Yes and no. It would be nice to be there, but not nice enough to forego my own wedding trip."

He smiled in the way that always made her stomach flip and she blushed.

"Why did you think Jane would not stand up with you? I know it is usual for it to be a maiden, but married women sometimes perform the office. And she would not necessarily marry first just because she was the eldest," he asked.

Elizabeth chuckled. "It is *Jane*, Fitzwilliam. She is the sweetest, most beautiful creature in the world. Why would I ever think I would marry before her? Or marry at all?"

"And yet you did." He shot her a meaningful look and she looked away. "Why did you think you wouldn't marry at all?"

"I simply didn't think it very likely. I am not as sweet or as pretty as Jane, I have very little money and few connections, and I am not nearly docile enough for most men."

He rose and walked toward her. "Good thing I am not most men," he growled as he slipped onto the settee next to her.

She laughed. "You should never be given a docile creature. You would eat her alive in minutes!"

By this point he was nibbling at her neck and his hand was wandering dangerously high on her thigh.

"I was of the opinion some women liked being eaten alive," he murmured before he nipped her ear.

She gasped and smacked his shoulder lightly. "Fitzwilliam Darcy! How could you say such a thing to a lady?" She tried to look indignant, but it was difficult when her eyes were filled with mirth and her shoulders were shaking with suppressed laughter.

"When the lady is my wife, I believe the rules differ," he said huskily before rising and throwing her over his shoulder, causing her to shriek loudly.

"Put me down, you brute!" she cried as forcefully as she could while laughing uncontrollably.

"Never!"

The servants in the house looked the other way when a laughing mistress thrown over the shoulder of a running Mr. Darcy rushed into the master suite and slammed the door behind them.

EPILOGUE

Spring, 1823

"Come, Robin, we're almost there," called Elizabeth as she crested the hill.

"I'm coming, Lizzy," returned her ten-year-old brother.

They reached the top of Oakham Mount and he looked out at the view surrounding him.

"I never tire of this view," she said wistfully.

"Do you miss it when you are away in Derbyshire?"

"I am not away in Derbyshire. It is my home now."

"But you said this morning that this would always feel like home," he said, perplexed.

"Yes, because I grew up here. I know every tree and stream and farm. But the lot of women, or most women, is to move to their husband's home, as I did when I married Fitzwilliam."

"Will this always be my home?" he asked.

"Yes. Longbourn is yours already. We're just helping you look after it until you're older."

He nodded thoughtfully. "When do you think I'll be old enough to look after it on my own?"

"I don't know. Perhaps two and twenty? Papa was five and twenty when he began managing Longbourn."

"I wish he was here now," said Robin.

Elizabeth sighed. "As do I. But we were very lucky to have him with us as long as we did."

Robin sighed and agreed, absently kicking a stone on the path.

"When will Kitty come back again?"

She ruffled his hair and repressed the urge to pinch his round cheek. "She will return in six months, and then you will live with her and Mr. Thurston at Netherfield until you are old enough to live here alone." She squeezed his soft hand. "Are you nervous about her being gone so long?"

"A little," he said softly. "I am happy to stay with you at Pemberley and with Jane, too, but I have never been away from her so long before."

"I know, dearest. It cannot be easy. But Bennet and Alex and Charlie will keep you so busy the time will rush by, and she'll be back before you know it."

He smiled shyly and she led him back down the hill. "Come. I want to visit our parents before the wedding."

The two made their way into Longbourn's small graveyard and Elizabeth placed the flowers she had picked on her mother's grave. She said a few words and touched her fingers to her lips before placing them on the headstone, then left Robin to himself. She knew he liked to tell their mother about his goings on and had visited her grave weekly since she passed four years ago. She traced the year on her father's headstone, 1817, and sat with her legs stretched in front of her, leaning back against the cold stone and settling in for a good chat.

"Well, Papa, Kitty is finally marrying tomorrow. I know we thought it would never happen, but Thurston is a good man. He must be, for he has waited for her long enough." She laughed lightly. "You would be very proud of her, Papa. She has taken excellent care of Robbie. He is a good boy. I know he is only ten now and much will change soon, but I think he will be a fine man. Fitzwilliam says he has an excellent head for numbers and believes he will manage the estate admirably. He took him along when he was riding the estate with Bennet when we were last all at Pemberley. Who knew that would become a holiday tradition? Anyway, the boys are more like cousins than uncle and nephew, you saw that, but as they've gotten older it has only become more pronounced.

"They remind me of Fitzwilliam and his cousin Richard. I nearly fainted when I saw them racing around the lake." She sighed. "He is so like you, Papa, but I see Mama in him, too. He has her liveliness and your mind. And of course her blue eyes. The bluest eyes in Hertfordshire." She laughed lightly as she remembered her mother and her constant boasting about her children's beauty. "He shall be very handsome, I'm sure of it. He has your nose and hair. It was blond when you last saw him, but it has gotten quite dark now and I believe it will be as dark as mine when he is grown.

"I will have another babe in the summer." She rubbed her swollen belly absently. "Fitzwilliam desperately hopes this one will be a girl. He has never said it, but I believe he worries how he will provide for so many sons. Obviously, Bennet will inherit Pemberley, and Alex can take over Everbrook, the small estate to the north his grandfather bought. Fitzwilliam purchased a small estate in Staffordshire recently that is planned for Tommy, but that still leaves Jack and Peter without. I've told him that Peter is not yet two; there is time to save, and of course there is the Kympton living, but you know how he worries and plans."

She sighed. "He takes such good care of us; I cannot believe I almost didn't marry him all those years ago. Thank you, Papa. I know I've said it before, but thank you for seeing in him what I didn't and convincing me to give him a chance. I cannot imagine my life otherwise."

She looked up as a shadow fell across her face.

"Are you finished talking to Papa, Lizzy?"

"Yes, Robbie, I am. Help your sister up?" She held out her hand with a smile and he pulled her to her feet. "Oh!" she cried. "Do you want to feel the baby?"

His eyes lit up. "May I?"

"Of course. The boys do it all the time. Here, put your hand here." She placed his hand on her abdomen and his eyes lit up when he felt a tiny kick on his palm.

"Oh!" he cried.

"Isn't it wondrous?"

He nodded. "Do you think it will be another boy?"

"You don't think five boys is enough?" she teased.

Robin laughed. "I suppose. It would be nice to have a girl, though."

"You think?"

"Mhmm. What do you think you would call her? If it's a girl?"

"I like Sophie or Helena. Or Jane, after our sister. What do you think?"

"I like Jane. None of her daughters have been named after her, well, Agnes Jane, but second names don't count, do they?"

"Of course they do!" cried Elizabeth. "You are Robin Thomas after our grandfather and father, and Bennet's second name is Fitzwilliam after his father, and of course Alexander draws his name from Fitzwilliam's second name, which was his grandfather's name. A name is very important, Robin. It mustn't be chosen lightly."

He nodded. "Would you name her Agnes if Jane hadn't already?"

Elizabeth smiled sadly. "I don't know. Mama was Agnes Jane, so I probably would have used it in some fashion, but as you know, I only produce sons. Well, until now." She looked at her belly.

"Are you sure it is a girl, then?"

"I have a very strong feeling."

He smiled her father's smile at her and they walked into Longbourn together.

THE END

ABOUT THE AUTHOR

Elizabeth Adams loves sunshine and a good book, hates asparagus, and often laughs at inappropriate moments. She has a slight chocolate addiction and can swim four laps on a good day, but makes up for it by being a great dancer.

Find more information, outtakes, and short stories at www.elizabethadamswrites.wordpress.com. You can also follow her on Twitter (@EAdamsWrites) or find her on Facebook (Author Elizabeth Adams).

Other books by Elizabeth Adams

The Houseguest

Green Card

Printed by Amazon Italia Logistica S.r.l.
Torrazza Piemonte (TO), Italy

56369072R00138